BLUSH

A NOVEL

BLUSH

A NOVEL

HELEN HARDT

#1 *NEW YORK TIMES* BESTSELLING AUTHOR

Entangled Publishing, LLC
644 Shrewsbury Commons Ave., STE 181
Shrewsbury, PA 17361
rights@entangledpublishing.com

Amara is an imprint of Entangled Publishing, LLC.

Visit our website at www.entangledpublishing.com.

Edited by Liz Pelletier
Cover design by Elizabeth Turner Stokes
Stock art by Shutterstock/Valentina Azhgirevich,
Shutterstock/JOGENDRA KUMAR,
Shutterstock/Pongstorn Pixs
Interior design by Toni Kerr

ISBN 978-1-64937-215-4
Ebook ISBN 978-1-64937-227-7

Manufactured in the United States of America

First Edition January 2023

10 9 8 7 6 5 4 3 2 1

For everyone at Entangled.
Thank you for your loyalty and support!

CHAPTER ONE

Amanda

My sister, Frankie—short for Francesca—has two settings. High and low. Either she's going to have incredibly good news or incredibly bad news when she calls. So when her name and number pop up on my buzzing cell phone, my stomach sinks and I assume the worst. If it ends up being good news, it's a relief. And if it's bad news, at least I'm a little prepared.

I sigh. I have a headache after staring at my computer screen for ten hours—an average day on the job for me, but now that I'm mentally playing "guess that phone call," the pain feels sharper.

Relax. It can't be worse than when she called to say Mom was rushed to the hospital.

Can it?

I look at her name pulsing on my phone screen in time with my pounding head and pick up the call.

"Hey, Frank," I say into the phone, trying to keep my voice light.

"Mandy, you're never going to guess what happened!" she squeals.

Good news, then. *Thank God.* I lean back in my chair, relief washing over me in a pleasant rush.

"You're right, I'll never guess," I say and rub my temple. "So just tell me. What's up?"

"Penn proposed last night! We're getting married!"

And just like that, my relief turns to anxiety again.

Pendleton Berry is Frankie's on-again, off-again significant other. He's also an overgrown frat brat who sells software systems but actually lives off a trust fund from his grandfather. He and Frankie have been together for more than five years— but with all the breakups, they've probably only been together around half of that.

Am I supposed to take this seriously? Maybe, because this is the first time the man actually *proposed* to her.

Frankie is younger than I am by two years. Even so, she gets everything first. Seriously. She even started menstruating before I did. She was twelve and I was fourteen. Sure, I got the curse a month later, but still, she had to show me up. I was an awkward kid, introverted and hardly athletically inclined. Frankie even learned to ride a bike before I did.

I love my sister, but now that I'm pushing thirty? This shit is getting old.

She's going to get married, and I don't even have any prospects.

And if I'm honest with myself? I don't *want* any prospects, because I'm hopelessly in love with the one man I'll never have. But now's not the time to focus on that one problem. My sister just dropped a bombshell and is likely waiting on me to share her excitement.

"Aren't you going to say anything?" Frankie asks.

I inject as much enthusiasm as I can into my voice. "That's great, Frank. Really."

She scoffs. "Don't increase your heart rate or anything, Mandy."

"I'm sorry. I'm happy for you. Really." Do I sound sincere?

Part of me truly *is* sincere. I don't wish anything bad on Frankie. I adore my sister and want her to be happy. I'm just not sure Penn Berry is the man who can achieve that.

"I'm thrilled! We're so happy," she gushes.

"That's great, Frank."

"You just said that, Mandy."

"Did I? See? I really mean it."

And I do. Like I said, part of me is truly sincere. Part of me is jealous as all hell. Then that third part of me—the part that would fight to the death anyone who hurt my sister—is worried. She and Penn haven't had the most stable relationship.

"Sometimes I didn't think this would ever happen," Frankie continues. "Things have always been so volatile between Penn and me. But these last six months, everything's been so great."

"That's awesome."

"You'll be my maid of honor, of course," she continues. "And next, I have to call Isabella and Gigi."

Isabella and Gigi—Frankie's besties.

As an introvert, I don't make friends easily. I never have. And since my job as a virtual assistant keeps me behind a computer all day, I don't have a chance to remedy the situation. I'm happy alone, to be honest. Life is safer that way, and I have always taken the safe route. I don't need friends.

Well, except for one.

Jackson Paris has been my best friend since we were both in diapers.

He still is my best friend—on his side anyway. On my side? He's my closest friend in the world. But inconveniently, he's also the guy I've been hopelessly in love with most of my life.

To him, I'm as sexually interesting as a sack of potatoes. At least that's how it's felt over the years, when he's never once looked at me with an ounce of interest or heat.

Unfortunately, I began to see *him* as something more than a friend when we were in high school. He was busy growing into a gorgeous jock and captain of the football team who of course only dated cheerleaders. I used to tease him that he was a walking cliché, but he'd just wink and say that's not what he'd call what he did with *insert girl's name here* last night.

He continued with more of the same in college, where he played football again, majored in business, and landed an internship with Black Inc., under the tutelage of the blue-collar billionaire himself, Braden Black.

Now he's climbing up the corporate ladder at lightning speed as he works in marketing with Braden's brother, Ben Black.

And he still dates all the time. Well, anyone *not* me. I sigh.

Why would he want a bespectacled, no-makeup-wearing brunette with boring gray eyes? Plus, there's the fact that he's never dated a woman for more than three months. *I'm not the commitment type*, he always says. Perhaps it's a good thing he's never seen me as more than a friend. Do I really crave him enough to risk losing a lifetime best friend for only a few months of passion?

Sometimes, on particularly lonely nights, that answer is a hard yes.

Frankie babbles on and on. Engagement party, the bridesmaids' luncheon, the shower and bachelorette parties, and of course the wedding itself.

"It's not going to be a long engagement, Mandy. We both feel like we've wasted so much time with all our silly arguments and breakups. We want to get married right away. In three months or less."

I can't help gasping. "Three months?"

"Yeah, but we can do it. The ceremony will be at Penn's parents' house. You know how huge it is. It's an absolute mansion. And you don't have to worry about anything. You're the maid of honor, but Isabella and Gigi will take care of all the details, my shower and everything. They love that kind of stuff."

Good. That's fine with me. Isabella and Gigi are social animals. I'm not. I could probably put together a shower—how difficult is it to serve cake and punch and watch Frankie open gifts?— but a bachelorette party? Bridesmaids' luncheon? So not in my repertoire.

"That's great."

"Isn't it? Gigi has so many social contacts. Everything will be top-notch."

Top-notch. Great.

"I do need you to come with Isabella and Gigi and me to the gown fitting next week."

"Sure."

"I want all of you to be involved in choosing the dress you wear."

"Great. That's great, Frankie."

Sometimes I feel like I'm stuck on repeat.

Then my phone buzzes with another call.

My heart pumps wildly when I see Jackson's name.

"Frank? I've got another call. It's…work."

"Oh, sure, I understand. I'll keep you in the loop, okay, Mandy?"

"Yeah. Please do."

"Absolutely."

"I'm really happy for you, Frank. Truly." I do my best to sound sincere. I truly *do* want my sister happy.

"I know you are. Love you!"

I quickly end that call and take the other. "Hey, Jack."

"Hey, my little Mandy Cake," he says.

Mandy Cake. He's called me that since we could both talk. Pancakes were Jackson's favorite breakfast as a kid. His mom would make them in the shape of a bear, and his favorite bear was a panda. He called them pandy cakes, so I became Mandy Cake.

And I'm *still* Mandy Cake, which tells the truth of our

relationship. He'll never see me as anything other than that toddler in diapers who used to eat pandy cakes with him.

"I thought I'd come over and take you out to dinner," Jackson continues.

That's code for, *I don't have a date tonight.*

Don't get me wrong. I know Jack loves me as much as I love him. Just in a totally different way. In a "we've been friends forever" kind of way. And most days, I convince myself it's enough.

"Sure, that'd be nice."

"Dress up. There's a new sushi place I want to try downtown."

Jack and I love sushi. It's our guilty pleasure whenever we're together. "Sure."

"Great. Pick you up in an hour?"

"I'll be ready."

As the line goes dead, I can't help but feel the finality echo in my bones.

My sister is getting married...and I am going to be alone forever. Living for the occasional night Jack isn't hooking up with his flavor of the month and wants to try a new restaurant with his dorky best friend.

And just like that, I realize I can either feel sorry for myself...

Or I can do something about it.

On impulse, I pull up the app store on my phone. I need to swallow my fear and put myself out there—and move the hell on from this unrequited hole I've been napping in since *high school*, for God's sake. There are only about a thousand dating apps to choose from.

My hands shake as I type "lustr" into the search bar and pull up the app.

I create a profile quickly but then realize I don't know what to do after that. Nothing about me is remotely interesting. And a photo? God help me.

Jackson. I'll ask Jackson to help me. He's always finding

someone new to hook up with, so he'll know exactly how to help me set up my profile to get the most action.

I smile. This will work out after all.

. . .

"Lustr?" Jackson shakes his head as he spears a piece of spicy tuna roll with his chopsticks. "Seriously, Mandy Cake?"

We've had the "Mandy Cake" discussion many times. I've asked him to stop calling me that, and he's said, "Really? You'll always be Mandy Cake to me."

Lather, rinse, repeat.

Which is the problem. I'll always be Mandy Cake, despite the fact that he stopped being *Jackie Lantern* to me when I hit puberty.

I have to work to *not* stare at Jackson. He's gorgeous—all chiseled jawline, sandy-brown stubble, and dark-blond hair that swoops over his forehead in a way he hates but only makes him more enticing. And those long-lashed eyes—sometimes they're emerald green and sometimes they're the light brown of cognac.

He calls them hazel.

I call them spectacular.

I could gaze into them forever and never tire of their beauty.

I clear my throat. "Yeah, really. Frankie just got engaged. I'm not getting any younger, Jack. I'm a virtual assistant. I sit behind a computer all day. When am I supposed to meet anyone?"

"Anywhere. How about here?" Jackson glances around the dining room at Sushi Palace and then nods to a table of three guys. "How about any of those guys?"

I follow Jack's gaze and roll my eyes. "First of all, they all have gray in their hair. They're too old for me."

"I have a few gray hairs."

"Not enough to matter. Those guys are in their late forties, I'd bet."

Jackson takes a sip of his sake. "You don't know that. They dress well, look interesting."

"Exactly how can you tell they're interesting by the way they dress?"

He smiles his dazzling smile—the one that makes my heart soar.

"They dress like I dress. And I happen to think I'm a very interesting person."

The dazzling smile again.

My God, could I lust for this man more?

"I'm an introvert, Jack. Besides, what kind of woman walks up to a table of three men and starts flirting?"

He raises his eyebrows. "The kind of woman who's looking for a date?"

"I'm not that woman. You've known me forever. You know how shy I am."

He doesn't reply. Instead, he focuses his attention on popping the beans out of an edamame pod.

Doesn't matter. If I can't have the man I want, I can find one exactly like him on Lustr. Right? It's a virtual smorgasbord of eligible men, and one might be looking for Amanda Rose Thomas.

CHAPTER TWO

Jackson

Mandy Cake on Lustr? I can't see it. And then, when I think about it, I can't *un*see it.

She's too sweet and innocent to get messed up in that hunting ground. I hate the idea. And I hate it even more when—

"So will you help me?"

I nearly spit out the mouthful of sake I just drank. I swallow quickly.

"*Help* you?"

"Yeah. Help me with my profile on Lustr."

She's got to be kidding.

"How can *I* help you?"

"Well…I figure…you know me as well as *I* know me. Better in some ways."

"I'm not sure the time you had an accident in my sandbox belongs on your Lustr profile."

"For God's sake, Jack. Could you be serious for one minute?"

I *am* serious. She just doesn't realize it. Lustr is no place for Amanda Thomas. It's a fucking meat market.

"Jack?" Mandy prods.

I sip the last of my sake from my tiny cup. "You're serious about this?"

"Absolutely. My little sister's engaged, and I have absolutely no prospects. I can't wait around for life to start happening to me. I need to get proactive. I want a partner in life. A family."

Amanda has always underestimated herself. She's quite beautiful, with a luscious hourglass figure. Her silvery gray eyes are unique and sparkling, and she has some of the fullest lips I've ever seen on a woman.

If she weren't my Mandy Cake? Sure, I'd tap that. But Amanda is a white-picket-fence type. Sweet and innocent.

And I'm not.

Not even close.

I'm up at four a.m. every morning. I work eighty hours a week.

And I play.

I play *hard*.

I don't want Mandy on Lustr, but if she's going to be on the site, I can at least make sure she doesn't attract the wrong kind of man.

"All right, Amanda." I sigh and can't help thinking I'm going to regret this. "I'll help you."

. . .

The next morning—Sunday—I head over to Amanda's. She lives in a small one-bedroom apartment in the Village that's still in her great-aunt's name, so it's rent controlled. Me? I live in a larger apartment in Manhattan that's close to work and play.

I knock and then key in her code, pushing the door open. "Mandy, where are you?"

I kneel and pet her rescue pup, Roger. He's a Chihuahua mix and hates pretty much everyone except Mandy and me.

"What's up, Rog?" I scratch him behind his ears.

Amanda walks out from her bedroom, her hair wet and hanging in ringlets around her shoulders. She's wearing pink lounging pants and a white tank top. No bra. Her nipples poke through the cotton.

I'm a guy. I notice these things.

Mandy has really nice tits. Not that I've ever seen them. The closest I've ever gotten was when she lost her bikini top at my parents' pool the summer between our freshman and sophomore years of high school. She covered herself and ran inside before I got a good look. The nipples, though? They poke through the flimsy cotton fabric and give me an eyeful.

"Hey, Mandy Cake," I say.

"Sorry. I didn't hear you knock. Did you get a cup of coffee?" She points to the drip coffee maker on a kitchen counter.

"No. I stopped at the new Bean There Done That after my run this morning."

"You want anything else? I've got some glazed doughnuts, or I can make you some scrambled eggs."

"I'm good. Thanks."

Mandy always wants to cook me something. Every time I come over, it's, "Can I get you this? Can I get you that?" She once told me it's because I take her out to expensive dinners sometimes. She can't afford to do that for me in return, so she likes to offer what she can. She doesn't need to worry about that, but no matter how many times I tell her, she still tries to take care of me. To be honest, I don't mind. Not at all. It's comforting.

Her laptop is set up on the small table in the kitchen—or rather, the kitchen area. Mandy pours herself a cup of coffee and then sits down, motioning for me to do the same.

"I set up a profile yesterday, but it's not public yet. Should I call myself Amanda or Mandy?"

"How about Mandy Cake?" I wink.

"Not in this lifetime." She rolls her eyes. "Mandy sounds

a little more playful than Amanda. But do I want to sound playful?"

"Use Amanda," I say dryly.

"Okay. I'm trying to find the right picture."

"Let me look at my phone."

I scan my photos, looking for one of Amanda that would make a good Lustr profile picture.

And then I wonder... Maybe I *shouldn't* be looking for a good photo. Maybe I should be looking for a *bad* photo. The idea of Amanda on Lustr... She's just too sweet and innocent for this. If I set her up with a lousy profile, no one will respond.

But that's a nasty thing to do. It's not me. Still...I can't help thinking about it. The last thing I want is for my best friend to get involved with some troll or womanizer on this silly app.

There's no shortage of good pictures of Mandy on my phone. The best one is from a year ago from a party at my parents' house. It was a semiformal affair to celebrate their thirtieth anniversary. Mandy showed up in a black miniskirt and a pink silk camisole. And yeah, her nipples were showing.

I had some very non–Mandy Cake thoughts about her that night.

But I pushed them away. Amanda and I? We'll never happen. There's way too much history there, and my tastes? They're *definitely* not for her. Besides, she deserves more than I'm capable of giving her.

I sigh. I have to let her do this, no matter my feelings about it. I pass my phone to her. "What about this one?"

She smiles. "Wow. I didn't know you took that."

"Don't you remember? It was right after the champagne toast, and you were standing by the bar, getting a refill. You had taken your glasses off. I don't know why. But you looked so...serene."

And sexy, but I keep that to myself.

"This doesn't even look like me."

"Mandy Cake, it looks *exactly* like you."

Her cheeks pinken, giving her a rosy blush, and she looks back to her laptop screen. "I did a little research last night after you dropped me off after dinner. Apparently, on Lustr, the idea is to make a good first impression quickly. That means a good photo."

"This *is* a good photo."

"This is the *best* photo. It almost looks professional. How did you manage the lighting like that?"

"It's my parents' house. It's well lit. But, Mandy Cake, you looked good that night. This is what you looked like. This is what you *look* like."

She blushes further. "So I can use this one? It's not…lying? I mean, in real life I wear glasses."

"Why don't you wear your contacts?"

"Because you know I can't stand touching my eyes." She makes an adorable scrunched expression with her nose.

"Right."

"I've tried, Jack."

We've had this conversation many times. Mandy has this weird phobia about touching her eyes, but her unique silvery gray eyes are her best feature. Or maybe it's her full lips. Or her nipples that make themselves known at the slightest whiff of cool air.

"Do you want me to try to find a picture this good where you're wearing your glasses?"

"God, no. This is the best picture." She sighs. "I'll try the damned contacts again."

"Okay. Yeah, let me airdrop it to you."

I send her the photo against my better judgment. She needs me to be a friend right now, not an overprotective best friend.

"Okay. Thanks." She taps on her computer. "Profile pic is uploaded. Now…my bio." She sighs. "I'm a virtual assistant who loves Jane Austen novels and Japanese food. My God, I'm a boring person."

I shake my head. "That's not boring. Everyone loves Jane Austen and Japanese food."

"That's what makes it boring, Jack. There's nothing unique about me. Nothing that stands out."

I'm honestly not sure how to help her here. I've never been on one of these apps.

I run a hand through my hair. "All right, I guess you want to appear normal, right? I mean, no one goes on these apps looking for someone strange. So…what are some other facts about you?"

"I've watched all the Star Wars movies a million times, but that just makes me a nerd."

"Actually, that's kind of cute. But say something like, 'I can quote Princess Leia from every Star Wars movie' or something."

She starts tapping notes on her laptop but then pauses.

"That's not too dorky?" she asks, her big eyes blinking up at me behind her glasses.

Maybe a little. But if she attracts Star Wars nerds, I won't have to worry about her.

"Not at all. Who doesn't love Star Wars?"

"You, for one," Amanda says.

"I'm just not really into sci-fi. But plenty of men are."

"All right," Amanda says. "So far I have, 'Twenty-nine-year-old virtual assistant, college-educated, loves Jane Austen and Japanese food, can quote every line of Princess Leia from the Star Wars movies.'" She clears her throat. "Shouldn't I say something…sexy?"

"No," I say with a firm shake of my head, shoving my hands deep into my front pockets. "Not unless you're looking for a hookup. That's not what you're looking for, is it, Mandy Cake?"

She doesn't reply right away, which makes my stomach clench a little. Mandy hooking up? One-nighters? Quick fucks?

I can't stand the thought of it.

"No, of course not. I want something long-term, something that may lead to a lifetime."

A lifetime.

That is so far from what I'm ever after, it's hard to consider it for someone else. Especially for Mandy. I guess I never imagined she wouldn't be there for me forever. What if she *does* meet someone? Someone she gets serious with? Starts a family with?

What will that do to our relationship?

I'm being selfish. Part of me has always been a little bit selfish with Mandy. She's my best friend. She always has been, even when our paths diverged starting in middle school and then further when we went to high school. She was a brain who played the clarinet in the marching band. I was a jock who started for the football, baseball, and basketball teams. We both took AP classes, so that's how we maintained a relationship. We studied together, usually one or two nights a week after dinner and after all my practices were over. Though she did come to all my games to cheer me on. At football games, she was the loudest voice from the marching band section.

Amanda and Jackson. Even when we didn't run in the same circles, we never let our friendship suffer.

But a serious relationship for either of us?

How can our friendship *not* suffer if that happens?

Stop being selfish, I say to myself.

"It's all right to say that, isn't it?" Amanda asks, her front teeth digging into her plump bottom lip. "That I'm looking for something serious?"

"Sure. I suppose so. Christ, Mandy Cake, I don't know how this all works."

"That's because you've always been the center of attention, Jack. Always hordes of women around you. It's been that way since we went through puberty fifteen years ago."

Amanda's not wrong. I shot up six inches between seventh

and eighth grade. Once my testosterone kicked in, all my sports workouts gave me the physique I still have.

"I don't know," Amanda continues. "If I say I *am* looking for something serious, I'm going to scare off half the men."

"Yeah, the half you don't want. Look, most guys are on this app for hookups."

"You really think so?"

"I don't think so, Mandy. I know so."

She bites her bottom lip again. "But you're not on Lustr? How would you know?"

"Because I'm a *guy*. That's what guys are looking for. Most of them anyway. They're all horny, and they're all looking for a quick fuck."

She casts her gaze downward.

Crap. I've upset her.

"Not *all* guys, Mandy. I'm sure there are some who are where you are. Who want more than just a quick hookup."

"Yeah, but I'm not going to find them on this app, am I?"

"You don't know that. I suppose you start by being honest and then seeing if anyone matches with you."

She nods and taps a few things into her computer.

"What are you writing?" I ask.

"Just some stuff. What I'm looking for."

"Good."

Perhaps she'll find someone. Someone to fall in love with, to make a life with.

That's what she wants, and that's what she deserves.

I try to ignore the lump in my stomach.

CHAPTER THREE

Amanda

I went against Jackson's advice. I used Mandy as my name instead of Amanda. Apparently, your name and age are the two things you can't change on Lustr, so if I want to change them, I'll have to create an entirely new profile.

I went against Jackson's advice on something else as well.

Yes, I want to find someone long-term, but if Jackson really thinks this app isn't going to have guys looking for the same, I had to remind myself why I was *really* taking such a bold step.

To get over Jackson once and for all.

And to do that, I don't need to fall in love with some forever guy. I just need *someone* to replace my best friend in my fantasies. To that end, the app will work just as well.

Besides, if I'm eventually going to find a permanent relationship, getting some experience isn't a bad idea, either. I'm not untried, not in the technical sense, but I may as well be. I lost my virginity in college with a fumbling Tracy Fredrickson, a guy in my freshman psychology class. We weren't involved, but we got paired on a group project about sexuality. During the investigation phase, we found out we were both virgins, so we decided to remedy the situation. Good deal, right?

Wrong.

The coupling of two virgins is something no one should have to live through. If I had it to do over again, I'd find somebody with a lot of experience and knew what he was doing.

Tracy knew nothing, and I knew nothing.

Sure, we were both nerds. We had both read all the textbooks about human sexuality. Hell, I'd even read several graphic romance novels.

Tracy Fredrickson was no romance hero.

Far from it.

From high school on, I always imagined losing my virginity to Jackson. He had never looked at me that way. Not even once. Why should he, when he has always had women hanging on him like the ivy that crawls up the brick chimney on his parents' massive house?

He and I aren't going to happen. He's made it very clear that I'll never be anything more than a friend and that he's not into commitment. I can walk around half-naked, and Jackson doesn't even notice. Hell, I doubt he even knows I have boobs. Since I can't have what I want, I'll look for what I *need*.

A teacher. Someone to teach me the art of seduction and lovemaking. And once I learn…maybe I can find someone who wants a real commitment. Maybe I can settle for someone *not* Jackson. And if not, at least I won't be lusting after my best friend anymore. I'll have new fantasies to occupy my thoughts.

The minute Jackson left to go to the office—yes, on a Sunday—I rewrote my bio.

I'm twenty-nine years old—a virtual assistant who hides behind a computer screen most days. I love sweet cherries, pink roses, sushi, Jane Austen, and Princess Leia. I'm looking for a man with experience. A man who's willing to teach me the art of kissing, of seduction, of lovemaking. Let me be your willing protégé.

I purposefully say nothing about my looks and let the photo

do the talking. I read over the bio again. Then I read it out loud.

And I'm so damned thankful that Jackson is not on Lustr, so he'll never see this.

I let my finger hover over the Submit button.

If I do this, I *will* get matches. That bio combined with the photo Jackson gave me will definitely lead to something. Probably multiple somethings. I draw in a deep breath. Hold a few seconds.

Then—

Submit.

• • •

Eight o'clock Monday morning. Time to begin my day. I work for a romance author as her assistant. Sure, it's a lot of busywork— sending out packages, arranging her schedule. I also take care of her social media, basically pretending to be her as I post. I was an English Lit major, so I do light editing sometimes, and I proofread all her work after it comes back from content editing.

I love my job. As an introvert, I adore pretending to be someone else. Someone way more interesting than Amanda Thomas. I can take on a different personality and be Lily Jade, *New York Times* bestselling author of the Rock Hard Steel series.

In real life, Lily Jade is Lorraine Stuckey, a fifty-year-old librarian. Online? She's a svelte thirtysomething-year-old who uses a stock photo as a profile pic and introvert Amanda Thomas as her personality.

My Lily persona is the persona I've decided to use for Lustr.

Except Lily Jade knows *everything* about sex. How else could she write such steamy novels? I'm well-versed in her novels. I have to be in order to *be* her online.

She can write sex like the best of them. Her readers call

her the "Steinbeck of Steam" because her style is both literary and smutty.

I scan my email quickly to see if Lily has any special instructions for the day. Nope, nothing new, so it's business as usual.

Which means...

I can check my Lustr.

I log into my account and—

"Oh my God," I say out loud.

Matches. Lots and lots of matches.

I'll be the best teacher you've ever had, sweetheart.

Hmm. Seems a little overconfident. Next...

We can learn from each other.

Since I basically know nothing...um...no. Next...

You're drop-dead gorgeous, baby. I can't wait to feel your lips around my hard cock.

What about teaching me anything? Sounds like he read a Lily Jade novel, or he just wants a blow job. Next...

I've been looking for a protégé. Will you be my bitch?

I'm no one's bitch. Next...

On and on, and nothing strikes my fancy. Only then do I realize I'm only giving the profile photos a cursory look. Interesting. I'm not searching for the best-looking guy out there. I'm searching for the one who—

I pull up the next match.

This time? I take a look at the profile pic first. He's wearing a black mask that covers his eyes and most of his cheeks. Not only that, the photo is black-and-white, so I can't ascertain the color of his hair or his eyes.

I'm instantly intrigued.

You're beautiful. And sexy. And interesting. I love classic literature and sushi and the sweetness of a cherry on my tongue. I love to scatter pink rose petals on the bed before making love. You say you want a teacher? I can teach you what I know, but are you ready? Because I like things dark. Dark and rough and sexy. I can take you places you never knew existed, and in those places, you will find pleasure like you've never known... though I fear you're way too innocent for what I have in mind.

The sweetness of a cherry on my tongue. Is that a double entendre? Doesn't matter. It gives me goose bumps either way. Seriously. Goose bumps actually skitter over my flesh.

Is this guy truly for real?

His profile name is simply Mr. Dark.

To me? He's Mr. Dark and Sexy.

Mr. Dark and Sexy who can make a woman squirm with words alone.

And I *am* squirming. More action is going on between my legs at this moment than has in a long time.

When I say I lack experience, I'm not overexaggerating. I'm not even sure I've ever had a real orgasm. After the fumbling attempt with Tracy in college, I had a few dates here and there, but I stayed celibate until I was twenty-four. That was the year I dated Seamus Murphy for nearly a year. Seamus was a gorgeous red-haired Irishman who was a lot of fun to hang out with but didn't have a lot of interest between the sheets. I found out why six months after we broke up. He's now married to the love of his life—John Richards. I see the two of them around at the market every now and then, and even though I know it has nothing to do with me that his sexual orientation doesn't include a person with a vagina, it still stings a little.

That's about it. I've dated here and there, none of which ever amounted to anything. I've only been to bed with two men—an inept virgin and a closeted gay man.

So when I say I'm inexperienced? I'm not blowing smoke up anyone's ass.

I'm sure as hell *not* ready for Mr. Dark and Sexy. He got that right. I'm innocent.

But you know what? I made a decision yesterday to be

proactive, so proactive I will be.

Good morning, Mr. Dark. I'm intrigued by you and your offer, and I'd like to know more.

After considering several other things to say, I leave it at that and hit Send.

I'm about ready to check Lily's socials when my computer dings with a response from Mr. Dark and Sexy.

Tonight. If you're ready.

Tonight? It's a work night. I rarely go out on weeknights. It's not like I have girls to hang out with. I don't have an Isabella or a Gigi of my own. All I have is Jackson. He's all I've ever needed—in more ways than one.

I rise and pace around my small apartment. I pour myself another cup of coffee, take one sip, and then set it on the counter. I'm already on edge. The last thing I need is more caffeine.

A pinball seems to be ricocheting over every part of my insides. My nipples are hard, and the tickle between my legs is so intense, I can't stand it.

The only other times I've felt this way? During my fantasies about Jackson.

But those are just that—fantasies.

This could be a reality.

Sure, I fantasize about Jackson. I fantasize about him doing to me all the things I read about in Lily's books. I fantasize about him doing the things to me I've seen the few times I've watched pornography.

Still, that doesn't mean I have any experience. My experience—other than Tracy and Seamus—is all imaginary.

Before I can overthink further, I sit back down at the table in front of my laptop.

Okay. Tonight it is.

My finger drops on the key, hitting Send.

Okay, Mr. Dark and Sexy. Let's see what you've got.

CHAPTER FOUR

Jackson

"Hey, Mandy," I drawl into the phone.

"I did it, Jack."

"Did what?" I say with as much innocence in my tone as I can muster.

"I responded to one of my matches. On Lustr."

"Oh?"

"Yeah. He wants to see me tonight."

"Tonight? Sounds a little overeager to me."

She pauses a few seconds. "Yeah. I suppose you could be right."

"Of course I'm right, Mandy."

"Thank you, Jack."

"For what?"

"For not calling me Mandy Cake."

Huh. No, I didn't call her Mandy Cake, which is unlike me. Why didn't I? I force out a chuckle. "You've only been pestering me about that our whole lives."

"Can it stop now, Jack? For real?"

No, it can't stop. It can't stop for one simple reason. If I stop thinking of my best friend as Mandy Cake and start thinking of her as Amanda, I may start to want more from her than just friendship. There have been a few close calls over the years, but I've always been able to shove my attraction down deep. Kill it with a well-placed "Mandy Cake." Besides, my Mandy Cake is not ready for the kind of relationship I like—which isn't a relationship at all, since I don't do relationships.

It's sex. Dirty sex that can get rough and nasty and painful.

But God...the pleasure.

I clear my throat. "How many matches did you get?"

"Lots. More than I could believe."

What the hell did she expect? When you go on Lustr and basically ask for someone to teach you sex, every horny guy in New York is going to respond.

Yeah, I joined Lustr just to stalk her profile.

I couldn't freaking believe it.

"I see. And one of them wants to get together with you tonight?"

"Is that so surprising?"

No, it's not surprising at all. But I keep this to myself.

"You really shouldn't go," I tell her.

"Are you serious?"

I sigh. "Fine. If you go to a public place and meet him there, there's no reason to be apprehensive."

"Really, Jack, you treat me like a three-year-old sometimes. Of course I know better than to go someplace private with someone I've never met."

"All right, all right. Don't take anything the wrong way. To me, you're innocent. A little naive. I don't want you to get taken advantage of."

"Maybe that's what I need. Maybe I need someone to take advantage of me. Maybe I need to *give* him the advantage. How the hell else am I going to—"

I run a hand through my hair. "Please don't go out and do something you may regret just because you're angry with me."

"There you go again. Giving me no credit at all. I'm twenty-nine years old. I graduated summa cum laude. I make a good living, and I'm—"

"I'm sorry," I interrupt her. This whole situation makes my chest feel tight, but that's not her fault. "I'm sorry, Mandy. You know I didn't mean any of it that way."

She pauses a moment. "I know."

"You also know how much you mean to me," I tell her. "I'm just concerned."

"Well, you don't have to be," she huffs out. "I'm perfectly capable of taking care of myself."

"So...what are you going to do? Have I talked you out of meeting this guy tonight?"

"I don't know."

"All right." I check my watch. "I've got a meeting in five minutes. You okay?"

"Fine," she says tersely.

"Call me if you need anything. Always."

"Sure, Jack. Bye."

After ending the call, I shove my phone in my pocket, grab my laptop, and head to the conference room.

If she responded to one profile, she may respond to another. And another.

I shake my head. I have no choice—I have to erase the thoughts from my mind and concentrate on this meeting with several important executives.

I just hope I can get through it without worrying about Mandy.

Besides...I have a date tonight.

CHAPTER FIVE

Amanda

No sooner do I hang up from Jackson when Frankie calls. "Yeah?" I say a little more harshly than I mean to.

"Great news, Mandy. I got a private fitting tonight at the bridal shop. Isabella and Gigi can make it. Can you?"

"Tonight? Really, Frankie?"

"Yeah, tonight. You're not busy, are you?"

Am I really that predictable? I lift my chin. "Actually, I *do* have plans. I have a date."

Frankie doesn't respond right away. What would she do if she knew I actually have a date with Mr. Dark and Sexy? Although he hasn't gotten back to me yet with any information. So perhaps I don't have a date.

"I guess I can try to reschedule..." Frankie eventually says.

Oh, jeez. This is my sister. Not some Lustr hookup. Of course she takes priority. "It's all right, Frank. I can be there. Text me the information."

"No, it's fine," she says. "I didn't mean to imply...you know."

I sigh. No, I don't think she meant to be rude. She never does. And I don't think she meant to just assume I would be available. She's on cloud nine. She's getting married. And the truth is that I'm usually available on short notice.

"I know," I say. "And I apologize. I'm a little on edge. But it's no big deal to reschedule my evening out. I want to be there for you."

"I can help with that. Isabella, Gigi, and I are going out for a drink afterward. We'd love for you to join us."

"I'll see how I'm feeling at the time."

After all, going out with Frankie and her two besties, all of whom are beautiful and built, may lead to meeting someone *not* on Lustr.

Maybe I'll even put those dreaded contacts in.

After ending the call, Frankie texts me the information for the bridal shop. I'm lucky that my sister has amazingly good taste. She won't choose one of those goofy lime-green dresses for her bridesmaids.

Time to update Mr. Dark and Sexy.

Sorry. Something came up. I can't make it tonight. Some other time, I hope?

This time, he replies right away.

You're not ready.

What? He just assumes I'm not ready? Does he really think I'm lying? Something *did* come up. My sister is getting married in three months, and I have to go to a fitting.

I let my fingers hover on the keyboard as I try to compose something in my head. Do I tell the truth? That I have to go to a bridesmaids' dress fitting?

Always a bridesmaid, never a bride.

Isn't that the truth.

Nope, I'm not telling Mr. Dark and Sexy that I'm going to a bridesmaid dress fitting. That'll make me look kind of pathetic.

Maybe you're the one who's not ready.

Part of me can't believe I actually typed those words.

Before I change my mind, I hit Send.

Then I exit out of Lustr. I can't let this consume me. I do have work to do, after all. Time to check Lily's social media.

...

I knew I could count on Frankie to choose a lovely bridesmaid dress. It's dusty plum satin, mid-length, with spaghetti straps. I could totally wear it again. You know, for all those cocktail parties I'm invited to.

Still, it's classy and gorgeous, and it looks great on all three of us. My curvier hourglass figure, Isabella's long and lithe body, and Gigi's large posterior. Frankie also showed us—and modeled—her wedding dress. Basically the same dress as ours, except floor length in ivory satin with some intricate beading. Perfect for a less formal wedding at a home.

I decide to join Frankie and the others for drinks after the fitting. I didn't touch my eyeball for nothing, after all. My eyes are already dried out from the contact lenses.

We end up at a hotel bar with a dance floor—not a club, thank God—a few buildings down from the bridal shop. We're lucky to snag one of those high tables that seats four.

It's early yet, only eight thirty. I had a sandwich before the fitting, but it's wearing off now.

"Do you want to order some food?" I ask the others.

"Not for me," Gigi says. "I'm on a diet."

"Me neither." From Isabella.

"I can't gain a single pound before the wedding," Frankie adds. "I can't risk having to do my fitting all over again."

I resist an eye roll. They all look fine. Sure, Gigi has a large booty, but it works for her. Men love it.

In fact—

She's the first one of us to get approached. She's a beauty—naturally light blond hair, big blue eyes, and of course that posterior for which privileged women pay plastic surgeons thousands.

"Would you like to dance?" an Armani-clad gentleman asks Gigi.

"I'd like that very much."

She rises and heads to the dance floor. Even in her casual leggings and tunic, Gigi looks great dancing with a gentleman in a suit.

A server approaches us. "What can I get you, ladies?"

"I'd love a martini," Frankie says.

Her drink of choice. Personally, I think it tastes like rubbing alcohol.

"Cosmo for me," Isabella says in that bored tone that works for her.

"And you?" She glances at me.

"Sidecar. And an order of seared ahi nachos."

"Good enough. I'll be back with your drinks soon. The nachos will take a few minutes longer."

"Thank you," I say.

Isabella and Frankie both glare at me.

"What? I told you I was hungry."

"Mom and Dad aren't going to pay for an extra fitting for your dress," Frankie warns.

I roll my eyes at her. "One order of ahi nachos is not going to make me gain a size."

In truth, I haven't gained a size since I was fourteen. I've had the same body forever, and Frankie knows it. That's the one thing I have on her. I don't have to watch my weight. As much as I'd love to be tall and slim like Isabella, genetics didn't make me that way. I have our mother's cute little figure. Frankie takes after our father. She's taller, with a tendency to gain weight around the middle.

After one dance, Gigi makes her way back to the table just as our drinks are being served. "You didn't order anything for me?"

"Sorry," Frankie says. "We didn't know what you'd want."

"Don't worry about that," the man with her says. "I'll get you something from the bar. What would you like?"

"What are you drinking?" Gigi bats her eyes.

"Jack on the rocks."

"Sounds wonderful. I'll have the same."

The man exits quickly and heads to the bar.

"Gigi," Isabella says, still in the robot tone. "You hate hard liquor."

"I'll suffer through. Isn't he luscious? He works for Braden Black."

I perk to attention. Jackson works for Braden Black.

"What's his name?" I ask.

"Dylan something or other. Andrews or Anderson or something like that. He's meeting someone here. A coworker. But he's not here yet. All the better for me."

I take a sip of my sidecar. It's my drink of choice. Lemon juice and cognac with a sugared rim to add just a touch of sweetness.

Dylan returns with his and Gigi's drinks.

"Why don't you pull up a chair?" Gigi says.

Dylan looks around. "I don't see a spare one anywhere. But there are two seats at the bar if you'd like to join me."

"You don't mind, do you?" Gigi glances around our table.

"Of course not," I say.

Isabella and Frankie don't look as thrilled.

Really, Frank? You're engaged, for God's sake. Let Gigi have her fun.

Frankie, Isabella, and Gigi have been in a perpetual competition for men since I can remember.

"What's up with her?" Isabella says after Gigi leaves. "This is your night, Frank."

"Oh, it's okay."

Right. Frankie wants to sulk, but she's engaged. She's supposed to be happy. Penn Berry better make my sister happy or he'll answer to me.

"Why don't we toast?" I hold up my sidecar. "To Frankie and Penn."

That brings a smile to Frankie's face.

"Yes," Isabella says monotonously. "To Frankie and Penn. And to many happy years."

We clink glasses, and I take another sip of my sidecar when—

"Hey, Mandy."

My heart jolts. I'd know that whiskey-toned voice anywhere.

"Don't mind if I do." Jackson sits down in the empty chair at our table.

"Oh," I say, willing my voice not to shake. "Yeah. Please join us, Jack."

"What are you ladies up to tonight?"

"Are you the coworker Dylan was meeting?" Frankie asks.

"Guilty. But I see he found someone else to occupy his time." Jackson waves to our server, who nearly takes out two customers getting to our table.

Yeah. Jackson has that effect on women.

I should know.

"What can I get you, sir?" she asks, smiling.

"Tanqueray and tonic, please."

"Absolutely. Coming right up."

Jackson turns back to us. "So...anyone going to answer me?"

"What?" I say.

"I asked what you ladies were up to this evening."

"Oh, right. We had to get fitted for our dresses for Frankie's wedding."

"Mandy told me the good news." Jackson nods to Frankie. "Congratulations, love."

"Thank you. The wedding's in three months. I hope we can count on you being there."

"Wouldn't miss it."

Our server—I think her name is Jane—brings Jackson's drink and sets it on the table. In record time.

"Thanks, love," Jackson says and gives her that dazzling smile.

Jane blushes and whisks away.

Love. Jackson calls everyone *love*. Everyone except me. I get to be Mandy Cake.

Jackson is a world-class flirt. He has been since puberty. It drives me up the wall. Not only up the wall but across the ceiling and back down the other side.

He has no feelings for the server. He has no feelings for any of the women he calls *love*. I'm not even sure he's ever had feelings for anyone he's dated seriously. And by seriously, I mean a maximum of three months. I rarely even get to meet any of them. In fact, I'm glad when I don't. The few times he's introduced me to a date, he's been more serious than normal. Which of course makes me feel terrible, since I'm hopelessly in love with him.

Luckily, none of them have lasted, even the ones he's introduced me to.

Isabella stands. "You want to dance, Jack?"

Really, Isabella?

To be fair, Isabella and Gigi don't know my true feelings for Jack. Neither does Frankie, though I'm sure she suspects. It's not something I talk about. Not to anyone.

It's my own private hell.

Jack takes a drink of his gin and tonic. "Sure, love." He leads Isabella to the dance floor.

It's a weeknight at a hotel bar, so the floor is hardly crowded. About five other couples besides Isabella and Jackson are dancing. It's a fast song, so they're not touching. Does Isabella have a thing for Jackson? I can't blame her if she does, but she's never mentioned it to me. Maybe she just wants to dance. Sometimes a cigar is just a cigar, after all.

Gigi and Dylan join them on the dance floor, and I finish my sidecar. I motion to Jane to bring me another, which she does, along with my nachos and four plates. I guess she thinks I'm sharing.

I'm not a big drinker, but I tend to have more than one when I'm forced to watch Jackson interact with other women.

"Do you want to try these?" The obligatory offering to Frankie.

She grabs one of the small plates and helps herself to a nacho. "I shouldn't. But these look fabulous."

I heap several nachos onto a plate for myself and take a bite. Yum. Seared ahi is sublime, and with green onions, soy sauce and wasabi, just a touch of crema, piled on deep-fried flour tortilla chips?

Wow.

Frankie and I have nearly depleted the nachos, and I've placed another order, when Isabella and Jackson return to the table.

"Eating without me, Mandy?"

At least he didn't add the *Cake* this time. "Don't worry. Another order's on the way. Seared ahi nachos."

"Sounds great." He downs the rest of his gin and tonic. "How is…everything?"

"Fine. We just talked on the phone today, Jackson."

He raises an eyebrow, and it dawns on me. He's asking about Lustr.

I raise my eyebrow back at him, mentally saying, *Do not speak of that in front of my sister.*

He seems to get it as he turns to Frankie. "Where's Penn tonight?" he asks.

"I've no idea. He knew we were doing the fitting tonight, and you know. He can't see me in my dress."

Jackson nods. "Three months?"

"Yes," Frankie says. "It'll be at Penn's parents' place. Invitations will go out soon. We don't have time to do a save the date."

Jackson nods again as Jane brings the second plate of nachos and another sidecar for me.

"I'll have another." Jackson jiggles his glass that is now filled with nothing but ice.

"Right away." Jane smiles.

Jackson grabs a plate and piles nachos onto it. "These look amazing."

"They are." I grab a few more for my own plate. "Frankie?"

"No more for me. I'm full."

"Isabella?" I ask.

"Thank you, but no." Although she eyes them longingly.

Jane brings Jackson's drink, and he hands her his credit card. "Put all of this on my tab, love."

"You don't need to do that," I say.

"I know. I want to."

"Thank you, Jackson." Frankie smiles. "I'm strapped right now with the wedding and all. I appreciate your generosity."

"Yes, thanks." This from Isabella, who I swear to God doesn't know the meaning of intonation.

Seems to work for Jackson, though. After he finishes the food on his plate, he takes Isabella back to the dance floor for another spin.

While I order a third plate of nachos.

CHAPTER SIX

Jackson

Dylan Andrews won't be getting a promotion anytime soon. Going out for drinks tonight was his idea, not mine, and I agreed, since my date fell through. He works under me, and he's gunning for a recommendation to the IT department. I'm in marketing management. So was he, until he finished his master's degree in computer information systems. Now he wants to switch departments, and they want my recommendation.

Fine. Maybe I'll give the recommendation just to get him the hell out of my department. If he thinks asking me to have drinks with him and then picking up a woman instead of talking to me will get him where he wants to be, he's deluded.

Isabella Phillips is tall and great on her feet, and she's not a big talker, so I can concentrate on the music.

I've danced with Mandy on occasion, but it felt…weird.

Both right and wrong.

In truth? Mandy's a beautiful woman, and if she weren't my Mandy Cake…

I've had some very un-best-friend-like thoughts about her lately.

But I can't allow myself to go there. I don't want to ruin her.

In her sweet and innocent way, she's so perfect, and nothing should taint that.

Least of all me and my limitations.

The song ends, and a slow dance begins. Before I can stop her, Isabella entwines her arms around my neck and we're moving gently to the music. I glance over to the table. Mandy is noshing on more nachos, and if she sees Isabella and me, she makes no indication of it.

The next time I look back at the table, Mandy's gone.

. . .

I call her an hour later.

"Jack?" she says into her phone. "It's eleven o'clock."

"I just wanted to make sure you're okay. You seemed to leave the bar in a hurry."

"Didn't Frankie tell you? I have an early meeting in the morning with Lily."

"She didn't mention it."

In truth, I didn't ask Frankie or anyone else where Mandy had run off to. Once I disentangled myself from Isabella, I took care of the tab and left. When I got back to my place, I called Mandy.

"Oh," she says. "Well, I do."

I don't call her out on the lie. She never has an early meeting with Lily. Lily lives on the West Coast, so she's on Pacific time. Here in New York, we're on Eastern time so even a six o'clock a.m. meeting would be nine o'clock for Mandy.

Why is she lying to me?

More and more, we seem to be growing apart.

I suppose it had to happen sooner or later. We're different in so many ways. I want Mandy to be happy, and I know I'm not the one who can give her that.

Maybe I could try fixing her up. I work with some young men who might be right for her. Maybe someone in HR.

"Jack? You still there?"

I clear my throat. "Yeah, I'm here. I'm sorry I bothered you. You want to have lunch tomorrow?"

"Sure. Just text me where and when."

"Will do."

I end the call, and just as I'm about to jump in the shower and get ready for bed, my phone buzzes again.

It's Dylan.

"Yeah?" I say, not kindly.

"Jackson, bro."

First, he's not my bro.

"I wanted to apologize for tonight. But you know..."

"Yeah, I know. You saw a pretty face with a great ass."

"When the man's right, the man's right."

"Not a problem, Dylan. See you at work tomorrow."

Feminine laughter permeates the background. Gigi Frost. Not that I'm surprised. I knew damned well where Dylan was heading tonight.

He is, however, *not* heading to the IT department on a recommendation from me. He's on his own. I like to get laid as much as the next person, but I've worked hard to get where I am in Black Inc., and I didn't let any hot piece of ass keep me from getting there—and plenty tried.

Into the shower.

And I find myself with a rock-hard dick.

I'm not exactly sure why. A few dances with Isabella Phillips didn't do that for me. At any rate, the shower I take is a cold one.

When I'm done, I'm still horny as hell.

I could go to the club. It's open until three a.m. I'm sure someone would be up for a scene. I even go so far as to dress in my club gear. I stand at the door of my apartment, ready to open it, but my hand doesn't quite get to the knob.

I'm not sure how long I stand there—or what I think about—
before I head back to my bedroom, peel off my black jeans,
and go to bed.

•••

Four a.m. comes early, but I love it. I mix myself a protein shake
and head downstairs to the gym on the first floor of my building.
Today is arms and abs day. After a forty-five-minute workout, I
hit the treadmill. Normally, I like to run outside, but the weather
is drizzly and dreary this morning, so the treadmill it is. I plug
myself into some hard rock that keeps my blood pumping, set
the machine to a steep incline, and begin.

I don't think during my workouts—not about work, not
about women, not about anything in particular. I listen to tunes
and concentrate on physical fitness. I've been an athlete most
of my life, and this is my *me* time.

Once my workout is complete, I head to the showers and
then the steam room. Then back up to my apartment to dress
for work.

Once at the office, who's waiting for me but Dylan Andrews.

"Hey," he says, following me into my office. "I want to
apologize again for last night."

"Not a problem."

I don't make eye contact. It's a little trick I picked up when I
first interned for Braden and Ben Black. They both do it. Some
people will think it's because you're too insecure to look them
in the eye, but in truth, it's showing them they're not important
enough to bother with.

Will Dylan get it? I honestly don't give a rat's ass.

"Can we arrange a do-over?"

This time, I look up from my phone and deliberately meet
his gaze. "No. We can't."

His cheeks redden slightly. "Look, man, I said I was sorry."

"Mr. Andrews—"

He reddens further at my use of his surname.

"You need to decide what's important. Is it your career? Is it drinks with someone whose recommendation you want? Or is it a quick lay?"

"You're out of line, man. I'm allowed to have a social life." His voice cracks.

Just a bit, but I notice.

"Not if you blow off a coworker after *you* set up the meeting." I shake my head. "I hope Gigi Frost was worth it."

"Frost? Is that her last name?"

I pick up a report off my desk, scanning the numbers in the spreadsheet. "Mr. Andrews, leave my office."

"Wait, wait, wait. Does this mean I'm not getting your recommendation?"

"Figure that one out for yourself."

He slinks out of my office with his tail between his legs.

I sit down at my desk, return several phone calls, and then…

I check the Lustr website.

CHAPTER SEVEN

Amanda

Lunch. Lunch with Jackson.

He texted me, wants me to meet him for sushi at one of our favorite dive sushi bars. I haven't checked my Lustr account again. The thought is kind of daunting. And now? I have to meet Jackson for lunch, so Lustr will have to wait.

I take the subway, and when I reach the sushi bar, Jackson hasn't arrived yet. I find a seat at the bar next to a single woman who is finishing up. I figure she'll be done by the time Jack gets here.

"What can I get you?" one of the chefs asks me.

"Salmon skin roll and a dragon roll, please. Plus an order of nigiri unagi."

"Any sake?"

"No, thank you. Just some water will be fine."

I don't drink during the day. That's not exactly true. I don't *prefer* to drink during the day.

Then the text from Jack.

Can't make it. Something came up.

Damn it all. And I've already ordered. I catch the chef's attention. "Could you make that to-go?"

"Leaving so soon?" Warm breath caresses the back of my neck.

I turn on my stool and meet the gaze of a strikingly handsome dark-haired and dark-eyed man. He seems familiar in a way, and lord, is he good-looking.

But my heart doesn't do a flip-flop. My heart flip-flops for one man only.

"Yes," I say. "Do you want the seat?"

"Sure, I'd love the seat." He takes the spot next to me that the single woman has vacated. "But only if you stay."

"I've already asked the chef to pack up my rolls."

"Not a problem." He motions to the chef. "The lady will be staying after all, and put her order on my tab."

"Of course, sir."

Before I can object, the man is sitting next to me, and he holds out his hand. "Ben Black."

I hold back a gasp. No wonder he looks so familiar. I've only seen his face plastered all over the news a thousand times. Ben Black. The brother of Braden Black, the blue-collar billionaire from Boston. Also Jackson's employer.

And a known womanizer.

"I'm Amanda Thomas." I shyly put my hand in his large one.

"Were you waiting for someone?"

"I was, but he just canceled on me."

"His loss is my gain."

"What can I get you?" the chef asks Ben.

"What is the lady having?"

"A salmon skin roll, a dragon roll, and unagi."

"I'm not much into the salmon skin myself, but a dragon roll sounds good. Plus a few pieces of yellowtail sashimi." He turns to me. "Really, my poison of choice is oysters on the half shell. I'm from Boston."

"I know."

"You do?"

"Of course. Everyone knows who Braden and Ben Black are. My best friend works for you."

"Does he?"

"Yeah, Jackson Paris. Do you know him?"

Ben's eyebrows rise. "I do indeed. Good man. Very intelligent."

The chef plates my two rolls and slides them in front of me.

"Thank you," I murmur.

"How long have you known Mr. Paris?" Ben asks.

"My whole life."

"Really. Best friends forever, huh?"

"Something like that." Warmth floats into me. Already I feel a blush rising to my cheeks. Just at the mention of Jackson.

Best friends forever. That's all I'll ever be to Jackson.

Yet here is not only a great-looking but also richer-than-God man talking to me at a sushi dive.

Why is he even here? Ben doesn't live here. He lives in Boston, although he and Braden spend a lot of their time here at their New York office—at least according to Jackson.

What are the odds that Ben himself would show up at this tiny little sushi place?

Not good.

Which makes me wonder...

"Why are you here, exactly?" I ask.

"Well...lunch, for starters."

Another surge of warmth touches my cheeks. Why would I ask why he's here? I'm being overly presumptuous. No way was this orchestrated by anything—or anyone—but fate.

Besides, Ben Black has no interest in the likes of me.

"A friend of mine recommended this place," Ben says. "Do you come here often?"

"Yeah, it's one of my favorites. The portions are so much larger than the bigger sushi restaurants."

"Then maybe I found a new favorite as well." He smiles.

And as dazzling as his smile is, it doesn't make my heart nearly stop like Jackson Paris's does.

"Would you excuse me for a moment?" Ben rises and walks out the door of the restaurant, staring at his phone.

My moment for escape has come. I'm able to catch the eye of one of the chefs. "Could you just give me a to-go box, please?"

"Sure."

A moment later, I'm shoving what's left of my two rolls in the box, and I make a quick getaway out the back door.

. . .

Get a grip, Mandy.

I've been sitting in front of my computer, staring at the takeout container holding the rest of my lunch, too frightened to get back on Lustr.

I swallow down my fear, or at least attempt to, and pull up the site.

More matches and more matches. All as ridiculous as the ones I saw yesterday. Then—

Still think you're ready?

Mr. Dark and Sexy.

Goose bumps erupt. So strange. Normally, I only feel this way when I'm thinking about Jackson.

What is it about this person? This masked man behind my computer screen?

My heart pounds. Just when I'm convinced it's going to fly right out of my chest, another message arrives from him.

I won't wait forever.

Normally I'd tell someone who said those words to me to go screw himself. Sure, I may be inexperienced and innocent—Jackson's words, not mine—but I don't take ultimatums lightly.

I'm about ready to move on when—

Don't venture out if you're not ready for the consequences.
Damn.

Damn, damn, damn.

This is what I want. I want experience. I yearn for it. With experience, maybe I can be something more than Mandy Cake to someone. Maybe I can finally get over lusting for my best friend.

Tonight?

I hit Send without thinking about it.

He responds.

Nine p.m.

Where?

An address follows. Oddly, it's one of the buildings owned by Black Inc., though it's a residential building, not their office complex.

Just outside the building? I write.

Tell the doorman you're meeting someone at the bar. It's on the first floor. Have a seat and ask for Alfred. I'll take it from there.

Apprehension surges through me. Fear...but also excitement.

Tonight.

Tonight I will begin my education in the art of sex and seduction.

CHAPTER EIGHT

Jackson

"Found her," Ben says to me.

"How did she look?" I ask.

"She seemed shy. And then, when I had to leave the restaurant to take a quick phone call, she disappeared."

Icicles poke the back of my neck. "What do you mean, she disappeared?"

"I mean, when I got back to my spot at the bar, she was gone."

"That doesn't sound like Amanda. She's never rude."

"I think she was just shy. I mean, here I am, coming up to her in a tiny little sushi bar. She just freaked out a little."

"Amanda doesn't freak out."

"I'm a strange man—a famous, strange man—coming up to her and starting a conversation. Of course she freaked out."

"Well, thanks for checking on her. I hated having to blow her off at the last minute. She's a special woman."

"She seems special. Very pretty but definitely an introvert."

"She is."

"And you haven't..." Ben raises his eyebrows.

"No, I haven't. We're friends. Just friends."

"And you think you can always be just friends?"

"Sure. Why not?"

"Because, Jack, she probably already has feelings for you."

"No. She doesn't."

I've wondered from time to time whether Mandy thinks of me in that way, but I've always concluded that she doesn't. She hasn't given me any hint that she does. Besides, we're just too different. I don't want a relationship—I'm clearly not capable of it—and she wants a white picket fence and 2.4 kids.

But then I wonder...

Does she?

Mandy and I have never really talked about it.

Or rather...*she* doesn't talk about what she ultimately wants. She knows damned well I'm not looking for a relationship—I make no secret of it—but she doesn't know the kind of sex I like.

The kind of sex she could never go for.

The club I frequent is called Black Rose Underground. It's owned by Braden Black, and membership is by invitation only.

When I first started working for Black Inc., the leather club I had been a member of for several years closed.

Braden Black, it turned out, owned a small piece of the club, and he invited a few of the former members to Black Rose. I was one of them. The dues are expensive, but the club is elegant and mysterious. Full confidentiality and elite clientele. As a gold member, I can invite guests, though only one at a time.

I've only exercised that privilege a few times. Normally I play in scenes with members who are already there and available. Sometimes it leads to a date or two after that. Sometimes three months of dating.

The club will scare the pants off Amanda Thomas.

Which is what I'm counting on.

After reading her profile, I decided someone had to scare her off that app. I don't want to keep her from dating, just trying to hook up with random strangers. It's not safe.

Besides, despite what her profile says, she told me she's

looking for someone who wants a long-term relationship. She's being very naive if she thinks a date with anyone on Lustr is going to lead to anything remotely *resembling* forever.

So really, I'm doing her a favor. She'll take one look at Black Rose—and the kind of dark and kinky sex within its walls—and go running back to wanting a sweet man to settle down with and not someone interested in *educating* her.

I swallow hard.

Tonight, Amanda is going to get a very different kind of education.

CHAPTER NINE

Amanda

After putting on and taking off several outfits, I finally decide on simple skinny jeans, black pumps, and a tight black T-shirt. And of course, the contact lenses. I've been wearing them all day. This morning, it only took me ten minutes to get up the courage to touch my eyeball. Last night it took a half hour.

The bar is on the first floor of the Manhattan building. That's where I'm meeting Mr. Dark and Sexy. He gave me no guidance as to what I should wear, but I know how to dress for a bar.

I go all out on my makeup. Even false eyelashes, which I don't normally wear, but they really make my eyes pop. Red lips, too. I'm normally a dusty rose kind of girl, but red?

This seems like a red night.

Mr. Dark and Sexy likes red.

At least in my mind he does.

After a long Uber ride in traffic, I'm a few minutes late. I rush out of the car and into the building.

I walk into the bar, scan the room, but nowhere do I see anyone who might be Mr. Dark and Sexy. Would I even recognize him if I did see him? Between the black-and-white photo and the mask, I'm not sure.

No matter. He may not even be here. After all, I'm supposed to sit at the bar and find someone named Alfred.

Alfred. Is *he* Mr. Dark and Sexy?

No. Mr. Dark and Sexy would have a name like Rock or Talon or Dante. Certainly not Alfred.

I find an empty seat at the bar and sit down.

"What can I get you?" a handsome bartender asks me. He's tall, blond, and muscular. Definitely not an Alfred.

"Nothing."

A sidecar would take the edge off, but I have to be in charge of my faculties. This is a blind date. Anything could happen, and I need to take care of myself. Keep myself safe.

"Then I'll need you to give the seat to someone else," the bartender says. "Nothing personal, just the rules."

"Then give me...a Virgin Mary."

He smiles. "Coming right up."

A Virgin Mary. I have to laugh at myself. I'm not a virgin, but I may as well be.

Then again, isn't that why I'm here? To get experience? To find a teacher?

He slides the Virgin Mary in front of me. "Tell me," he says. "Are you Mandy?"

"Depends on who's asking." I take a sip of the spicy tomato juice and try to ignore the warmth of a flush on my cheeks. I'm seriously trying to flirt with this sexy barkeep? I'm way out of my league.

"Mr. Dark is asking."

My pulse races. "Are you... Are you Alfred?"

"Guilty as charged."

"I guess I just expected..." Damn the heat in my face! "I... you know..."

"I'm afraid I don't know. But it doesn't matter. I'm supposed to give you some information before Mr. Dark finds you."

"Oh?" My pulse races.

"First things first," Alfred says. "I've known Mr. Dark for years. You will be completely safe with him."

"Okay." Just those words make me feel completely *not* safe with him.

I gaze over my shoulder. The exit is near. I can jet out of here right now and go home, delete my Lustr profile, and continue with my mundane life.

My life... My existence...

Damn, my existence.

I'm sick of simply existing. I want to *live*. I want to have sex. I want to learn to please a man and be pleased in return.

"At any time," Alfred continues, "you may leave."

What the hell? Of course I can leave at any time. It's a blind date. That's it. However, I don't reply.

Alfred slides a folder in front of me. "Take a look at these."

I open it. Inside is a nondisclosure agreement for a place called Black Rose Underground.

"I'm afraid I'm not understanding."

"It's a private club. In this building. Read through the agreement. Make sure everything's okay."

"I'm sure everything's fine, but—"

"Look, it's my understanding that you're meeting Mr. Dark for...you know."

"What do you—" I stop abruptly.

I'm the one who wrote that bio. I'm the one who asked for a teacher, asked to be someone's protégé. How did I think that would happen? In a freaking nursery?

Sure, I know how to keep myself safe. But if I want a teacher, I'm going to have to be alone with the guy. I'm going to have to let him...do things with me.

I read through the document. I'm no legal expert, but it seems like a standard nondisclosure agreement. I can't tell anyone about the club, who I may see in the club, what I may see anyone doing in the club. If at any time I feel unsafe, I may leave the club with the help of one of their security people.

Etcetera, etcetera…

"Do you have any questions?" Alfred asks.

Yeah. What is the quickest way to hightail it out of here?

But I stay seated.

Damn it! I've taken the safe route my entire life. Didn't I say I was done existing? Didn't I say I wanted to *live*?

Yes, I'm frightened. But I'm also intrigued.

Anyone who wants to rape me isn't going to ask me to sign something agreeing that I'm allowed to leave at any time with the help of security.

"Your safety is guaranteed," Alfred says. "Above everything else."

"How can anyone guarantee my safety?"

"Mr. Dark will explain."

As usual, I'm overthinking.

This is what I asked for. This is what I joined Lustr for. This is what I wrote that bio for.

I want experience.

With experience, maybe I can get Jackson to see me as something more than just Mandy Cake. And if not? With experience, I'll be able to move on.

I hastily scribble my signature at the bottom, close the folder, and push it back toward Alfred. "Now what?"

"Now…you wait."

All righty, then. I take another long drink of my Virgin Mary and then munch on the celery stalk. I grab my phone out of my pocket, check my email. Nothing important.

How long will I be waiting here?

Then—

I jolt when something silky slides over my eyes.

"Don't be frightened." A whisper caresses the back of my neck.

"Mr. Dark and Sexy?" I ask timidly.

"Mr. Dark," he whispers. "Are you sure you want to do this? You don't have to."

I gulp.

He's giving me a chance to back out.

I should probably take it.

"I'm ready," I say.

"Then come with me."

"But won't people wonder why I—"

"Shh," he whispers. "No one will see you. There's an entrance to the club behind the bar."

"But why am I blindfolded?"

"Doesn't that make it more exciting?" he whispers.

I shiver. He's right. It does.

"I figured it had more to do with the fact that you're taking me to a private club—a place I had to sign an NDA just to enter."

"That's another part of it. Since you're not a member, I can't let you see where the entrances are. But really, don't you think the mysterious aspect is a better explanation?"

He's still whispering. Probably because we're still in the bar. He pulls me into a standing position and then puts an arm around my waist.

"Just walk forward. I'll let you know if you need to turn or anything."

I listen, my ears on alert, for anything out of the ordinary. All I hear are normal bar sounds—the clinking of glasses, the din of conversation. Until—

"We're going to walk down some stairs now," Mr. Dark and Sexy whispers. "Just follow me. Here's the first step."

Carefully, I step down.

"There are fifteen more," he says.

I count to fifteen and then stop, making sure I'm on level ground.

"We will walk down the hallway."

He's still whispering, which has me slightly confused. Everything's quiet now.

"Remember, Mandy," he whispers. "You may leave at any time. If you're feeling unsafe, or if you're frightened, you will be escorted back up to the bar."

"I understand."

"All right." The sound of a door opening. "Welcome to Black Rose Underground."

"May I take my blindfold off now?"

"You may."

"Why are you still whispering?"

"Just setting the mood."

I slip the blindfold off my eyes. Mr. Dark and Sexy stands next to me, wearing black jeans and a leather vest. His entire face is covered by a mask except for his mouth. His hair is dark and slicked back. And his eyes... They're dark as well—as well as I can see in the dim light of the club.

People are dancing on a large dance floor, and along the back wall is a bar. The bartenders—both male and female— are topless. The entire large room is shrouded in a dim red light.

A security guard sits at the desk at the door. "I have your paperwork, ma'am." He turns to Mr. Dark. "Here's her collar and her pager."

"Thank you, Claude." Mr. Dark and Sexy is still whispering.

"Collar? Pager?" I ask.

"He'll explain everything inside," Claude says.

"Okay."

Mr. Dark and Sexy takes my hand—I burn at his touch—and we enter the large area. It's like a ballroom—except no one is dressed for a ball. Some are dressed casually, as I am. Others are clad in sexy leatherwear. Still others in nothing at all.

This is a sex club. A BDSM club. A leather club.

What have I gotten myself into?

My body tingles all over, and I don't know whether it's from fear or desire.

Something about Mr. Dark and Sexy seems familiar to me, but I can't quite place what it is. Whatever it is, I feel safe with him. Protected.

Maybe it's the agreement I signed—the agreement that ensured my safety at all times. But a piece of paper doesn't offer protection. Only *I* can ensure my own protection. Still…I feel safe with him.

He leads me through the room to the bar. Though I hesitate to order any alcohol, I need to do something with my hands. This is definitely *not* the place to order a Virgin Mary.

Mr. Dark and Sexy hasn't said anything since we left Claude. "Mr. Dark?"

"Yes, Mandy?" Still a whisper but a harsh one. It has to be for me to hear over the music playing.

"What did Claude give you?"

He hands me a small pager—it reminds me of the pagers Jack and I get when we're waiting for a table at our favorite sushi place in the Village.

"You'll keep this at your fingertips at all times. If you ever feel unsafe, you simply press the button."

I swallow. "Isn't that what a safe word is for?"

"Yes. But if your mouth is bound, you won't be able to say your safe word."

"What if my mouth *and* hands are bound?" I gulp out.

"That won't happen your first time at the club."

My nerves skitter. Pager. Safe word. *Your safety is guaranteed at all times.* I can leave now. Simply tell Mr. Dark and Sexy I've changed my mind.

All it will take is a couple of words…

"You can leave now, Mandy, if you choose to."

What? Is he reading my mind now?

He nods toward the entrance. "There is no shame in admitting this scene isn't for you."

He turns as though to lead me out, and I reach up and grasp his arm. Yes, I'm scared witless, but not about what might happen next. I'm afraid if I leave, I'll never have the strength to move on from waiting for Jackson to notice me.

"No. I want to stay."

He holds my gaze, the muscle in his jaw clenching before he offers a single nod and ushers me toward the bar.

Mr. Dark and Sexy motions to one of the bartenders—a female with average-size breasts and nipple rings. She's beautiful. Everyone is beautiful here.

But are they? Honestly, I don't really notice any physical characteristics. Everyone is just so...

I can't find a word.

A few minutes later, two drinks slide in front of us.

"What is it?"

"Taste," Mr. Dark and Sexy whispers.

Willing myself not to shake, I pick up the glass of orange liquid and take a sip.

Then I laugh. "It's orange juice. Just orange juice."

The bartender smiles. "We don't serve a person alcohol unless that person specifically asks for it."

Mr. Dark and Sexy picks up his glass—his is clear with a twist of lime—and takes a sip.

"Are you ready?" he asks, still in a whisper.

"I can't be ready," I say. "Not until I hear your voice."

He takes another sip of his clear liquid. Is it just water? Seltzer? Or does his have booze in it? I can't tell by watching him.

Nothing. Nothing for the next few seconds until I feel like he may not even possess vocal cords.

But then—

"Are you ready, Mandy?"

My jaw drops.

That clear drink with a twist of lime? It's a Tanqueray and tonic.

Does Mr. Dark and Sexy truly think he can hide himself from me? I'd know that whiskey-toned voice anywhere.

CHAPTER TEN

Jackson

U h-oh.

For a split second, she appeared to recognize my voice, but from one blink to the next, the look of surprise is gone. I must have imagined it. This won't work if she knows who I am.

She doesn't say anything, her gaze bouncing around the room nervously as she bites her lower lip.

Why is she still here? Just one look at this place should have scared the hell out of her.

And her red lips? Those aren't Mandy, no matter how fucking hot they look.

I clear my throat, lowering my voice again. "I said, are you ready?"

Amanda smiles. Actually smiles. "I came here to learn, Mr. Dark and Sexy. What do you have to teach me?"

Mr. Dark and Sexy? God, she's killing me. She can't possibly be serious. Black Rose Underground is *not* for Amanda. I can't believe she allowed me to put a blindfold over her, not knowing who I was.

What is happening? Are the planets out of alignment?

How is my Mandy Cake even *here*?

I look around. I know about a third of these people personally, and they are good people. Businessmen and -women who share my tastes in the darker and kinkier side of sex.

This is the place where we act out our deepest fantasies. Where we don leather, where we act out scenes with each other, where we...

Mandy can't be here.

She just can't.

Here in the main room, sex acts technically aren't allowed—except oral sex is common and security turns a blind eye. Members can wear what they want—including nothing at all—and they can touch each other as they dance, they can kiss, but when it's time to get down and dirty, they go to the back.

Several large rooms exist behind the main dance room for exhibitionists and voyeurs. Anything goes in those rooms as long as there's consent—with the exception of edge play. Edge play isn't allowed at Black Rose.

God. How am I even thinking about edge play when Mandy's right next to me?

Fine. I haven't scared her off Lustr yet. Doesn't mean I won't.

"What's your pleasure, Mandy?" I ask.

"My pleasure is your pleasure," she says, her voice totally calm. "I'm here for you to teach. Where do I start?"

Where do I start? Seriously? Probably with a kiss on the cheek. Mandy doesn't belong here. Vanilla sex doesn't belong here. But at the same time, I'm hard as a rock just looking at her in this place.

God, something about her here—her innocence and sweetness, her unassuming beauty—seems totally at home.

Which makes no sense at all.

I'm not ready to take her to the back. Hell, I never expected her to get this far. "Why don't we dance?"

She nods. "I'd love that, Mr. Dark."

I lead her out to the dance floor. Again—like the time at my parents' anniversary party, like the photo on her profile—I can see her nipples protruding through her shirt. God, she has great nipples. I've trained myself not to think of Mandy this way, but in this place? With her nipples showing?

I find myself wanting her.

I can't have her. This is my private place where I indulge my darkest desires. So why does she seem so at home?

She doesn't know who I am yet. I made a mistake before. I imagined her jaw dropping. But thank God she's acting like she doesn't know me, which is good.

I'm not using my actual voice. I've added a rasp to my low tones.

She wraps her arms around my neck, looks into my eyes.

I'm wearing colored contacts. A brown so dark it's almost black, to conceal the hazel I know she would recognize. The black mask covers most of my face except for my mouth and chin.

Normally, I go shirtless when I come to the club, but tonight I'm wearing a leather vest that covers my chest. Mandy knows I have a tattoo of an eagle over most of my back. She'd recognize me in an instant if my upper body were uncovered.

She moves against me, and I wish I didn't have this vest separating us. I want to feel her hard nipples abrading my chest.

Where the fuck did that thought come from?

We dance together through two songs, and then I have to pull back. I'm so hard, I'm almost sure she can feel the bulge in my jeans.

Am I really supposed to be her teacher? She was supposed to be scared. She was supposed to run the hell out of here.

I'm not used to going slowly at this club. When I find someone who's willing to share a scene with me, we go all in. I'm a natural Dominant. I like to tie women up. Bind them, spank them, bring them to their knees.

And now…

Never before have I thought of Mandy in that position, kneeling before me, taking what I give.

Damn it, I want it. I want it more than anything.

But I can't.

Except then I have to reject her. I can't do that to her.

I never expected this to get so far. I assumed she'd whip those hands to her hips with a "hell, no!" once she saw the NDA.

Once I slipped a blindfold over her.

Once she saw the inside of the club.

But she hasn't. She's still here, and I won't reject her. She has to reject me, and she will.

I answered her Lustr when she was looking for a teacher, so perhaps that's what I should be. The teacher. I could teach her the kind of sex I like, take her to her limits, because no way will she go through with it.

Not Mandy Thomas.

Not my sweet and innocent Mandy Cake.

But I can't stop myself from lowering my head, touching my lips to hers…

Sparks. Sparks that shoot through me, landing in my groin.

And when she parts her lips… Touches her tongue to mine…

I nearly explode.

I've known this woman most of my life, and this is the first time our tongues have touched.

The kiss is wet and slow and fills me with desire. Mandy… Oh my God, Mandy.

Her tongue is like silk and her lips like maple sugar.

I feel like a high school kid, making out at the school dance with the girl of my dreams.

Except…this isn't the girl of my dreams.

This is Mandy. My best friend. No matter what she wants, I can't do this to her.

I end the kiss.

A soft whimper escapes her throat. "Please…"

My attempt to scare her away hasn't worked so far, so I'm going to have to get a little more proactive.

"Come on." I take her hand and lead her off the dance floor to the door next to the bar—the door that leads to all the playrooms, both public and private.

"You ready?" I say as we stand in front of the closed door.

She nods. "I'm ready, Mr. Dark."

Good. This ought to do it. I lead her through the door into the hallway, and then I open the first door on the left. It's a large room, and whips, cuffs, floggers, and other tools hang from the walls. Several scenes are taking place. Closest to us is a threesome—two men and a woman—the woman's mouth is held open by a spider gag, and one of the men is fucking her mouth. The other is behind her, ramming his cock into her.

Mandy goes rigid next to me.

Good. This should end soon.

In the next scene, a man is bound, trussed up like a turkey, while a woman sits on his face and forces him to eat her.

And then a scene I know will send Mandy running for the hills. A woman's wrists are bound to a pole, her ass being whipped by a masked man dressed very similarly to how I'm dressed.

Yes, she's rigid. Freaked. Frightened.

It's only a matter of seconds before she leaves.

Except she doesn't move.

So I have to make the move for her. "See anything you like?" I ask.

She nods.

Shit. Really?

Not my Mandy. Not my Mandy Cake.

"Teach me," she says. "Teach me how to please a man."

Fuck. It. *All.*

How have I been such a fool? Here I thought I was keeping

Mandy safe from a random hookup with a guy from an app—and instead I've turned *myself* into that guy.

Because that's not fear I see burning in my best friend's eyes. That's interest. And if I turn her away, now that I've sparked her curiosity? She's going to find someone else to introduce her to this world. Someone who won't respect her as much as I will.

Fine. She wants a teacher? I can be her teacher.

"Let's go," I say.

"No. You said you'd teach—"

I silence her with two fingers over her lips. "Not here. In a private suite."

I lead her out of the larger room, down another hallway, to the room I've reserved. I reserve it each time I come to the club, but I honestly didn't think I'd use it tonight.

I key in the code and urge her inside.

She inhales. "Smells good in here."

I nod. The rooms are always scented with lavender. It's relaxing, and it helps everyone feel at ease.

She looks around, her eyes wide. "What...exactly do you do in here?"

"Whatever I want," I say gruffly.

She tenses again, but her lips quirk upward. "I want to learn it all. Every single thing."

"All right," I say. "We'll start with the basics, then. Take off your clothes."

"Don't you want to undress me?" she teases.

"First thing to learn, Mandy, is that you do what I tell you in here. Undress yourself. Slowly. Sensually."

She blushes. A striking rosiness spreads over her cheeks. How have I never noticed her blush before?

Amanda Thomas is beautiful. Not just beautiful but damned sexy. Why have I never seen it?

No, the truth is, I *have* seen it. But I haven't let myself dwell on it because she's Mandy Cake. Mandy Cake, who played in my sandbox, whose mother changed my diapers. Mandy Cake, who has remained the only constant in my entire life.

Which is why I can never tell her who Mr. Dark really is. We *both* value our friendship more than any other relationship in our lives. She wouldn't want me to tell her if it would change things between us.

She carefully removes her black pumps, and then she lifts her shirt over her head.

Her bra is simple white lace. In the moment, it turns me on more than the most intricate leather binding. My cock throbs.

She unclasps it in the back and then shimmies out of it, letting her breasts fall against her chest.

They're perfect, I'd say between a B and C cup. A little more than a handful, and I have big hands. Her nipples stick out like pencil erasers, and they're pink. Dark pink.

"Keep going," I say with a rasp.

She peels off her jeans, stumbling a bit. I suppress a chuckle. Then she stands in her white cotton panties.

White cotton has never been so sexy.

"The rest." My voice cracks. Damn.

She slides her panties over her hips, down her legs, and steps out of them.

And I suck in a breath.

CHAPTER ELEVEN

Amanda

Jackson.

Did he really think I wouldn't recognize him? What has he done to his gorgeous eyes? Must be colored contacts.

He's trying to disguise his voice, but I know him too well. He's using the same voice he used when he dressed up as Thor for Halloween a few years ago.

He doesn't even have a Lustr profile. How did he—

Of course. He opened a Lustr account. Or maybe he's had one for a while and never told me.

All I know is that kiss... That kiss we shared on the dance floor...

It was more amazing than I've ever imagined in my fantasies.

It was...

Me.

I *am* that kiss.

I am a person standing naked in front of Jackson, the man of my dreams, whom I've loved from afar for as long as I can remember.

Why is he doing this? Is it possible he shares my feelings? After all this time?

And all this time... All this time I thought I knew him. I thought I knew Jackson Paris better than anyone, and I had no idea...

No idea he was into all this...*kink*.

I should be frightened out of my mind, but I'm not. I'm not because this is Jackson. And Jackson would never harm a hair on my head.

In fact...

If this is what he likes, I want to please him.

I look around the private suite. A king-size bed, something that looks kind of like a massage table, a wall full of whips and cuffs and ropes, most of which I've never seen before.

I inhale the relaxing fragrance. "Teach me."

"We begin at the beginning, then," he says, leading me toward the bed. "Lie down."

I obey. The red silk comforter is like a cool breeze on my blazing body—a sensual contradiction, and already I'm sizzling between my thighs.

"Spread your legs," he says.

No one has seen that part of me. Not in lighting like this. All my experiences have been in the dark, and neither Tracy nor Seamus ever went down on me.

I prepped the area. Shaved my pubes into a thin triangle. Will Jackson like it? Am I pretty down there? I have no idea, and my nerves are doing a polka beneath my skin. But I'm determined to see this through.

"Don't make me say it again," he growls.

This time I obey him. I spread my legs.

And he draws in a breath.

Does that mean he likes what he sees? I know so little about men. I truly *do* need a teacher.

"Cup your breasts," he says.

Again, I obey, though I'd rather he be the one cupping my breasts.

"Touch your nipples," he says. "Lightly."

I flutter my fingers over my hard nipples. Jolts of desire arrow through me at warp speed. Just from my fingers. My God...

"Now pull on them," Jackson says. "Tug on them softly and imagine it's my lips."

"I'd rather it be your lips," I say, tossing my shyness to the wind.

God, if that isn't the truth.

How often have I fantasized about this? How often have I imagined Jackson sucking on my nipples, sucking between my legs?

Will it happen tonight? Or will I only touch myself?

My clit is throbbing. I'm so wet. I hate to think what my juices are doing to this beautiful silk comforter.

"Keep touching yourself..."

I continue to pull on my nipples, and my eyes close, seemingly of their own accord. A soft sigh escapes me.

"Yes," he says. "Keep those eyes closed, Mandy."

"Oh..."

"Good. Now take your right hand, remove it from your nipple, trail it down your belly, and stop between your legs."

I obey him once more, sift my fingers through my trimmed pubic hair.

"Are you wet?"

"Yes," I breathe.

"Smooth your fingers through those wet pussy folds," he says. "Then circle your clit."

My God, I'm so slick. I slide my fingers through my pussy and then back up to my clit. Just one touch, and I'm almost ready to explode. I should feel self-conscious, but somehow, I'm not. In fact, Jackson telling me what to do next evaporates my usual indecision and worry that I'm not doing something right. He'd tell me if I weren't.

"Slowly," he says. "Slowly circle your clit with those wet fingers, Mandy. Make yourself feel the fire."

The fire? I'm already a freaking inferno.

Moans vibrate out of me as I circle my clit slowly, deliberately, my eyes still closed.

"Good," he says. "Very good."

I pinch my left nipple harder as I quicken my strokes on my clit.

He's supposed to teach me to please a man. Instead, he's teaching me how to please myself. I can't complain, though. I'm ready, ready, ready—

"Now stop," he says harshly.

My eyes pop open as I let my fingers drop from my left nipple. My right hand is immobile, still touching my clit.

Fire. Fire everywhere. All over my skin, and it's heating the blood in my veins into boiling honey.

Stop? Stop *now*?

"For God's sake, Jackson. What the hell are you doing? Would you just fuck me already?"

CHAPTER TWELVE

Jackson

Fuck.

No way. No fucking way.

"I don't know what you're talking about," I say, making my voice rumble.

"Of course it's you, Jack. I'd know your voice anywhere. I'd know that stubbly jawline anywhere. Those lips. And for the record, I don't know how much dark grease you put in your hair, but it's going to take at least three shampoos to get it all out. And what the hell did you do to your eyes?"

"Damn it." I rip the mask off my face. "They're contacts, of course."

"I don't have any idea why you did this," she says. "At the moment, I honestly don't care. I'm so freaking hot and bothered. Would you please just take care of what you started?"

I'm more than ready. I have to keep myself from adjusting the bulge in my pants.

"Mandy, I—"

"Please, Jack. Just fuck me. Fuck me hard and fast. Fuck me the way you like to fuck. If you won't be my teacher, at least ease the ache between my legs. I've never been so horny before, and I swear to God, I'm not sure I can take it."

My God. Those dirty words from her apple-pie lips... Her apple-pie lips painted red...

I'm going to fucking explode.

I want to do everything to her. I want to bind her wrists. Force her mouth onto my dick. Spank her sweet little bottom until it's fire-engine red.

I want to tie her up, suspend her from the ceiling, let her hang there, and take my pleasure.

I want to kiss those lips—those red lips that taste like honey crisp apples and brown sugar with just a touch of sweet cream.

My God... If her lips taste that good, what must her pussy taste like?

I inhale. Even over the aromatherapy fragrance, I can smell her. Scent her. Her ripeness and her sweetness. She's ready for me.

I should ask her. I should ask her if she's sure. I should give her a chance to say no. A chance to leave. A chance to go back to the way everything was before—the comfort of it all for both of us.

I should do all those things.

But I don't.

Instead, I dive between her legs, slide my tongue inside her pussy, taste her cream.

Her hands. They're in my hair, and she's right about the product. Her hands will be full of oil, but I don't care.

All I care about right now is tasting her pussy, eating her, licking her, making her go wild with desire.

Her texture is like slick satin on my tongue, and the flavor... Oh God, the flavor.

Sweet, tart, unique.

Amanda. I'm tasting Amanda. I'm eating the pussy of my best friend in the world.

And damn, I'm liking it. I'm liking it a lot.

I suck and slurp and pull her labia between my teeth. She tastes so good, and I could bury my face in her forever, except...

I need to give her clit some attention. I want to make her come. I want to make her come so hard that she never forgets who did it to her. That every time she looks at me, sees my mouth, she remembers it on her pussy, eating her, giving her pleasure.

I can't stop. Don't want to stop. I flick my tongue over her clit once, twice, three times...

"Jackson! Oh my God!"

She squeezes her thighs around me as she pulses. I feel every contraction as if it were my own.

God, yes. She's coming. Sweet Mandy is coming. All over my face. *My* face.

I keep licking her, my cock throbbing inside these damned black jeans that I wish would just dissolve into nothingness at a mere thought.

I suck, I eat, I kiss her wet thighs...

Until I can stand it no longer.

I force myself away from her pussy, and I ignore her whimper of loss.

These damned jeans. They're tight, and they take some time to get off. I nearly fall to the floor trying to wiggle out of them, but finally I'm free. My cock is free and hard and ready.

I return to the bed, climb on top of Mandy, and thrust into her heat.

God, she's so tight, and she lets out a scream as I invade her.

Is she a virgin? It's not something we've talked about. I never thought...

And then I don't care.

All thoughts cease.

And all I do is fuck her. Fuck her tight little pussy. After a few thrusts, I realize my eyes are closed.

Do I keep them closed? Do I look at her? Do I face what

I've done? What I'm doing?

Mandy makes the decision for me. "Please, Jack. Open your eyes. I want to see your eyes."

She won't see *my* eyes. She'll see the contact lenses. But I open them, and I look into hers. That lovely blue-gray.

And I feel something. Something unexpected. Something that frightens me.

But it's not enough to stop me from fucking her amazing pussy.

I grunt, I groan, I go quickly, slowly, quickly again.

She wraps her thighs around my hips, squeezing them and making herself even tighter.

Oh my God.

I can't take it. Can't take it all. I fuck her, fuck her, fuck her. Thrusting, and thrusting, and thrusting... And then—

Nirvana. Ecstasy. Stars and sparks and flames all at once.

I empty myself into her, and I feel...

I feel...

Like I've come home.

Relaxation sweeps through me, and for one moment—one amazing fucking moment—I feel lighter than air.

Until reality hits.

I'm on top of my best friend. My cock is embedded inside her.

And now I don't know what the hell to do.

CHAPTER THIRTEEN

Amanda

My eyes are squeezed shut. I can't open them for fear this has all been a lovely dream.

Except it was better than it's ever been in my dreams, and I've been dreaming about Jackson Paris since... Well, since we both hit puberty and my hormones started racing.

My love for him has been unrequited for so long...

And now?

Now what?

I'm still not exactly sure why he did this. Why he stalked my Lustr profile and made a date with me.

Does he finally return my feelings?

I want to believe that. I want to believe it so badly. But though he likes to call me innocent, I'm not all that innocent. Not all that naive. I don't believe for an instant that he's suddenly realized he's in love with me.

He must have an ulterior motive.

I open my mouth to say something, but no words emerge. What can I say? That it was amazing? Magnificent? Better than anything in my dreams?

Jackson is my best friend, and I've talked to him about so much.

But I can't talk to him about this.

It's too...

Personal?

Of course it's personal. We just had sex. Sex like I've never thought possible. Granted, my experience is limited, but even *I* didn't imagine it could be as good as it was.

All we did was kiss. Then he licked me, and then we had sex.

Still so much we didn't explore. I didn't get to touch him all over with my lips. I didn't get to feel him suck on my nipples.

And we didn't use any of the...implements in this room.

And oddly? I'm intrigued by every single one of them.

I want to learn more. Not just about how to please a man but how to specifically please Jackson Paris.

He rolls off me then, lies silently at my side. I finally open my eyes and turn to look at him. His are closed, his arm over his forehead, and he looks...

Upset? Regretful?

The truth is that I don't know, and I can usually read Jackson like a book.

But all this time... All this time I thought I knew him as well as I knew myself. I had no idea he had a kinky side.

I had no idea *I* had a kinky side.

I'm on the pill. He knows that. I've been on it since I was in high school because of irregular periods. Not only that, but Jackson would never put me in harm's way, which means he's clean. Heck, I'd bet this place requires testing every month or so. After all, they all but guarantee your safety here.

So no worries there. Now my worries are limited to the fact that I may have just ended my friendship with Jackson.

And I don't know what I'll do without him.

Ambivalence rolls through me. This is what I wanted. This is what I've dreamed of for years and years. But he's regretful. I can see it in the way his body is stiff when he should be relaxed.

"Jack..." I finally eke out.

"What?"

I don't think he means to sound terse. Maybe I'm imagining it.

"I...I think I'd like to go home now."

It's not what I want. At least it's not *all* of what I want. What I want is to escape from this feeling—this feeling that we just did something wrong. Why do I feel this way? We're two consenting adults. We did nothing wrong. In fact, I immensely enjoyed every second of it.

All those years when I was worried I'd never had a real orgasm? I was right. I've had one now, and there's no doubt in my mind about what I was missing before.

Still...it's weird. I never imagined this weirdness in my fantasies about Jackson.

"Okay," he finally says.

But he doesn't move.

What is he waiting for? Does he want me to say something? Does he want me to assure him that this is okay? That I understand it can never happen again?

I'm not going to do that. I *want* it to happen again. What I *don't* want is this feeling of unease between us.

If only he would look at me, meet my gaze, tell me he loves me and he always has.

I can't wait for that. Besides, his gaze won't be his, not with those colored contacts that cover the green-and-gold beauty of his eyes.

That's not how I want to hear his profession of love.

Besides, he clearly regrets all of this.

Which still doesn't make sense, since he started it all. He's the one who looked up my Lustr account. He's the one who sent me those messages.

And he's the one who brought me here. To this club. To this private club I didn't even know existed. Pretended to be some mysterious Mr. Dark.

Why, then, do I feel like *I've* done something wrong?

I haven't. This is all on him.

I could take control here. I could tell him it was a mistake. But as far as I'm concerned, it *wasn't* a mistake. It's everything I wanted and so much more.

Except for how Jackson is acting now.

He should be holding me, kissing my face, whispering sweet nothings to me in our afterglow.

But he's not. My body is still warm and relaxed from the orgasms he gave me, but my mind? My mind is a mess. A big mess.

"Jackson?" I say again.

"Right." His eyes are still closed, his arm still over his forehead. "Home."

Again, he doesn't move.

I don't need his permission for anything. I can get home on my own. I just have to go back up to where the bar is, and I can grab a cab.

I swing my legs over to the side of the bed and rise. I gather my clothes and quickly dress. Make sure my phone, ID, and credit card are still in my pocket, and I leave the room.

Only then does Jackson appear behind me, grabbing me and pulling me back into the room.

"What do you think you're doing?"

"I told you. I want to go home."

"You can't go out there alone."

"Why not? I signed their disclosure thing. And besides, I'm leaving. Anything I see on my way out, I'll pretend I didn't."

"No, you don't understand," he says. "You can't go out there without *me*."

"Why? Because you're a member here?"

"No. Because you're not collared."

I wrinkle my forehead. "What the heck is that supposed to mean?"

"Claude gave me a collar for you, and I—" He shakes his head. "Damn. How was I so careless? And with you, of all people."

"Jack, what the heck is a collar?"

He rubs his temples. "Any submissive—"

"Excuse me? *Submissive?*"

"For God's sake, Mandy, you have submissive written all over your face."

Now I'm angry. Pissed off and angry and still turned on. "Right. I'm innocent Mandy Cake. That's me."

"Look, I'm being serious. Without a collar—something designating that you're mine—"

His? God, if only... "Excuse me? *Yours?*"

"I don't have time to explain right now. Let me get dressed, and I'll give you the collar and escort you out."

"No. You'll explain right now. You're going to explain to me why I can't go out alone and walk through the club to the door and exit."

"Because any Dom who sees you uncollared—"

"I really hate the term 'collar.' It sounds like you want to lead me around on a leash like a dog."

He doesn't reply at first.

"Oh my God. You *do*."

He shakes his head. "No. I don't have any desire to lead anyone around on a leash. A collar simply designates that you're taken. That you're the property of—"

"Property? What the hell, Jackson?"

"Not like ownership or anything. But in a place like this, if you're not collared or accompanied by a Dom of your own, any Dom in the club will think it's okay to approach you."

"So what if someone approaches me? My safety was guaranteed here. Remember?"

"I know, but some of these Doms can be very persuasive, Mandy."

I set my hands on my hips. "And you think I don't have the ability to say no?"

"No. That's not it. This is all coming out wrong." He shakes his head again. "Just let me get my pants on, and I'll put the

collar on you and take you out. Okay? Would you do that one
thing for me?"

I finally relent. But not without a sarcastic scoff.

Jackson dons his jeans, and I can't help checking out his
ass both before and after. The man has one tight ass. I swear
to God, he must've been carved in heaven by angels.

I try not to look at him too wistfully.

He takes a velvet ribbon from his pocket and Velcros it
around my neck. He escorts me then, his arm around me at all
times, as we leave the private room, walk down the hallway,
and enter the main room where the dance floor and bar are.

Only a few couples are dancing now, as it's later.

We walk through the entryway, where Jackson says goodbye
to Claude, who appears to be the bouncer, and then we're in a
hallway. A simple hallway.

"I'm supposed to blindfold you again so you don't know
where the entrance is."

"I already know what building it's in," I say.

"I know. I can trust you, Mandy. You won't tell anyone you
were here and what's in the basement floor of this building."

I shake my head. "Of course I won't. I signed the NDA."

"I know that." He fixes the blindfold over my eyes. "This is…"

"What?"

"Never mind." He leads me toward the door, and then we
ascend the staircase. A few twists and turns later, we enter the
back of the bar, and he removes the blindfold.

"I'll just grab a cab," I say.

"No. I'll take you home."

"That's not necessary—"

"I said I'll take you home, Mandy." Jackson's voice is firm.

And for some odd reason that I don't understand—and that
irks me a little—I want to obey him.

So I do.

CHAPTER FOURTEEN

Jackson

We're silent during the cab ride to Mandy's place. Once we arrive, I ask the cabbie to wait, and I walk up to her apartment.

"I don't have long," I say, "because the cab driver's waiting."

"Of course," she says dully.

"Mandy Cake..."

"Seriously? After what just happened between us, you're going to revert to Mandy Cake?"

I sigh. "Mandy...this was a huge mistake."

"You're telling me," she says.

"It's not...what I wanted," I say.

"Then why did you take me there?"

"I was trying to convince you that..."

"That what?"

She's really going to make me say it. She's really going to make me say that I don't think she should be on Lustr. That these things should happen organically. Tha—

"I'm aging here, Jackson. Just say it."

I open my mouth, but nothing comes out. The truth? Tonight was amazing. Mandy was amazing. Sure, I didn't get a chance to see any of her moves—if she even has any; she wants a teacher, after all—but the way she took off her clothes... For a moment, I thought she was going to climb up a stripper pole once she got naked.

"It just can't happen again," I say.

Why not? I wait for the words.

They don't come.

"Fine."

"Mandy, please don't be angry."

"Why should I be angry, Jack? You got on Lustr just to stalk me, you brought me to your sex club, you screwed me in a private room, and now you hardly want to speak to me."

"It's not like that. I just wanted to..."

"You wanted to convince me that I shouldn't be on Lustr. That I shouldn't be asking someone to teach me. What if that's what *I* want, Jackson?"

"Not every man out there is like me, Mandy. Not everyone out there is concerned with your safety."

"*I'm* concerned with my safety, Jack. Me. A fully grown woman who's perfectly capable of taking care of herself."

"You don't understand these kind of people. You go on Lustr and ask for someone to teach you? You're going to get all kinds of creeps."

"And you don't think I can tell a creep from a good guy?"

"For God's sake, Mandy, you agreed to go to a club with me without knowing who I was."

"I agreed to meet you in a public bar. That's what I agreed to. The rest I agreed to after reading the disclosure and signing the agreement. My safety was assured."

"That particular club is very concerned with everyone's safety," I say. "But I could've easily been some degenerate who had you sign a fake document and dragged you down the hallway and out into an alley to rape you."

She goes rigid then. That beautiful blush that's usually

present on her cheeks? It's gone, replaced with a pasty white.

Thank God. I got to her finally.

"So now you understand."

She nods, trembling. "Yes. I suppose I should get off Lustr."

"I think that would be a good idea."

She changes her stance then. Becomes more willful. "Or maybe I just change my bio. Lots of people find meaningful relationships on Lustr."

Something twists in my gut. *Do* I have an ulterior motive? Is there a reason, other than her safety, that I don't want Mandy on Lustr? Or any other similar app?

I've tamped down all my sexual feelings for Mandy for so long that I'm used to it. It's like they don't exist. But Mandy is a very attractive woman. Not only physically attractive but beautiful on the inside as well.

She may have enjoyed tonight. Hell, I enjoyed it too. What we had tonight was pure vanilla sex. Even so, it was extremely satisfying, even though it wouldn't satisfy me long-term.

Mandy didn't seem to be scared off by all the tools and toys hanging on the walls. Or by watching the scenes in one of the large rooms.

Maybe she's not as sweet and as innocent as I thought.

So what does that mean for me?

It means I must make a decision. Do I want to bring Mandy into my world? Or do I want to keep her as she is—the sweet, innocent best friend I adore. Because I can't have both. Being with her this way will destroy our friendship. I'll get tired of her, and I'll move on. It's what I do.

But damn, tonight was so amazing that in this moment?

I'm not sure.

Mandy walks to her door, slides her key through—something I usually do for her. Roger's whines leak through the door.

"Leave. Please leave, Jackson."

She's pissed. Probably hurt. I can't blame her. I'm pissed,

too. Not at her but at myself.

What was I thinking? Did I really think I'd get away with this? Did I really believe Mandy wouldn't know me?

My eyes are dry and parched from these damned contacts. No wonder she hates wearing her own. I need to get home and get them out. And the hair product... Yuck.

So I follow Mandy's lead. I walk down the hallway without so much as a goodbye.

CHAPTER FIFTEEN

Amanda

I wake the next morning, pad into my bathroom, and gawk at my red and swollen face. My eyelids are double their size, and my nose is red and nearly bloodied from all the blowing.

I cried myself to sleep after Jackson left.

But damn it, those are the last tears I'll shed over him.

I have a busy day with work, and I'm determined to get right to it. After a shower and two cups of coffee, I log in, check Lily's social media, and settle into my daily tasks.

I'm in the midst of proofreading a book when a knock sounds on my door and gets Roger yapping.

It's the middle of the week, and I'm not expecting a delivery. I'm at a loss. I have no idea who it could be. Maybe a neighbor?

I get up, go to the door, open it, and—

"Jackson, what are you doing here?"

His dark-blond hair is back, and his eyes… Those spectacular eyes.

He walks in as if he owns the place, Roger scampering around him for attention. This is no different from any other time, but today it disturbs me. Especially since I was up all night crying about him.

And now…he's going to see my face.

But he hardly looks at me. He heads to the kitchen, grabs a mug out of the cupboard, and pours himself a cup of coffee, which I'm sure is now cold.

He takes a sip, wincing a bit.

Yep, it's cold.

"Listen, Mandy," he says, pacing around my apartment—again as if he owns the place. "Last night… It can't happen again."

"I think we already went through all this," I say.

He doesn't meet my gaze. "No. We didn't. I made a mistake. I should've never taken you to the club."

"You can say *that* again," I agree.

"I just… I can't feel that way about you, Mandy. It was a mistake, and it *won't* happen again."

"Okay, Jackson. You've made your point. Now throw that disgusting cold coffee down the drain and get the hell out of here."

He doesn't move and instead takes another drink of the cold coffee. "All right, Mandy. As long as you understand." He sets the cup down on the counter.

"I understand fully. But let me be clear as well." I gather my courage, determined to break out of my introverted shell. "I enjoyed myself, Jackson. I enjoyed what I saw. I'm intrigued. I honestly had no idea a place like that even existed. A place where people can explore their baser instincts. I enjoyed it because I needed it. I've been out of circulation for too long, Jackson. Far too long. I deserve better. You know what? I *do* need a teacher. I realize it can't be you, and that's fine. I never wanted it to be you in the first place. I didn't even know you were *on* Lustr. There were a lot of other men in the club. Men who aren't attached, or you wouldn't have been so worried about me being uncollared. I'm betting there's someone there who might be willing to tutor me."

He stiffens, leaning against my counter and gripping it, his knuckles white. "The place isn't for you, Mandy."

"Not for me? I think it was *you* who took me there. How can you say that?"

"We've been through this. It was a mistake. I'm not sure what I was thinking."

"I know exactly what you were thinking, Jack. You were thinking that I was too sweet and innocent for something like that, and that I'd go running out screaming."

He says nothing.

Yep. Nailed it.

"I didn't run out screaming."

"You told me to take you home."

I can't deny it. I did tell him that, but not for the reason he thinks. I loved what happened between us, and I was intrigued by the club. I wanted to go home because he got quiet and sullen after we had sex.

He has a lot of regrets, clearly.

I do not.

But it's time to let my unrequited love for him go. He's made it very clear that he doesn't feel the same way, and that's okay. Well, it's *not* okay. It sucks a big donkey dick, but what choice do I have?

Now that I know the place exists, I can find it again. They won't let me in, of course, but maybe I can meet some other people who go there. Maybe get another invite.

The bartender last night—Alfred—clearly works for the club as well as the bar. Maybe the bar is part of the club.

"I have to get to work," Jackson says.

"Don't let me stop you. I have work to do as well."

"Mandy..."

"Can we please just not go there again? Please, Jack? I had a nice time last night, but I agree with you. It was a mistake."

He walks toward me slowly, trails a finger over my cheek.

"Then why have you been crying?"

Why, indeed? *Because I've been in love with you for fifteen years and you don't see me that way. Because you think I can't handle the kind of sex you like. Because, because, because…*

Because what I want most in the world will never be.

My cheeks burn where he touched me. "It's nothing. I had an allergy attack in the middle of the night."

"All right, Mandy."

He doesn't believe me. I know this, but he's letting me off the hook. He's still Jackson. And he still loves me as a friend. As a damned *friend*.

"This won't affect our friendship, Jack," I say.

A breezy sigh pushes out of him. "Thank you. I don't know what I'd do without you, Mandy Cake." This time he makes it to the door. He drops a chaste kiss on my forehead. "Love you."

After he closes the door, I lean against it for a moment.

"I love you, too, Jack."

CHAPTER SIXTEEN

Jackson

Back at the office, I'm preparing for a meeting when my secretary buzzes me.

"What is it, Jenny? I told you I couldn't be disturbed this afternoon."

"I'm sorry, Mr. Paris, but Mr. Black wants to see you."

"Ben? Sure, what does he need?"

"Not Ben Black," Jenny says. "Braden Black."

I work directly under Ben. I don't see Braden much. He's quieter than Ben and keeps to himself for the most part. He's engaged to be married and spends what little free time he has with his fiancée.

Why would he want to see me? One thing's for sure—no matter how busy I am, I can't say no when Braden Black calls.

"All right. Send him in."

"He's not here. He wants you to go up to his office."

Jeez. "Okay. Tell him I'll be right up."

So much for preparing for the meeting. I'll be fine. I've had to wing it more than once. It won't be the first time. It's not my standard MO, but I can do it.

Braden's office is on the floor above mine—a lush corner

office that's even bigger than Ben's. Braden is the CEO of Black
Inc.—the brains behind the innovative construction goggles
that put the company on the map.

I'm not nervous exactly. More...apprehensive.

"Hey." I clear my throat. "Mr. Black wants to see me."

Braden's assistant nods. "Go ahead in. He's expecting you."

I walk toward his door. I haven't done anything wrong. Ben
loves me and my work. So what the heck is this about?

I knock.

"Come in."

I open the door. Braden sits behind his giant desk, his tie
loosened. He pushes a folder out of his way and meets my gaze.

"You wanted to see me?"

"Yes, Jackson. Sit down." Braden motions to one of the
chairs facing his desk.

I take a seat.

"I understand you were at the club last night."

Okay. This doesn't have anything to do with work. It's about
the club Braden Black owns.

"I was."

"And you brought a guest?"

"I did."

"All the necessary paperwork was signed, so your guest is
bound by our nondisclosure agreement."

"Of course. I've invited guests before."

"You have. We've never had a problem. But this time, you
didn't make sure she was collared."

He's right. I didn't. Claude gave me the collar, but I didn't
put it on Mandy until we left the private suite. Perhaps I knew,
if I tried to collar Mandy, she would balk at it.

Which she ended up doing when we left the suite.

"The members of the club are decent people," Braden
goes on. "I'm sure you know this. However, when you bring a
submissive—or even just a guest—to the club, you are required

to collar them for their own safety."

"I'm aware of that. Claude gave me the collar, and I realized my mistake before the evening was over. I did not let her walk around the club alone."

"I understand. We all make mistakes now and then, but I have to ask why."

"Just a mistake. It won't happen again."

"Good. I'm glad to hear it. I don't normally call employees into my office on personal matters such as these, but I tend to be overly cautious where the club is concerned."

"I understand." I rise. "Was there anything else?"

"No. You've always been a responsible member of the club. We're done here."

I nod. "Thank you. I appreciate your concern. And your discretion." I turn, until—

"Jackson?"

I look over my shoulder. "Yes?"

"Be careful."

I raise an eyebrow. "Are we still talking about the club?"

"We're talking about the woman you brought to the club. I was there last night, and you seemed more...*taken* than normal."

A sliver of warmth hits my neck, and I bristle at the suggestion. "I think you were seeing things."

"Maybe I was. But if you feel something for this woman, make sure you never bring her to the club without a collar again."

I nod.

Then I turn to leave without saying goodbye.

I'm not sure if I should be pissed or flattered. I guess I'm both. I'm flattered that Braden thinks highly enough of me to speak to me about a club issue without simply canceling my membership. I'm also pissed that he's sticking his nose into my personal business. Then again, he owns the club, and that makes him responsible for everyone's safety, including my own.

He's wrong, though.

Mandy *is* gorgeous. She's the only one who doesn't see herself that way. And I'd be lying if I said I didn't enjoy every minute of our interlude last night. Why did I neglect the collar? It's unlike me, and Mandy means more to me than anyone I've ever taken to the club, so why wasn't I *more* cautious instead of less? I thought about it last night, so much that I couldn't sleep.

And I realized it's because I don't think of Mandy in that way—as a submissive. But damn...she acted like a submissive last night. My body is reacting just thinking about it.

But Braden doesn't have to worry.

Mandy will never step foot in the club again.

I'll make sure of it.

The best way to make sure of it? I need to find someone new. Someone I can slake my desires with. Someone who is *not* Amanda Thomas. Someone whose innocence and naivete were taken long ago.

And I know just the one.

Once I'm back in my office, I send a text.

You going to the club tonight?

The three dots and then her reply—

Absolutely. See you there at nine thirty.

CHAPTER SEVENTEEN

Amanda

Five o'clock. On Friday.

As usual, I have no plans for the evening.

No problem. Once I'm free for the day, I pull up my search engine and type *Black Rose Underground* into the bar. Then I add quotation marks around the words.

And…nothing.

Well, it's a private club—a private BDSM club, so of course it wouldn't have a huge website or anything like that.

But it seriously is *nowhere* on the internet. No one even mentions it on a blog or a journal or anything.

Of course they don't. They all signed a nondisclosure agreement.

So how do I find out more about it? The only way I know how. Since I have no plans for the evening, I'll dress up, go back to the bar where I met Jackson, and start my investigation there. Maybe Alfred is working tonight. I can interrogate him. Bat my eyes and get him to show me the entrance.

Gag me. Did I really just imagine batting my eyes? I am so *not* that woman.

Okay. No eye batting. But I *am* going back to that bar.

At least that's my plan until I get a text from Frankie.

Girls' night! Can you meet Isabella, Gigi, and me at Rossi's? I want to hang with all my bridesmaids.

A wave of relief saturates me. I'm glad to have an excuse *not* to go back to that bar. I have nothing to wear anyway.

I text Frankie back quickly. *Sure. What time?*

Nine.

See you there.

Rossi's is a dance club a few blocks away from my place. Some call it a dive, but Frankie and her pals love it. Probably because they can always get in. You won't see a lot of celebrities there, but the drinks are expensive enough that you won't see a lot of deadbeats, either.

I've never been into the clubbing scene, but what the heck? It won't hurt me to be a little more social. If I seriously think I'm going to find someone to teach me the art of seduction and pleasure, I need to learn not to be so introverted. Getting out will be good practice.

I don't have to leave for another hour or two, so I take the extra time to continue work on Lily's proofreading. Her new book is a scorcher. I'm completely into it when I realize I've forgotten about Frankie and the others.

It's nearly nine o'clock already, and I haven't even started getting dressed.

I wash my face and put on some makeup. Definitely no false eyelashes tonight. I don't normally do much with my eyes other than a little bit of eyeliner and mascara, but I have this huge eye shadow palette that Frankie gave me last year for Christmas. What the heck? Let's do some experimenting.

I pull up a smoky-eye tutorial on my phone and follow the instructions.

And...I look like...well...not me.

Oh well. Let's do it. Let's go all out.

I add blush and a red lipstick. Then I head to my closet to

see if I have anything that might go with my newfound look.

Nothing.

I have jeans. I have a couple of camisoles. I have my black pumps, which will blister the heck out of my feet if I dance in them. Good thing I'm not much of a dancer. Jeans, pumps, and a purple camisole it is. Should I go without a bra? God no. The smoky eyes and red lips are enough for one night.

Once I'm ready, I shove a credit card, my ID, and a few bills into my phone case and then shove that into my pocket. It's always best not to take a purse to these places.

One cab ride later, and I make it to the club just before ten.

Rossi's is crowded, but it's not horribly dense. I can actually see through the hordes of people.

I once went to one of the big clubs with Frankie and the others, and the crowds were ridiculous. You couldn't move. If a fire had broken out, we would've all been stampeded to death. For the life of me, I don't know why people enjoy that.

The bar is crowded, with no seats available. Most of the tables are packed as well. Frankie and the others have snagged a table near the back. I walk toward them.

Isabella must be out dancing because only Frankie and Gigi are at the table.

"So you finally decided to grace us with your presence," Frankie yells over the music. But she's not being sarcastic. My sister isn't a rude person.

"Sorry. I got involved in some work and lost track of time."

"Classic Mandy." She smiles. "Glad you're here."

"Wouldn't miss girls' night," I say, hiding the sarcasm that wants to creep out of me. "Is Isabella dancing?"

"She couldn't make it," Gigi says. "Said she had a bit of a headache."

I nod. That's Isabella-speak for, *I got a better offer.*

I don't say this, though. Frankie may not take it too well. This is supposed to be a night with her bridesmaids.

"What are you two up to?" I ask.

Before they can answer, though, a cocktail waitress appears with two froufrou drinks for Gigi and Frankie.

"We're on our second round," Frankie says. "What do you want, Mandy?"

"Sidecar," I say.

Frankie laughs. "I should've just ordered one for you. I always know what you want."

"No worries."

The server scribbles a quick note. "I'll have that for you as soon as I can."

My stomach growls. This place doesn't serve food, and I'm pretty sure I forgot to eat dinner.

"We've been flirting with that table of guys over there." Frankie gestures.

"Flirting? When you're engaged?" I point to the ring on Mandy's finger—

Only to find she's not wearing it.

"Frankie! Where's your ring?"

"I couldn't wear it. What if I got mugged?"

"You've never been mugged in your life."

She huffs. "No one's going to ask me to dance if I'm wearing a rock on my left hand."

Then I get it. She's having her last hurrah. "Okay."

"It's not like I'm looking to go home with anyone," Frankie continues. "I just want to do some dancing. Have a nice time. Feel attractive."

"Frank, you've always been attractive."

True that. I was the ugly duckling of the two of us.

"Still...I just want to have some fun."

"Are you going to be doing girls' night a lot, then?" I ask.

"Whenever I can. Even after I'm married, for that matter. Marriage doesn't mean you have to stop having fun." She giggles. "It just means you have to stop having sex with other guys."

Sure. I nod, and then I look over to Gigi...who's staring at me.

"What is it?" I ask.

"I don't know. You look...different."

Frankie turns her stare on me then. "You do. It's your eyes. You're wearing eye makeup."

"Guilty."

"That's not what I'm talking about," Gigi says. "Something else is different. I can't quite put my finger on— Oh my God. You had sex!"

Thank God my natural flush is being covered up by the cheek rouge I applied rather liberally. I somehow keep my jaw from dropping to the floor.

"Mandy?" Frankie says.

"I don't know what you're talking about." I'm so warm, I think my sweat glands may explode.

"Gigi has sex radar," Frankie says. "If she says you had sex, you had sex."

"Well, I hate to tell you this, Gigi, but your radar has failed you."

Except her radar hasn't failed her. Not only did I have sex, I had the most amazing panty-melting sex with the unrequited love of my life.

"Seriously?" Gigi shakes her head. "I'm never wrong."

"You are this ti—"

"Excuse me?" Someone taps my shoulder.

I turn to see a tall and handsome man standing next to me.

"Would you like to dance?" he asks.

"Sure." I rise, secretly thanking this guy for putting an end to a conversation I did not want to have.

He leads me to the dance floor, which is crowded but not unbearable. It's a fast song playing, so I don't have to get close to him or anything.

He's nice-looking. Blond hair, some scruffy brown stubble,

and dark-blue eyes.

"I'm Michael," he yells over the music.

"Mandy," I yell back.

"Brandy?"

"Mandy!"

"Mandy, nice to meet you."

"You too."

And…we've effectively run out of things to talk about. Good thing we're dancing, and we can pretend to be really into the music.

When the song ends, I hold out my hand. "Thanks, Michael. Nice meeting you."

"Can I get you a drink?" he asks.

"I should have one. The waitress should've brought it by now."

"No problem. I get it."

He's a nice guy, and I think I just hurt his feelings. God, I'm so bad at this.

I smile at him. "Tell you what. Why don't I get *you* a drink?"

He brightens then. "I'm a gentleman. I don't let a lady buy my drinks. But would you like to join me at my table?"

"Sure."

We walk back to the table where Frankie and Gigi are sitting. Sure enough, my sidecar is at my space. "This is Michael," I say. "Michael, my sister, Frankie, and her friend Gigi."

"Nice to meet you ladies," he says.

"Would you like to join us?" Frankie asks.

Michael beams. "If you don't mind." He waves to a table where a couple of guys are sitting and then takes the empty seat at our table.

"Are those your friends?" Frankie asks.

"Yeah."

"Why don't you invite them over here?"

"Because this is a four-top table," I say to Frankie.

"We can all scoot," she says.

Gigi agrees. "Absolutely. We'll scoot."

"Okay." Michael heads to his original table, and soon the two other guys are bringing chairs over.

Now we're squeezed, six people—including three pretty large men—at a table meant for four.

"This is Ryan and Morgan," Michael says. "Mandy, Frankie, and Gigi, is it?"

Gigi blushes. "Short for Gianna."

I take a sip of my sidecar. One good thing about having three men at the table with Gigi and Frankie...I don't have to talk at all.

Which turns out not to be a blessing...because Jackson invades my thoughts.

He's probably at his club...doing things to someone who isn't me.

CHAPTER EIGHTEEN

Jackson

Mariah Sandusky—known as Blossom—practically lives at Black Rose Underground. She's always ready for a scene, and she especially loves being bound in leather, which happens to be my binding of choice as well.

I meet her outside the club, give her a temporary collar for the evening, and then lead her to my reserved suite. She sheds her black trench coat and is wearing nothing but some candy-apple-red panties. She walks to the bed in the corner and lies down on her side—a seductive pose of hers that I know well. Her hair settles on her milky-white shoulders.

"Hello, my dark prince," she says.

I do not reply to her.

That lets her know that I don't want her to talk. She understands.

Blossom is a good sub.

But she's not *my* sub.

I don't have a sub.

I don't want that kind of responsibility.

Right now, the only responsibility I have to Blossom is to keep her safe while the two of us participate in a scene together.

Once we are outside the doors of the club, she's no longer my responsibility.

I'm in the mood for a pretty dark scene tonight. I need to get my aggression out, try to forget…

I have to try to forget about Mandy and the time we spent together.

It was hot and amazing and soul baring, but it will never be enough. I know myself too well. I'll never be satisfied with simple vanilla sex, and I won't be able to commit to her.

I'll only hurt her in the end, and I can't risk that.

I gather some leather rope, glide my fingers over the sleekness of it. Leather and nylon rope are better than cotton rope. They're easier to unbind in case of an emergency.

But I'm good at what I do. I've never had an emergency. Still, I'm careful. My sub—tonight it's Blossom—must be safe at all times in my care.

I remove my jacket so I'm wearing nothing but another pair of black jeans.

"Kneel before me," I say gruffly.

Blossom ambles off the bed—not too quickly—and drops to her knees before me, her head bowed.

"Thank you," I say. "Thank you for trusting me this evening. Thank you for agreeing to do a scene with me."

She nods, her gaze still on the floor.

Normally, I'm turned on by now. My cock is usually pulsating, my skin usually tingling. Just the thought of a submissive kneeling before me, trusting me…

Blossom and I have played scenes together many times in the past. She's good at what she does, and she knows how to please her Dom.

Tonight, though, I'm not even starting to get hard.

Blossom is a beautiful woman. She has flaming auburn hair and deep brown eyes. She's taller than Mandy, has bigger breasts and more slender legs.

And why am I comparing her to Mandy?

Damn.

I've got to get this out of my system.

"Rise," I say to Blossom.

She obeys, and I bind her wrists with the leather. Then I lead her to the pole in the center of the room and fasten her wrists to the top so she's standing, her arms elevated, tied to the pole.

I turn to the wall, study the tools on display, and choose a whip.

I don't use a whip often, but tonight it feels right. I hold the leather grip, let it become part of me. Through this instrument I will feel the warmth of Blossom's flesh as I flog her.

Blossom loves being spanked, flogged, and whipped. Many times, I've taken her ass from creamy white to cherry red, and then I've fucked her as she stands like she is now—bound by leather to the pole, completely at my mercy. I've only used an actual whip with her once, but she and I both ended the evening with raging climaxes. I need that tonight.

Snap—

I bring the whip down upon her milky flesh.

Snap. Again. *Snap.* Again.

Yes, the globes of her ass are pink now—pink and beautiful and delicious.

But nothing from my cock.

Normally I have to restrain myself. I have to stay in control so I don't fuck her too quickly. I give her the pain she requires, the sting she craves, before I take my own pleasure.

Snap! Snap! Snap!

How much more before I find arousal?

I continue to whip her for another minute. Then another.

Snap! Snap! Snap—

"Tesla!" she yells.

I go rigid, and the whip falls to the floor with a dull thud.

Tesla—the car of Blossom's dreams. The car she's saving for.

The car whose name she chose for her safe word.

My heart thunders, and remorse surges through me. What have I done?

Never before has a sub needed to use a safe word with me.

I drop my gaze to her ass.

Oh my God. One of the lashes has drawn blood.

"Blossom, forgive me." I unbind her quickly and lead her to the table where I help her lie down on her stomach.

In the bottom drawer of the chest in the corner are first aid supplies. I've never opened the bottom drawer in any of these suites before.

What is wrong with me?

Quickly, I pull out antiseptic wipes, antibacterial ointment, gauze, and bandages.

"I'm okay, Jack," she says.

"You used your safe word. You're not okay."

"No, I am. This isn't the first time someone has drawn blood."

"But it's the first time *I've* drawn blood."

She says nothing more. Just lets me tend to her. I've drawn blood on occasion with other partners. Partners who want it.

But it's one of Blossom's hard limits. She does not want broken skin. Ever.

I've violated her trust. I've violated the agreement between us.

This will be my last scene with her. We both know this.

And normally? I'd be grieving the loss. Blossom is an excellent partner. We're attracted to each other, and we enjoy each other.

I have effectively ruined what we had.

Guilt eats away at me, as if it's inside me, like a scorpion trying to claw its way out. How could I do something so rash? How could I have violated Blossom's trust this way?

I wasn't thinking of her, and that's on me.

I was thinking only of myself. I was trying to get Mandy

out of my mind.

And Blossom had to pay the price.

I could be kicked out of the club for this. I won't be. I know Blossom, and she won't report me. This is why subs have safe words, after all. She'll accept my apology, and we will move on.

I dress her wound. It's not serious. It's barely oozing blood at this point. Still, I hate myself for it.

And I know the truth now.

If I could do this to Blossom...who knows what I could do to Mandy?

Perhaps I need a break from Black Rose. Perhaps I need a break from sex altogether.

Biggest thing of all?

I need a break from Mandy.

CHAPTER NINETEEN

Amanda

Michael asks for my number and offers to take me home. I give him my number but decline to let him take me home. I'm not ready for him to know where I live, and I'm certainly not ready to get into a car with him alone.

I don't ask if he has a car. Most likely we'd share a cab, he'd see me up to my apartment, and then leave. He's been a gentleman all evening. I have no reason to think he'd act otherwise. However, despite what Jackson thinks of me, I'm *not* innocent and naïve. I know better than to let a man see where I live when I just met him.

"I need to be going, then," he says. "I have an early appointment tomorrow."

"On a Saturday?" I ask.

"Yes. I'm a personal trainer."

Funny. I haven't asked him what he does until he just volunteered. Frankie and Gigi were talking up such a storm at the table, I didn't ask anyone anything.

"That's so interesting," I say. "Where do you work?"

"At the gym around the corner. Body Flex."

"I go there every once in a while," I tell him. "I don't have a membership, but that's Frankie's gym. She gives me a free pass every now and then."

"That's strange. I've never seen her there."

"Honestly, I think she just goes and sits in the steam room. I mean look at her. She hardly needs to work out."

"Neither do you," he says.

"I could lose a few," I say.

"You know," Michael says, "I think you look perfect the way you are. But if you want to tone up a little, I can help you with that. I won't even charge you for the first session." He smiles.

That's not a bad idea, especially with Frankie's wedding coming up. I wouldn't mind my arms and legs looking a little more buff as I strut down the aisle in that plum dress.

"Okay. I'll see if Frankie has another pass."

"You don't need to. I've got your phone number. I'll email you a few passes. Just give me a call when you want to come in. Free first session."

"Actually…how about tomorrow? I'm free."

"Sure. I'm free after two p.m. Want to meet at the gym then? Around three?"

"I'd like that."

He fiddles with his phone. "I just texted you a pass. See you tomorrow. I'm sorry I have to leave so early, but I have this one client who loves to start at six in the morning."

"I understand."

He gives me a chaste kiss on the cheek and then walks toward the exit.

His friends are still at the table with Gigi and Frankie. I should probably leave as well. I start walking toward the door to hail a cab when I hear Frankie.

"Mandy! Come back. We're going to do a toast."

I head back to the table.

"What are we toasting to?" A fresh sidecar sits at my place. "Did I order this?"

"The guys bought a round," Frankie says.

"Oh? That's kind of you. Thank you. But still...what are we toasting?"

"I got a promotion," Morgan says.

"Oh? What do you do?"

"I'm a financial adviser."

Gigi holds up her glass. "To Morgan's new promotion!"

We clink glasses. Did we talk about careers? It was all just a din of conversation to me. Poor Michael. What the heck does he see in me anyway?

"I'd love a dance." Morgan rises and leads Gigi out to the dance floor, leaving just Frankie, Ryan, and me at the table.

Ryan quickly asks Frankie for a dance, so here I am.

Alone with my sidecar. I take a sip. It's too sour. The bartender forgot to put the rim of sugar on it.

It's okay. I feel kind of sour.

I don't have to feel sour, though. I made a date tomorrow for a training session with Michael, who seems like a good guy. A guy who I probably should've let escort me home.

But you can never be too careful in New York.

I down my sidecar in one large gulp.

Then I wave to Frankie on the dance floor, letting her know I'm leaving.

Outside, I catch a cab home.

It's nearing midnight, and I walk up to my apartment and gasp.

Jackson is sitting next to my door. He's wearing a jacket and... Damn. Black jeans. Three guesses where he's been.

"Jack, what are you doing here?"

"Waiting for you."

"Why didn't you use your key card?"

Jack and I always have keys to each other's places.

"I didn't want to be presumptuous."

I scoff. "Since when has that ever stopped you? You could

have at least let Roger out. Jeez, don't you hear him scratching?"

"Mandy," he says, "please, just let me in. I need a place to crash."

"What about your place?"

"I can't. I can't be alone tonight."

Only then do I notice the look of sheer desperation on his face. Something is bothering him. Disturbing him. Frightening him, even.

I unlock my door quickly. "Of course. Come on in."

CHAPTER TWENTY

Jackson

So much for staying away from Mandy.

When I got to my place, after escorting Blossom home and making sure she was okay, I couldn't bring myself to go in.

Who do I always turn to when I need to talk?

Mandy.

But I don't talk to her about my dark and dirty lifestyle. She wouldn't understand.

Still...this is where I came tonight when I needed someone.

I came to my best friend in the world. Mandy. My Mandy Cake.

Only...

She doesn't look anything like my Mandy Cake.

Her makeup is different. Her hair is different. Hell, her whole demeanor is different.

She looks...

She looks like she's been...

"Where have you been?" I demand.

She grabs Roger's leash and affixes it to his collar. "I was at Rossi's with Frankie and Gigi."

"Oh." Relief surges through me.

I'm not sure what's with the smoky eye, but hey, not my business, right?

No. None of it is my business. If I don't want her in my bed, I don't have any say in whose bed she ends up in.

Except I don't want her in *anyone's* bed.

I want her here. At my beck and call. To be my best friend the way she's always been.

God, I'm a dirtbag.

If only I could tell her about Blossom. About how I went overboard. About how I lost trust not only in myself but in everything I believe in.

All because…

All because of the woman standing before me. The woman who will take care of me. I don't even have to ask her to.

I grab the leash from her. "I'll take him out."

"Thanks."

After Roger has christened a fire hydrant, I bring him back up to the apartment.

And there's Mandy, taking care of me. Already, she's making the couch into a bed. She walks to her closet, pulls out sheets, grabs a pillow.

All the while, I simply watch her.

"Are you hungry? I can make you a sandwich. Ham on rye?"

I shake my head.

"Glass of water? Or I can brew a pot of coffee."

I shake my head again. I don't need coffee. I haven't been drinking. I never have more than one drink at the club. I feel very strongly about having all my wits about me when a sub is under my care.

"A drink?" Mandy asks. "I've got some bourbon. Vodka. I'm sorry, but I'm out of gin."

She's out of gin—Tanqueray—because she buys it for me and always pours me a gin and tonic when I'm here. That's okay. I need something a little stronger to soothe me tonight. "Yeah, if it's not too much trouble. Bourbon. Neat."

She nods.

"Join me?" I say.

"I had two sidecars at Rossi's. I'm good." She pours a finger of bourbon into a glass and hands it to me. Then she sits down on the edge and motions for me to sit next to her. "Spill it," she says. "What's wrong, Jack?"

"Nothing."

"Right. Because you show up at my place after midnight on a Friday night when nothing is bothering you. Happens all the time."

"Maybe it *should* happen more often, Mandy Cake."

"Didn't we talk about Mandy Cake?"

She's right, of course. I've eaten this woman's pussy. My dick has been inside her. I can no longer call her Mandy Cake.

"So what's going on?" she asks again.

I sigh, take a sip of my bourbon, let the smooth silkiness burn my throat. "This is good. What is it?"

"You don't recognize it? It's the Basil Hayden's you got me three years ago when you came over for dinner with Frankie and Penn."

It comes back to me then.

How much I've taken this woman for granted.

"I thought it was funny at the time," she continues, "because you know I don't drink bourbon, and you don't normally drink it, either, but you *do* drink it when something's bugging you."

She's not wrong. What a self-absorbed bastard I've been to her.

All this time...

She was always here for me.

I didn't mean to be so self-absorbed. I love this woman.

God, I love her. I've always loved her, but what I'm feeling now...

It's more frightening than what happened between Blossom

and me tonight.

I'm feeling…

More than sexual desire. More than animal urge and want. More than…

More than something I can even describe because I've never felt it before.

And I can't be feeling it. I absolutely can't, because Mandy will never accept the darker side of me.

And even if she could…she deserves more than what I'm capable of giving. She deserves forever.

"You're obviously not in the mood to talk, Jack. If you won't let me help you, I can at least let you rest." She nods to the bed she just made for me. "Finish your drink. I'm going to bed."

She heads to her bedroom. A few minutes later, I hear the whoosh of the shower.

Mandy. Naked. Warm water dripping over her body, meandering over every curve, every valley.

My cock responds.

The way it should have responded with Blossom earlier.

I take another sip of bourbon. Then I stand, shed my jacket and jeans until I'm wearing only my boxer briefs.

For a moment, I consider joining Mandy in the shower.

But only for a moment.

I can't give in. I can't risk Mandy. My Mandy. If we continue down this path, I'll lose her. Maybe not tonight. Or tomorrow. But eventually. And that's not fair to either of us.

I slip between the sheets of her sofa bed and close my eyes.

CHAPTER TWENTY-ONE

Amanda

My eyes pop open.

It's still dark outside. Why did I wake up? Roger, lying at the foot of my bed, perks up his ears.

I'm warm. I thought Roger would be snuggled up to me, but—

"Oh!"

The gasp comes from my throat before I can stop it. My eyes have adjusted, and a man stands by my bed.

For a moment, I freeze. This is the end of my life. He's here to—

Until I recognize Jack. Of course. Jack is here. If it were a stranger, Roger would be barking up a storm.

"God, Jack, you scared the daylights out of me. Why are you here?"

"Couldn't sleep."

"So you decided to watch me sleep?"

"I didn't think you'd mind?" He chuckles half-heartedly.

"Not mind you hovering over me while I sleep? Uh...yeah, I mind. Go back to bed."

He clears his throat. "Can we talk?"

"Look. I gave you the chance to talk last night. You clammed up. I can't be your…"

He yawns. "My what?"

"Your…consolation prize, okay?"

"Mandy Cake…"

I shake my head. "Damn it!"

"Sorry," he says, a yawn splitting his face once more.

"Get out."

Did those words just spew from my mouth? Never in my life have I imagined giving Jackson that command. But you know what? I mean it.

He stills. "Out of your room?"

"Out of my apartment, Jack. Go."

"It's the middle of the night, Mandy."

"So? You've got a car. You've got a place—which, by the way, is about three times the size of this one. Go home, Jackson."

"Mandy…" He closes his eyes, rubs his forehead.

"I mean it."

Still, he doesn't move.

And I begin to relent. My God, I have the world's biggest soft spot for this guy.

"Fine. You don't have to leave. But you do need to get out of my room. I made a perfectly good bed for you in the other room."

"Fine. You're right. See you in the morning." He shuffles out.

And I feel…

I should feel empowered. I stood up for myself. Made it clear that he couldn't use me when he's upset. That if he's not going to tell me what's wrong, he can get the hell out.

But all I feel is…

Loss.

Profound fucking loss.

...

Roger wakes me up the next morning—Saturday—to let me know it's time for him to go out.

I sit up and stretch my arms above my head. Is Jack still here? Why didn't he take Roger out?

I want to talk to him about what's bothering him, yet for the first time, I also don't. I'm angry. So angry that what happened between us meant nothing to him.

"Okay, boy," I say to Roger. "Come on, sweetie."

I rise, shove my feet into my slippers, and head into the main room. My bedroom is kind of the size of a large closet.

Make that an average-size closet. The bed takes up most of the room.

"Morning, Jack," I call as I grab Roger's leash from the side table.

No response.

Of course. He's still freaking asleep. He's not bothered at all by the fact that I kicked him out of my room in the middle of the night.

Then I glance toward the sofa.

He's gone.

My heart dives into my stomach as sadness sweeps through me.

Then I suck it up.

"Who needs him anyway?" I say to Roger as I attach his leash to his collar. "Let's go."

I shove a plastic bag into the pocket of my coat, and then I walk downstairs with Roger. After he does his business and I clean up after him, we return to the apartment.

Because I work at home, there isn't much difference between weekends and weekdays. After I brew some coffee, I sit down at my laptop to check Lily's emails and social media.

Then I remember—

I have an appointment this afternoon at the gym. With Michael whatever his name is. He's going to train me. He's going to help me get svelte and sexy for Frankie's wedding.

Ugh. I should cancel. I don't particularly want to leave the house today. Not when things aren't right between Jackson and me.

Which is a good reason *not* to cancel. Why should I let this thing with Jackson keep me from the gym? He's being an ass.

Yes, he can be an ass, but he would give you the shirt off his back, and you know it. He's your best friend. And you love him.

All true. He just doesn't love me back the way I want him to. And now that I've kissed him, had sex with him… God, I want him all the more. Even though he's being a dickhead.

Somehow, my fingers end up taking me to the Lustr site.

I haven't changed my bio, and of course I have match, match, match, most of which I won't touch with a ten-foot pole.

Clearly, trying to be someone's protégé isn't working.

I think again about where I was headed last night before Frankie texted. I was going back to that bar to try to get into Black Rose.

Thank God Frankie called.

What was I thinking? Although…I can't say I'm not intrigued by the concept of being tied up. Being helpless and at a man's mercy.

The thought makes me tingle all over, especially between my legs.

And thinking about that place between my legs…

Jackson was there. Jackson's face was between my legs. His dick was between my legs.

My God. No wonder he left.

How can our friendship ever be the same?

Maybe it's time to let Jackson go. I mean, he'll always be in my life, but he made it very clear that he and I will never happen again, despite how amazing the sex was.

Maybe it wasn't that amazing for him. Maybe it was just… mediocre.

My God, maybe it was *bad*.

That can't be possible. He was into it. I could tell.

Wasn't he?

"For God's sake," I say out loud.

I exit out of Lustr, and I get back to work on proofreading Lily's latest novel.

And of course that only leaves me more hot and bothered.

Still, it pays the bills, so I continue. After a few hours, I get up and get ready to meet Michael at the gym.

And I realize I have nothing to wear. The few times I go with Frankie, I wear an old college sweatshirt and some baggy sweatpants. I do, at least, have a decent pair of walking shoes. But nothing else.

Okay, no problem. I'll simply go out, buy some workout clothes that don't make me look like a middle-aged housewife, and *then* head to the gym.

Easy peasy.

I'm ready to leave when I get a phone call.

It's Frankie. In tears. "Penn didn't come home last night."

Quickly. Think of something to soothe her quickly. Penn's an ass, but he's not a cheater. Right? "He was probably out with the guys. And now he's couch surfing at one of his friends' places."

"I know. Should I call his friends?"

"Oh my God, no, Frank. That'll make it look like you don't trust him."

"I *do* trust him. I'm just worried."

"I understand, but that's what it'll look like to him."

She sighs. "You want to have lunch?"

"I have to go shopping for some workout clothes."

"Perfect. I'll go with you."

Frankie's help would be great. She got our mother's shopping gene and uncanny ability to know what will look good on my body simply by seeing it on the hanger.

"Okay. I'm working out at three, so if we do stop for lunch, it'll need to be something light."

"*You're* working out?"

"Yeah, remember Michael from last night? He's a personal trainer, and he's giving me a free session at your gym."

"He works there? Seems I would remember him."

"I don't know. Maybe he just started recently or something."

"Yeah, maybe. He seemed like a nice guy."

"He was. I think. I mean, how much can you know about a person after just hanging out at a club for a couple of hours?"

"True. Let's meet at Macy's. They have great workout clothes."

"Sounds good."

I take a quick shower, dress in jeans, my walking shoes, and a Las Vegas T-shirt, and I'm out the door.

And I haven't given Jackson Paris a thought.

At least not in the last five minutes.

CHAPTER TWENTY-TWO

Jackson

"I think you have feelings for this woman," Ben says.

"Of course I have feelings for her. She's my best friend. She's been my best friend since we were literally in diapers."

Ben laughs, taking a slurp of his protein smoothie. "Jack, you are in denial."

"You're wrong."

"Did you or did you not tell me you ended up at her place last night?"

"Yeah. She's my best friend."

"Right. Your best friend you fucked at the club several nights ago. And did you or did you not say you're determined to take a break from her?"

I don't reply. I have nothing to say.

"Look. You and I don't talk about this shit. But I have to ask. How was it? Fucking your best friend?"

"It was...adequate."

I hate myself as soon as the words leave my lips. It was so far from adequate. It was fucking magnificent. And I didn't even tie her up, didn't flog her little ass.

"Why did you take her there again?" Ben asks.

"Honestly? I was trying to scare her. She put up this dumb-ass Lustr bio asking for a teacher. I know Mandy. I knew exactly what would catch her eye, so I joined Lustr and I wrote back to her. Sure enough, she responded."

"I see."

Ben Black is my boss, but I'm right beneath him, and we work as equals most of the time. We're friends. Good friends.

"You see?"

"Yes, I see everything. Jack, you've got it bad."

"We don't think of each other that way. It's like *When Harry Met Sally*, that old Meg Ryan movie. They were friends for, like, twenty years."

"Right. Did you forget how the movie ends?"

Funny. I didn't forget how it ends. I just never think about that part.

"You're afraid she won't share your...proclivities," Ben continues.

"I don't *want* her to share my proclivities. Mandy is innocent."

"Is she now? Didn't you fuck her?"

"Yeah. But I didn't...you know...introduce her to any of the kink."

"So you fucked her at the club, but it was purely vanilla."

"Yep." I sip the last of my smoothie and throw a perfect arc into the wastepaper basket fifteen feet away.

"I'll say it again. You've got it bad."

"You're wrong."

"Have it your way." Ben rises. "You ready?"

"Yeah." Then I rake my fingers through my hair. "Seriously?"

Into the juice bar walks not only Mandy but her sister as well. They're carrying shopping bags from Macy's.

"You've got to be kidding me," I say.

Ben turns back toward me. "Speak of the lovely little devil."

Man. She's going to remember meeting Ben at the sushi place when I had to cancel. How can I get out of here without her seeing me?

Too freaking late.

"Jack!" Frankie waves.

Next thing I know, she's pulling Mandy toward the small table that Ben and I are sharing. Ben is still standing, and I join him.

"Hey, Frankie. Mandy. We were just leaving."

Ben seems to have other plans, though. "If it isn't the lovely lady who disappeared on me at lunch the other day."

Mandy blushes.

My cock responds.

"Something came up," Mandy says, not meeting Ben's or my gaze.

"I understand," Ben says. "Would the two of you like to join us?"

Frankie is pulling on Mandy's arm. Yup. She recognizes Ben. "Absolutely. We'll just go put in our order."

"Don't be silly," Ben says in that low voice that makes women fall all over him. "Let me get this for you. What would you two ladies like?"

"Mandy has a workout in an hour, so something light. But something that will give her energy."

"I know just the thing. And for you?"

"Whatever you get for her will be great for me." Frankie smiles. Then she plunks her ass down in the seat that Ben vacated.

Which means Mandy has to sit next to me.

It also means, once Ben returns, he will be sitting next to Frankie.

That worked out well. I'd think she planned it except she's engaged to be married. Why would she have any interest in flirting with Ben Black?

I have nothing to say to Mandy. Except that's a big-ass lie. But I can't say anything with her sister sitting here. And certainly not when Ben returns.

"How did you sleep?" I ask her.

"Like a baby," she says tersely.

"So you're working out today?"

"Yes. I have an appointment with a trainer."

"That's great. What are her qualifications?"

"I don't know his qualifications."

A sliver of jealousy spears into my gut. So what? So she has a male trainer. I've trained with men myself. I've trained with women, too. Doesn't mean I want to get in their pants.

Ben returns with two smoothies for Frankie and Mandy.

Mandy takes a sip of hers, and her eyes widen. "This is delicious. What is it?"

"It's something I have made special. It's a papaya and passionfruit base with a mixture of pea and whey protein flavored with vanilla and almond."

"It's amazing." Mandy takes another sip.

"Yes, I'm not sure I've ever had anything more delicious." Frankie beams at Ben.

I've had Ben's special pre-workout smoothie, and yes, it's delicious.

But it's not the most delicious thing I've ever tasted.

No. That would be Mandy's pussy.

And for some reason, I can't get that vision out of my head at the moment.

Mandy, her legs spread, my head between them as I lick every ounce of cream out of her.

Damn it.

Now she's going to go work out with some guy.

What the hell is wrong with me?

Is Ben right? Am I pining for Mandy on a subconscious level?

I mean...that night with her at Black Rose? It was fucking fabulous. Would she be open to kink? Even if she is, though, I'd eventually tire of her and everything would be ruined. I've never been able to commit to a woman. I've tried. Serena in high school. Susan in college. Julia last spring. Every single time, though, my interest eventually wanes. I start noticing things we don't have in common, imagining fights we'll one day have, wishing I were anywhere except with her. Some people just aren't meant to be with the same person forever.

"Where are you working out?" I ask her.

"At Frankie's gym. That one around the corner from Rossi's."

I chuckle. "Mandy Thomas, workout queen."

"What's that supposed to mean?"

"Just that…you're not really the exercise type, are you?"

"Says who?"

"Says you. You don't have a gym membership. You never played sports."

I'm not sure why I'm picking a fight with her. It's ridiculous anyway. Mandy does a lot of walking, so she gets plenty of exercise.

"What does playing sports have to do with it?" Ben asks, coming to her defense.

Now I'm getting angry. Why is he sticking his big nose into this?

"True," Frankie says, agreeing with Ben, of course. "I work out all the time, and I never played any sports."

"See?" Ben smiles at Frankie.

"I've been working out four times a week lately," Frankie continues.

"Right," I say. "To get in shape for your wedding."

Then I glance at Frankie's left hand. She's not wearing her engagement ring.

She reddens.

Ben doesn't seem to notice. He's not interested in Frankie that way, no matter how much she would like him to be.

"Mandy wants to get in shape for my wedding, too," Frankie continues.

I lift my eyebrows. "Oh?"

"Well, it won't hurt me to lose a few pounds." Mandy shrugs.

Except that her body is perfect as it is. I always thought it was, and now that I've seen her naked? I *know* it is. She's the only one who doesn't.

"I think you're both beautiful," Ben says, "but working out isn't just for looking better. It's for feeling better."

"Absolutely," Frankie agrees, dazzling him with her smile once more—or attempting to.

Mandy says nothing, just gives her total attention to Ben's special smoothie.

Within a few minutes, she's done. "Ready, Frankie? My appointment is"—she checks her watch—"soon."

"Your appointment is in forty-five minutes, Mandy."

"Sure, but I want to get there early. You know, I need to change. Maybe have a steam."

"You have a steam *after* the workout," Frankie says.

"I think I want one before my workout." She rises, walks the fifteen feet to the trash can, throws in her empty smoothie cup, and returns. "Thanks so much for the smoothie. And...I'm sorry for the other day."

"No worries. I totally understand." Ben smiles. "Maybe next time we can actually share that meal."

He's flirting with her, but Mandy doesn't seem to notice.

"Come on, Frank," she says.

Frankie smiles, though it's forced. Clearly she'd rather stay here and talk to Ben. "Okay, coming."

Once they're gone, I glare at Ben.

"You know, just because your brother signs my paychecks, I can still kick the shit out of you."

"I'd like to see you try."

Ben and I are pretty evenly matched. But damn, I'm pissed off.

"Now I'm *convinced* you have a thing for her," he says.

"You're full of it."

"Are you kidding me, Jack? I just witnessed the twenty-nine-year-old version of you pulling on her pigtails at recess. You've got it bad."

"You're wrong. I just look out for her. She's my best friend."

"She won't be your best friend for long if you keep treating her that way."

But he's wrong. Mandy and I will be best friends forever.

Well, as long as I don't fuck it up—and fuck her again.

CHAPTER TWENTY-THREE

Amanda

"Why didn't you tell me you had lunch with Benjamin Black?" Frankie demands.

I shrug. "I guess it didn't seem important."

"Not important? He's filthy rich and more handsome than a Greek god."

"And you seem to be minus your engagement ring...again..."

"It's in my purse. I took it off when we were trying on clothes."

I could catch her in the lie. It would be easy, but what would be the point? I saw her slip it into her purse as soon as she saw Jack and Ben at the juice place.

Is this wedding even going to happen?

Probably not. Penn and Frankie have been on-again, off-again so many times, and now she's worried that he didn't come home last night.

At least she's got someone. Sort of. I've got no one, and my best friend—my Jackson—has been treating me like complete crap.

Which means I go my own way.

I'll start with Michael and the workout. Then maybe I'll change the bio on my Lustr profile.

Or...maybe I'll try to get back into Black Rose.

Whatever I decide, I don't have to make my decision now. Now, all I have to do is go to the gym. Meet Michael. Have him work my butt off. I hope he's not one of those intense trainers who will kick my ass and make me sore for the next week. I hate that, though it's probably what I need.

"He is dreamy, isn't he?"

"Yeah, he is," I say absently.

"So what happened? When you had lunch with Ben Black?"

Right. She's talking about Ben. Not Jackson.

"I was supposed to meet Jack for lunch at our favorite sushi dive last week. He had to cancel at the last minute, and Ben Black walked in. He bought me some sushi. And then, when he went out to answer a phone call, I left."

"Why?"

Why indeed?

Jack had already blown me off. Why didn't I stay? Why didn't I get to know Ben?

And the answer hits me in the face with a cement block.

Benjamin Black is so far out of my league, I knew it would be best to escape before he let me down gently.

Not that it even matters.

I'm in love with one man and one man only. The man who thought it was a mistake to sleep with me, the man who wouldn't talk to me last night, the man who left my place without saying goodbye this morning.

Yeah, that man.

Why am I in love with him again?

Easy.

Because he's the other half of me. He always has been.

But never in a million years did I imagine he was into kinky sex. Dark sex. Dominant and submissive sex.

All this time, I thought I knew him better than anyone.

But this most intimate part of him was something I never knew.

On the other hand, he doesn't really know me any better than I know him. He's convinced I'm sweet and innocent.

Sure, I don't have a lot of experience, but I'm hardly sweet and innocent. Not the way he thinks I am. I loved being at the club. Part of it was because I was with Jack, but I loved the ambience. The atmosphere. The sheer liberation of it.

At the club, I felt…like *me*.

Like I could be me. I could express everything I felt inside, including how much I wanted Jackson.

And I did express that. At least I think I did.

The only problem? He doesn't want me in return.

Once we reach the gym, Frankie comes inside with me.

"Are you staying?"

"Yeah. I just bought new workout clothes, so why not try them out?"

"Okay."

"You think Michael would mind if I hijacked your training session?"

I should probably be pissed at Frankie. I should want to be alone with Michael, to get to know him better.

But I don't.

There's only one man for me. The man who doesn't want me.

"I don't know. You'd have to ask him. He's giving me this first session for free."

"Oh. I suppose I should just leave you alone, then. I don't want to make a faux pas."

"Okay." Once in the locker room, I change into my new workout clothes—a tight tank top and compression leggings. All in black.

"Black has a slimming effect," Frankie had told me at Macy's.

Yes, I've heard it all before.

I lock my clothes and phone in a locker, fill my water bottle, and pull Frankie out to the gym. I'm not exactly sure where I'm supposed to meet Michael, but he finds me right away.

"Hey, you're early," he says.

"A little. I'll just get on the treadmill while you finish up."

"Not necessary. My two o'clock bailed, so I'm all yours." He nods to Frankie. "Hey, nice to see you again."

"You all enjoy your session," Frankie says. "I'm going to do some cardio."

Michael doesn't ask her to join us, and I'm not sure how I feel about that. Frankie would have made a good buffer. Not that I need a buffer. This is a training session, not a date. Why am I trying to make it into more than what it is?

"So, Mandy," Michael says, "I thought we'd start with some cardio so I can find out your current physical fitness level."

"Sounds good."

He leads me to an elliptical and fiddles with the settings on the computer. "I want you to exercise on this for five minutes. The timer will go off when your time is up. Then I'll be able to see what your fitness level is, and I'll be able to figure out what exercises will work for you."

I hop onto the elliptical without telling him how much I hate ellipticals. They're supposed to be easier on your joints and everything, but I always feel weird on them—like my body isn't aligned properly or something.

I can suffer through the five minutes, though. Then I'll tell him how much I hate the elliptical, and if he wants me to do cardio, it will have to be on a treadmill or bike.

Surprisingly, I'm not terribly winded after the five minutes. Clearly he went easy on me.

"Okay, great job," Michael says. "Let me just stick these numbers into my handy-dandy computer."

His handy-dandy computer is his phone.

"Okay. You're in pretty good shape, Mandy. Your resting heart rate is about seventy-two. Not bad, but we can do better."

"Isn't cardio for weight loss?"

"Exercise, as a rule, isn't for weight loss. It's for body

strengthening. If you want to lose weight, you'll have to cut calories." He eyes me. "Frankly, I don't think you need to lose weight. Your body looks great. A little toning and firming, and you'll be ready for that wedding."

Did I tell him about the wedding? I don't remember. Frankie probably talked about it last night.

"And yes, you need cardio. Exercising the heart is the best way to keep it in shape and make sure you live a long and full life."

I sigh. "If you say so."

"We all hate cardio. I do mine first, because if I do my strength training first, I know I'll be tired and I won't bother to do my cardio."

"You mean personal trainers aren't all in love with cardio?"

"God, no. We're trainers, not professional athletes."

"Could've fooled me."

Indeed, Michael has an amazing body. Today he's wearing shorts and a tank top, so I'm getting a good look at his muscles. His calves look like he swallowed a couple of softballs.

Still...as attractive as I find him, I'm not feeling even a pinch of arousal.

Is he?

It's hard to tell. Maybe Jackson's right. Maybe I *am* innocent. I sure can't read this guy.

"I'm going to put you back on the elliptical—"

"No," I say adamantly. "No more elliptical. I took your test, but if you're going to insist that I do cardio, I need a treadmill or bike. I really hate the elliptical."

"I have to tell you that the elliptical is the most—"

"Yes, I know. I've heard it all before. I hate it. Stationary bike, treadmills, those I can handle."

"Okay." He chuckles and makes some notes on his phone. "Your choice, then. Which one?"

"Let's try the bike."

"Good enough." He leads me over to the line of stationary bikes, chooses an unoccupied one, and makes some settings on the computer. "Go ahead. I've got you set for half an hour. It's a pretty easy setting, but your heart rate should go up nicely."

"All right." I hop on the bike and start pedaling.

And then I really remember how much I hate working out at the gym and how boring stationary bikes are.

Which leads my thoughts—of course—back to Jackson. What is he doing this afternoon?

CHAPTER TWENTY-FOUR

Jackson

Back at my place, I think again about what happened with Blossom. I've never lost it like that before, and I'm not sure I can go back to the club until I figure out what's going on in my own head.

Playing squash with Ben this morning didn't help.

Running into Mandy and her sister at the juice bar *really* didn't help.

What's going on with me?

I went to Mandy's last night because she has always been my safe space. But can she truly be my safe space when I've kept such a significant part of my life from her? She knows now. Hell, I took her to Black Rose. I'm the one who thought I could scare her off random hookups forever, and she'd never know it was me.

Instead? She recognized me immediately, and she embraced it.

Embraced this part of me.

But we didn't do anything. I didn't do anything dark to her. I only thought about it. And damn, it was good. That simple sex with Mandy—it was good.

I haven't been able to admit it to myself until now, but it was *good*.

Is it possible it *wasn't* a mistake?

Could Mandy...

"No," I say out loud. I can't bring Mandy into my scene. She won't understand, and she'll ask a lot of questions.

Questions aren't a bad thing. I had a lot of questions myself, and I found some of the answers at Black Rose. I'm still searching for the rest of the answers. It's about the journey, after all.

Could Black Rose be part of Mandy's journey? Could *I* be?

Maybe I'm...

In love with her. You're in love with her, Jackson.

I ignore the words of my inner voice.

I'm not in love with Mandy. I can't be.

Why not?

Because we don't fit together that way.

Don't you?

And then I hurl backward in time, remembering...

• • •

I'm ready to leave for college, and I'm going far away—so far away that I won't be coming home until Thanksgiving. My D-II football scholarship awaits me, and I'm psyched.

I'm ready to leave.

Except...

Mandy and I already said our goodbyes last night. She choked up, and I pretended like I didn't.

But I want to see her one more time, so I hop into my car and drive to her home. She won't leave for college for another couple of months, not until the end of August. I have to go now because football practice starts next week.

I knock on the door.

Her parents are both at work, so I know she's home alone with Frankie.

Frankie answers the door. "Hey, Jack."

"Hey, Frankie. Where's Mandy?"

"She's in her room."

"Could you tell her I'm here?"

"Go on up." Frankie opens the door.

I walk in and head up the stairs. Mandy's family lives in a small three-level that was built in the seventies. Only three bedrooms upstairs, and I know which one is hers. It's been hers since we were little kids.

"Mandy?" I knock on her door.

She doesn't reply.

I crack the door open. "Mandy?"

"Go away."

Something's wrong. I open the door. Mandy is on her bed, under the covers, her head buried in her pillow.

I sit down next to her, rub her back through the covers. "Mandy Cake? You okay?"

"What are you doing here, Jack?" she chokes out.

"I'm leaving this afternoon. I just wanted to—"

"We already said goodbye."

"I know. I just…I needed to see you once more. I'm really going to miss you, Mandy Cake."

"I'll miss you, too. Now go."

"No. You face me. You tell me goodbye one more time."

"Jack, we already went through this last night."

"I know, but it wasn't enough. You're my best friend. How am I going to get along without you?"

"You'll be fine."

"You're the one I tell everything to."

No response. Just a sniffle.

"Mandy…"

She lifts her head then, turns to me. Her face is swollen and red, her eyes bloodshot.

My heart falls. "What's wrong?"

"Nothing, Jack. Nothing is wrong."

"Whatever it is, I'll fix it."

"You can't fix this, Jack."

"You have to let me try."

She shakes her head, tears rolling down her cheeks. "You, of all people, can never fix this."

"But that's what we do. You fix me and I fix you. We're two sides of the same coin. You're the other half of me, Mandy."

She chokes back a sob, and then she nods. "Don't forget that, Jack. Don't you ever forget that you're the other half of me."

She falls into me then and hugs me as I continue rubbing her back.

A few moments later, after we say goodbye again, I leave her house.

I drive to college.

• • •

I didn't give that conversation another thought for eleven years. Not until now.

The other half of me.

They were *my* words, not hers, and they were the words that made her stop crying.

It was always so easy to dismiss how much Mandy meant to me. She was always there when I needed to talk, but when things were going well—with football, with college, with my woman of the month—I didn't need her.

Only when things got tough.

She was there. Every single time.

She's been the one constant in my life—other than my

parents—for nearly all my twenty-nine years.

That's why I went to her last night. Because she's Mandy. Because I can tell her what's wrong, and she'll fix it. Or I can tell her nothing—as I did last night—and she'll take care of me anyway.

Maybe Ben is right. Maybe I feel more than I've been willing to admit all this time.

Maybe…

I grab my phone and call her.

Damn. Voicemail.

This is Mandy. You know the drill. I'll get back to you as soon as I can.

I clear my throat. "Hey, Mandy—" I stop myself from adding the *Cake*. "It's me. I…need to talk to you. It's important. Call me, okay?"

I'm still in my workout clothes from this morning, so I head down to the street and run. I run and run and run to clear my head.

And I wait for Mandy to return my call.

CHAPTER TWENTY-FIVE

Amanda

After Michael kicked my ass for an hour, he asked if he could see me again, not as a trainer.

I said yes.

I said yes because Jack and I are never going to happen. I said yes because I need to get on with my life.

I said yes because it was empowering.

Michael is the first magnificently good-looking man who has ever shown any kind of interest in me. I'm not going to screw it up. He didn't make a date with me yet, so I'm back at my place, and the workout has left me oddly euphoric. Oh, I'm going to feel it tomorrow, but tonight? I need to do something.

My gaze falls on my laptop sitting on the counter.

Lustr...

I want to go back to that club.

Of course, the chance of me meeting someone who will take me down there is in the one percent range, but why not try?

First, I need some better clothes. I was just at Macy's with Frankie this morning, but they don't carry the kind of garments I'm after. In fact, I have no idea where to get leather and lace and whatever else. But this is what the internet is for. Two clicks later, I find a store—a lingerie shop, actually, but they also stock leather goods.

Treasure's Chest. An interesting name. Two subway stops away, and I'm there. It's a tiny hole-in-the-wall that looks rather unassuming from the outside.

Inside, though? I feel like I just walked into a mannequin dungeon.

A smiling clerk with pretty auburn hair walks toward me. "Good afternoon."

"Hi."

"Are you looking for anything specific today?"

My cheeks are on fire. I'm sure my blush is candy-apple red. She's here to help, so I should just tell her what I want.

Except I'm not exactly sure what I want. Some of the women at the club were wearing pretty normal clothes. Others...not so much.

"I think I'll just look for a while," I say.

"Absolutely," she says. "If you need any help, my name is Mary."

Mary. I can't help a subtle smile. Mary is working in a lingerie and leather store. Mary—the most innocent and sweet name on the planet.

Mary, however, is dressed in leather pants and an emerald-green lace corset that has her boobs squeezed nearly up to her neck. She totally does *not* look like a Mary. Felicia, maybe. Samantha or Jessica. Definitely not Mary.

I wander through the store and stop at the lingerie section. Boy, this stuff is beautiful. And not even remotely inexpensive.

Still, wouldn't it be lovely to have a bra and panties that actually match? I'm drawn to a lacy set. It comes in all colors, and they have my bra size.

I grab a bra and boy shorts in both black and light pink.

I'm not sure why those two colors appeal to me. Maybe it's the contrariness of them. Pink for sweet and innocent. Black for naughty and not so innocent.

Naughty and nice. I feel like I'm making a list for Santa Claus.

Felicia—er, Mary—is right on my heels. "Can I take those up to the counter for you?"

"Sure." I hand the items to her. "I'm still looking."

"Absolutely no hurry. Let me know if you need any assistance."

I wander toward the back of the store—where the leather items reside.

Not only do they have garments, they have toys as well. Fur-lined handcuffs, floggers. None of the instruments look like they could do any real damage. They seem to be for show. Maybe for costuming.

I look over my shoulder, fearful that Mary has followed me here and will try to sell me some of these things. The warmth of my blush creeps up to my cheeks again at the mere thought of talking about these things.

And then…

Something I'm not expecting.

The warmth of a blush…down there.

I *like* the idea of this stuff.

Just like I like the idea of the club.

Was it Jackson? Or was it the club? The leather? The fucking?

A black-and-blue lace corset catches my eye. Or is it a bustier? I don't really know the difference. I've never worn a corset. I always figured they'd be very uncomfortable. I think of the Victorian women who were forced to wear them to make their waists look smaller, their boobs look bigger.

How restrictive…and how misogynistic.

So why am I thinking about putting this on my body?

I have no idea what size I would take.

But…Mary to the rescue.

"Do you know your size?" she asks as she thumbs through the corsets.

"I'm afraid I don't. I guess I'm a novice when it comes to these things." I let out a nervous laugh. I'm a novice at practically everything this store represents.

"You're far from the first one. Are you looking for a corset that cinches the waist only or one that also covers the bust?"

"Uh…definitely want to cover the bust. I guess."

"Perfect. Corsets are based on your actual measurements." She whips out a tape measure. "Here, let me show you. First we need to measure right under your bust."

Mary wraps the tape measure in a circle right under where my boobs fall and writes down some numbers. "Then your natural waist." She moves the tape measure, writes again. "Then your upper hip, and then we need to measure the length of your torso. You have a great hourglass figure."

Yep, the warmth of that blush again.

"This is your first corset, right?"

"Yes."

"Then let's go four inches smaller than your natural waist. That should give you some comfort. Once you get used to wearing a corset, you can go a little smaller." Mary searches through the rack and grabs a corset. "I'll help you. But this corset has its closures and laces in the front, so you will eventually be able to put it on yourself."

"Eventually?"

"Originally, back in the day, all corsets had their laces in the back, so the lady needed her maid to help her get into it every day."

I don't reply.

"Of course today, very few ladies actually have maids to do this." She giggles and rolls her eyes.

A maid. Right. In my tiny rent-controlled apartment.

Maybe I could dash past Mary and reach the exit quickly.

Instead, I follow her like a lemming back to the changing area.

"Take off your shirt and bra, and don't be embarrassed. I do this all the time. I've seen all shapes and sizes of women, and I've helped them all get into corsets."

Interesting that she says that before I make it known that I'm kind of shy. Except then I realize…she can tell. She does this for a living.

I disrobe quickly and Mary positions the corset, snapping it in place. "Okay. Now for the laces. I want you to breathe in and hold your breath for a minute."

I do, and she starts pulling on the laces.

And I feel like someone has shoved a hose down my throat to suck all the air out of me.

"You good? You still need to be able to breathe."

I let my breath out, and then I breathe in again. And oddly, I *can* breathe. In fact, I feel…good. The corset sucks in the flab of my stomach, and I feel like my posture is better than it's ever been.

"You need me to go looser? Tighter?"

"You tell me, I guess. I'm not uncomfortable."

"I can go tighter if you'd like."

"Actually…I think this is about right."

She laughs. "That's fourteen."

"Fourteen what?"

"Fourteen corsets in a row that I've tightened on first-time buyers who say I got it right the first time. When I get to twenty, I get a bonus."

"I guess you're pretty good at your job."

"Thank you. I actually design corsets. I'm hoping Chloe, the owner, will let me sell some of my designs here eventually."

"Really? That's fascinating."

"I love them," Mary says. "I'm not sure why we ever stopped wearing them."

"Probably because they're sexist."

"You have to get past that. I've fit men for corsets in here, too. They're great for your posture, and they help keep your internal organs in the right place. You just have to be careful not to go too tight."

"Interesting."

She hands me a book that was sitting on the shelf of the fitting room. "Have you read this book? It's all about corsets."

"I haven't." I mean really, who has?

Mary, apparently.

"I hope you don't mind," she continues. "I need you to sign a statement saying I got your fitting right the first try. That way I'm up to fourteen and only six more until I get my big bonus from Chloe."

"I'm happy to."

"Awesome. I really appreciate it."

"So…this covers the top of my body. What do I wear on the bottom?"

"Fishnets, thigh-high boots, and a thong?" Mary smiles.

Damn. The warmth of that blush once more. I'm going to burst into flames in another minute.

"I'm kidding. Well, maybe I'm not, but you seem like a newbie."

"A newbie?"

"I've never seen you in here before, and I don't get the feeling you're buying this for costuming."

"I'm… To be honest? I'm not sure why I'm buying this. There's this place…"

"A club?"

"Yeah, a club. I want to learn more."

"Really? We have classes."

"Classes?"

"Yeah. In the BDSM lifestyle. Figuring out whether it's for you."

Interesting. A class. Maybe that's what I need.

"How much do your classes cost?"

"There's no cost for the introductory class if you purchase two hundred dollars in clothing. With the corset and the lingerie you've chosen, you're close to four hundred."

I suck in a breath. And it's not from the corset.

"I know that seems like a lot," she says, "but our merchandise is top-quality. All made here in the USA."

"I see."

"Do you still want to look for something else?"

"Will skinny jeans and black pumps work with this corset?"

"The great thing about a corset is that it goes with anything. You can dress it up or down. If you're going clubbing, yes, skinny jeans go great. If you're into cosplay, it works great for anything steampunk."

"And if…"

"If you're going to a leather club? BDSM club? It's really up to you. The thigh-high boots, fishnets, and thong will help you fit right in. But if you're just beginning, jeans are fine, and the corset will look great no matter what."

"Thanks. I'll stick with the jeans for now. My credit card will thank you."

Mary laughs. "Like I said, our stuff is all top-quality. You won't find the seams ripping out of any of these anytime soon."

"Good to know."

"And if you do? Bring it in. We will repair it free of charge. Just be sure to save your receipt."

"I'll do that."

Mary rings up my purchases, and I hand her my credit card. I'm pretty sure I see it shiver as she slides it through the reader.

"I'm putting the flyer for classes into your bag along with your receipt. Is that okay?"

"Sure. Thanks."

"Don't forget that the intro class is free for you." She folds my items nicely, wraps them in tissue, and places all of them in a simple black paper bag that doesn't have the name of the store on it. "Our customers appreciate discretion," she says.

I understand. "Thank you."

"I hope to see you again soon. The classes are on weeknights, beginning at eight thirty. We close at eight."

"I'll look into it. Thanks again."

I leave the store, clutching my bag.

I'm freaking out more than a little over the fact that I'm thinking about attending a BDSM class.

And liking the idea.

CHAPTER TWENTY-SIX

Jackson

"Hey," Mandy says into the phone when I call her a third time.

"Where have you been? I left you two voicemails."

"Sorry. I had my phone on silent while I was working out this afternoon, and I forgot to put it back on. What's up?"

"Oh…nothing."

"For Christ's sake, Jackson. You called me three times for nothing?"

I clear my throat. "Where are you?"

"Walking to the subway. I just got done doing some shopping."

"Great. Can you meet me for dinner?"

"I don't know, Jackson."

"You've got to eat."

She sighs. "I guess I *am* pretty hungry. I haven't eaten since that smoothie I had with you this morning."

"Why don't I swing by your place and pick you up?"

"Sure. I'll be ready."

"Great. See you in about an hour."

• • •

My jaw drops when Mandy opens her door. I even ignore Roger, which I never do.

No. Mandy is totally *not* wearing a black-and-blue corset. Absolutely not. Not my Mandy Cake.

Except she looks completely gorgeous. Her tits are pushed up by black lace, and the blue brings out the lovely color of her eyes. I'm instantly hard.

"Cat got your tongue?" she asks dryly.

"What the hell is *that*, Mandy?"

"I think it's called a corset. Or a bustier. I'm not quite sure of the difference."

A corset cinches, while a bustier boosts. But I'm not about to tell her that. She'll want to know how I know.

Mandy's wearing a corset.

Mandy's wearing a goddamned corset. A goddamned corset that looks fabulous on her.

Fuck.

"You can't wear that to dinner."

"Why not? It'll keep me from overeating."

"That's not the point, Mandy."

"What is, then, Jackson? All my parts are covered."

"For God's sake, at least put on a jacket or something."

"Well, I was going to. It's a little chilly outside."

Thank God. "You'd really be a lot more comfortable if you'd put on something normal."

"Jack, I'm actually quite comfortable. It's the weirdest thing. I feel like my posture is better. Like everything is where it's supposed to be."

Everything is where it's supposed to be all right. My cock is noticing as much as I am.

My God…

Mandy grabs a white sweater that looks great when she layers it over the black-and-blue lace. Like something angelic over something dark and dirty. Damn. With her curves, the corset totally does its job.

Mandy's a beautiful woman.

You're the other half of me.

Damn those words.

Are they true? I certainly didn't say them with the intention of lying to Mandy. They just came out of my mouth that day. That day when I left her to move forward with my life.

"Where do you want to go?" she asks.

"Sushi?"

"Sushi sounds great. Even though I had it twice in the last week." She laughs.

"I love your laugh," I say. "You seemed… I don't know. Unhappy this morning."

"I *was* unhappy this morning, Jack. Because you were being an ass."

Touché. She's absolutely right. "I'm sorry."

"Look. You told me that what happened between us would never happen again. I accepted it then, and I accept it now."

"I know that."

Except part of me—a really big part of me, the part that controls my cock—doesn't want her to accept it. I'm having a difficult time accepting it myself.

Ben was right. I'm like a six-year-old boy chasing the girl I like around the playground.

Man, I never imagined…

Never in a million years did I imagine Mandy would be…

I don't let myself finish the thought.

Mandy and I leave her building and walk together to another little sushi bar a couple of blocks away. We know all the sushi places near her place.

We find two seats at the bar, and Mandy walks toward them, but I say, "Let's get a table."

"Jack, we always sit at the bar."

"I know. Let's do something different."

She shrugs. "Okay. Whatever."

We wait for the hostess to seat us at a two-top. I was actually hoping for a four-top, but since we're a party of two, I can't make a fuss. A two-top seems so…intimate.

The contradiction inside me is driving me to drink. For a moment, I feel like that mythical creature from *Dr. Dolittle*, the Pushmi-Pullyu.

Before I can say a word to Mandy, a waiter accosts us, asking for drink orders.

"Sake?" I say to Mandy.

She huffs softly. "You know I hate the stuff, Jack. I think I'll have a…dirty martini."

I widen my eyes. "Not a sidecar? I thought you said martinis taste like rubbing alcohol."

"It's a woman's prerogative to change her mind." she says coyly. "Make it a dirty vodka martini."

"Dirty vodka martini for the lady," the waiter says. "And for you, sir?"

"Konteki Tears of Dawn, please."

This time Mandy widens her eyes. It's an expensive sake, but it's one of my favorites. Mandy makes decent money working for her romance author, but I probably make four times what she does. Still, she winces whenever I buy something expensive.

It's kind of how we've always been. She grew up a lot more modestly than I did. Our mothers were best friends, and when they both got married, they lived in the same neighborhood on Long Island. But then my father made it big in a tech start-up, and we moved to a different neighborhood. A much more expensive neighborhood, but still close enough to Mandy that we went to the same schools.

Our moms were pregnant at the same time, too. Mandy came early, and she's actually a month and three days older than I am.

When I say we've been best friends since we were in diapers, I'm not exaggerating.

The waiter nods and heads to the bar.

Mandy picks up her pencil and her menu. "I'm in the mood for some unagi today."

"You're always in the mood for unagi."

"It's my favorite."

"But it's cooked."

"So what? Sushi doesn't have to be raw to be good."

"Let me guess. Dragon roll, right? Salmon skin roll. Plus a few pieces of nigiri unagi."

She shakes her head, sighing. "You know what? No. No unagi tonight. Just like no sidecar."

"Mandy…"

"It's time to expand my horizons, Jack. I'm wearing a corset, and I'm having a dirty martini. Let's change things up in the sushi area as well." She glances at her menu and makes several checkmarks with her small pencil.

And I'm ridiculously curious. I wait for her to tell me what she's ordering.

But she doesn't.

And for God's sake, it's driving me up the wall. Why? Why do I care what she's ordering?

I regard my own menu, check off all my favorites. Spicy tuna roll. Salmon, tuna, escolar. Chile yellowtail roll.

All the while, I have an obsessive desire to know what Mandy has ordered.

The waiter—Haru—returns with our drinks, and Mandy takes a sip of her martini. Her eyes widen slightly—only slightly, but I notice.

Did she forget that she hates martinis? Or maybe she hates gin martinis. By the look of her, she's not fond of vodka martinis, either.

"Delicious," she says.

The waiter grabs her paper. "Finished here?"

"Yes, thank you."

Then he lifts his eyebrows at me.

I hand him mine. "Here you go. Thanks."

"I'll get this started for you right away."

What did you order, Mandy?

The words sit at the tip of my tongue. Why do I care so much?

She doesn't seem to worry about what I've ordered. She already knows. She knows all my sushi favorites, just like I know hers.

"So...?" she says.

"So...what?"

"You called me three times today. You clearly want to talk to me about something. Maybe you want to explain why you left my house in the middle of the night?"

I have no answer. At least not one my conscious mind is going to let me say.

"It's nothing, Mandy. Everything's fine."

"Everything's not fine, Jackson. Something was bothering you last night. It was bothering you enough that you ended up at my apartment, standing over me while I slept. Now spill it."

Spill it. That's what Mandy always says when something's bothering me. Normally I can spill it pretty quickly.

This?

I'm not even sure what there is to spill.

Except I do know, and I'm just not willing to face it yet. My guilt about Blossom. My emerging feelings for my best friend. My knowledge that I can never commit to her and give her what she deserves. All this and then some.

"What made you buy a corset?" comes out of my mouth instead.

"I don't know. What made you buy those jeans you're wearing?"

"Okay. Who are you and what have you done with Amanda

Thomas?"

"I *am* Amanda Thomas. Who are you, and what have you done with Jackson Paris?"

"I am who I've always been, Mandy. I'm wearing the same clothes I always wear on a Saturday—jeans and a button-down."

"Don't give me that. You have a"—she clears her throat—"sex life I knew nothing about until days ago. And you came to me last night, and you weren't okay then."

"Maybe I got over it."

"And maybe you're lying."

"Tell you what… Let's make a deal. You tell me why you're wearing a corset, and I'll tell you why I came to your place last night."

She smiles. "Okay, if you want to play it that way. I bought a corset because I've never owned one before. I'm intrigued by the idea."

"You're intrigued by a corset?"

She glances down at the table. "Yeah. Is that so hard to believe?"

"It's absolutely hard to believe. Corsets went out of style about two hundred years ago. They're restrictive and really, really sexist." There. That ought to get her. Mandy's nothing if not an ardent feminist.

"It just so happens that Mary, the salesclerk who sold me this one, mentioned she's fit men for corsets before. And as for being in style, I seem to recall seeing a couple women wearing them at your club."

I jerk my head around. "Mandy, you can't mention that place here."

"I can't mention that I went to a club? I didn't say where it was. I'll never say its name. I understand the document I signed."

She's right, of course. Talking about a club is not against her nondisclosure agreement. And talking about it with me—the person who took her there—is certainly fine as well.

The damned place didn't scare her.

It didn't scare her at all.

But maybe it still could. Maybe I can get her off Lustr once and for all.

"Would you like to go back to the club, Mandy?"

She blushes. Oh my God, the tops of her breasts, very visible in the corset, are the same beautiful pink as her cheeks.

I never got to play with those breasts, never got to suck on those beautiful little nipples.

My groin tightens unbearably.

"I would, actually."

Fuck. Not the answer I wanted but the one I expected. I have to go all in now.

"Fine. Let's eat our sushi. Then we'll go back." We sure will, and I'll make sure, this time, that she never wants to return.

And we'll work whatever this is between us out of our systems once and for all. Surely that's possible. I don't question if it's really what I want. It is.

"You're not exactly dressed for it," she says.

"No, but you are. There's no required dress code at the club. Surely you figured that out after your time there."

"I did, and I felt very free. You can walk in wearing normal clothes, or you can walk around naked. Or you can wear a corset. Or leather. Or pasties and a thong."

Her blush is driving me senseless.

Mandy in pasties and a thong.

I've got to get a grip.

The waiter brings the miso soup I ordered. Mandy gets nothing, so apparently she didn't order soup. At least I know that now.

I inhale the savory broth, dip my ceramic spoon in, and bring it to my lips. I blow on it, all the while watching Mandy.

She's still blushing.

I bring the spoon to my mouth and—

Crap. Hot. Now I burned my tongue.

"You okay?" she asks.

"No, I'm not okay, Mandy. The soup is hot."

"I saw you blow on it."

"Apparently I didn't blow on it long enough."

Of course I didn't. I was too busy watching Mandy. Looking at that beautiful blush on her cheeks, her boobs pushing up from the stays in the corset.

"Get an ice cube from Haru."

"It's fine." I stir the soup, dropping my gaze.

"So now you're going to get all pissy," she says. "Pretty soon, you're going to think of some excuse *not* to take me back to the club."

CHAPTER TWENTY-SEVEN

Amanda

He doesn't respond.

Yep. I called it.

Until—

"No, Mandy. I'll take you. I'm nothing if not a man of my word."

When Haru brings our sushi, Jackson stares at mine.

"What is that thing?" He points to one of my pieces.

"Sea urchin."

He wrinkles his forehead. "Sea urchin? Seriously?"

"Yeah. I've never had it before."

"I haven't, either."

"Do you want to try it?"

He smiles. "Not even a little bit. But you try it. Tell me how it is."

Damn him. But hey, I'm trying new things, right? I'm done taking the safe route. I'm stepping out of my comfort zone. I'm drinking a vodka martini that doesn't taste much better than those Sapphire martinis Frankie loves. I'm wearing a corset, thinking about taking a BDSM class.

Scratch that. I *am* taking a BDSM class.

Tonight? Jackson is going to take me back to the club. He said so himself, and I'm not going to let him weasel out of it.

I bring the piece of sea urchin to my mouth and take a bite. The rest of it falls into a heap of seafood and rice on my plate.

Okay, not too awkward...

It tastes...like the ocean. Kind of briny, a little salty. Maybe even a touch of sweetness. Maybe a little metallic?"

"You like it, then?"

Do I? It's different, for sure. Creamy on my tongue. Creamier even than raw salmon, which is my favorite after unagi.

I look down at the mess on my plate. "I'm not sure how to eat the rest of this. My chopsticks certainly won't work."

Jackson laughs.

"What's so funny? You've never dropped a piece of sushi before?"

"Oh, it's not that."

"What is it, then?"

"You just ate gonads, Mandy. Sea urchin sex organs."

I drop my jaw but then shut my mouth quickly, trying to ignore the gag reflex at the back of my throat. So I just ate sea urchin ovaries. Or testicles. Or both. "Oh?"

"That's right. The only edible part of the sea urchin is its gonads."

I refuse to let him get to me. "Well, it was good. I might even order another."

He guffaws. "Be my guest."

"If I'm still hungry after I finish everything else, I'm absolutely going to order another."

"Please."

"Have you ever even tried it?"

"Nope."

"Why not?"

He laughs. "Because I found out it's gonads."

"How can you be so close-minded, Jackson? I've seen you

eat sweetbreads. I've seen you eat chicken livers."

"But you haven't seen me eat Rocky Mountain oysters."

"Can you even get them here in New York?"

"If you look hard enough. I don't have any desire for bull testicles."

He's being an ass again. What is wrong with him? Just for this, I'm going to finish the sea urchin. Yes, I'm going to eat sex organs. I gesture to Haru, who's walking back from another table.

"Yes?" he says.

"I've had a little faux pas with my sea urchin. Could I please have a fork so I can finish it?"

Haru smiles.

A great big smile, and he's quite good-looking with a marble jaw line. "Absolutely. I'll be right back."

I'll show Jackson Paris. I can eat gonads, I can wear a corset, I can flirt with a hot waiter, and I can go to Black Rose Underground. I am so done being sweet and virginal little Mandy Cake who always takes the safe route.

Haru brings my fork, and I gobble up the last of the sea urchin. I'll probably never order it again, but hey, I went out of my comfort zone. I finish the rest of my sushi, all of which is delicious, but I still miss my unagi.

Damn Jackson anyway. From now on, I'll order whatever I want, whether Jackson recites it to me or not.

The next time Haru comes by, I gesture to my martini glass. "Another, please?"

"Absolutely." He grabs the empty glass.

"Another?" Jackson says.

"Yeah, a martini is oddly good with sushi."

I'm not even lying. The vodka martini got a lot better after half of it went down, and it goes well with raw fish. Who would've thought? I don't drink a lot, though, and it's pure booze. This will be my last one. Especially if I do end up going to the club. I want to be fully alert there.

Jackson doesn't order another sake.

I'm not sure why that strikes me as strange. Jackson usually has two drinks. Sometimes even three. I've never seen him drunk, come to think of it.

He doesn't do anything that may make him lose control.

Interesting.

Very interesting.

Oh, yes. He's definitely taking me back to the club.

CHAPTER TWENTY-EIGHT

Jackson

The club opens at nine. It's eight thirty when we finish our sushi. Too early to go to the club yet.

"Well?" Mandy says.

"Well, what?"

"Are we going? To the club?"

"Are you sure you want this?"

God, let her say no. Please. Because if I take her to the club, I have to show her.

I have to show her why she doesn't belong there.

And why I can never have her.

I don't like this side of me. Not at all. I was a complete ass at dinner about the sea urchin gonads. I gave her shit that she didn't deserve, and she was a great sport about it.

Why can't I just walk away from this? Let her explore her sexuality in her own way? This doesn't have to involve me, so why...

I can't finish the thought.

"I'm sure, Jack," she finally replies.

"It doesn't open until nine."

"That's fine. I'll just have another drink." She gestures to Haru.

I grab her hand and bring it back to the table. "No more drinks, Mandy."

"Why not? It will take the edge off."

"That's just it. You can't take the edge off. If I'm going to take you to the club, you need to be fully aware of everything you're doing. You need to be able to tell me to stop if you want to."

God, that blush. Over her cheeks, the tops of her rosy breasts...

She's going to be the undoing of me.

And it dawns on me.

I'm not afraid that she won't like my dark side.

I'm afraid that she *will*.

That she'll like it and want it...and after three months, I'll lose interest and it will be over. But it won't just be another notch on my headboard for me. It will be the end of the most significant friendship I've ever had.

The other half of me.

"All right, Jack. No more drinks."

Good. No more drinks. For either of us. Except that now I have half an hour to fill.

"How about dessert?" I suggest.

"I couldn't eat anything more. The corset and all."

She's right. Plus... If I'm going to introduce her to the darker side of my lifestyle, I don't want her belly full and bloated. How can I get out of this?

I motion to Haru for the check. He brings it, and I throw my credit card on top.

"I can pay for my own," Mandy says.

"Don't be silly. I invited you."

Haru takes the card, brings it back quickly, and I add my usual twenty percent tip. For a split second, I thought about giving him twenty-five percent, as his service was impeccable, but I didn't appreciate how he was eyeing Mandy like a hot-fudge sundae every time he was at our table.

Of course, every man in the place is eyeing Mandy. She's wearing a damned corset.

I rise and offer my hand. "Ready?"

She declines to take my hand, which is unusual. "Ready as I'll ever be."

Her words aren't lost on me. She's not ready for what I have in mind, and no, she won't ever be. But it's best that she find out now.

Again, the fear pokes at the back of my neck—the fear that she is ready, that she'll like what I'm going to show her.

No. She can't. She has to hate it.

Then maybe I can get her out of my mind.

At least out of my sexual mind. Forever.

When we reach the building, I pull a silk blindfold out of my pocket. Funny that I thought to bring it along. Maybe somewhere in my subconscious, I knew we'd end up here tonight. "I'm sorry, but since you're not a member..."

"Right. I understand. Alfred told me last time."

"That wasn't Alfred. It was me. Remember?"

"Right. You whispered. You tried to hide who you were."

Yes. I did. And I didn't do a very good job of it. Was that on purpose?

"You look like yourself tonight, Jack," Mandy says. "No slicked-back hair, no fake contact lenses."

"I was trying to hide from *you*, Mandy Cake. Not from the people in the club. They all know me. And they've all signed—"

"Nondisclosure agreements, yes, I know. And quit calling me Mandy Cake."

"Of course."

Mandy Cake comes out automatically. To be truthful? She doesn't seem like Mandy Cake tonight. She hasn't in a while. I'm not even sure she seems like Mandy.

Amanda.

She's Amanda now. Amanda, wearing a fucking corset that makes her look *more* delicious than a freaking hot-fudge sundae.

I slip the blindfold over her, lead her to the staircase and then to a special elevator.

Once we're at the door, I remove her blindfold.

Then we enter.

"Claude," I say, "you remember Amanda."

"Yes. Your nondisclosure agreement lasts for a year. So you're good."

"Thank you."

"Enjoy yourselves." Claude smiles and hands me a pager and a velvet choker, which Mandy *will* wear this evening.

"Oh, we will," Mandy says.

I Velcro the black choker in place. God, she looks hot.

"What would you like to do?" I ask.

"Whatever you want."

Damn. Those are fighting words. Right now, I want to bind her wrists. Turn her around. Flog her sweet ass and then bury my nose between her cheeks and lick her asshole. Give her the rimming of a lifetime.

Has Amanda ever had a rimming?

I should be wary of flogging her ass after what happened with Blossom, but I'm not.

Already I know I won't go too far with Mandy.

Already I know I will get her ass to the perfect blush—matching her cheeks.

Then I'll slide my tongue between those cheeks, lick and suck at her asshole.

After that, I'll glide my tongue through her succulent pussy—that pussy that tastes like apples and vanilla and the sweetest cream.

"Jack?"

"Yeah?"

"Didn't you hear me? I said whatever you want."

"Why don't we start with a dance." I pull her close.

The sound system is playing a slow song, and she feels so right against my body. It's like her curves fill in every notch.

Even in the corset.

God, the corset. Has Mandy ever looked so sexy?

Yes. That night at my parents' house. In that pink camisole. When I had some very un–Mandy Cake thoughts about her.

Yet the thoughts I'm having now? They make the thoughts I had then feel like a schoolboy crush.

That night, I didn't think about rimming her perfect little asshole.

That night, I didn't think about tying her up.

Nope. That night, I just thought about her in a sexual way for the first time.

Now that I've had her?

I'm not sure I can let her go.

I have to. I must.

I dart my gaze around the room—

Blossom.

Damn.

Boner killer.

And I realize...

I can't do this.

I can't put Mandy in any impending danger. Look what happened with Blossom. And while I care about Blossom, like her as a person, she means nothing to me compared to Mandy.

I cannot risk Mandy being hurt. I absolutely cannot.

I brush her away from me. "We need to leave."

Her jaw drops. "What?"

"You heard me. I need to get you out of here."

She whips her hands to her hips. "I'm not leaving."

"Yes, you are. You're my guest. If I'm not here, you can't be here."

"You *are* here, Jack."

"Not for long." I head toward Claude's desk.

Mandy yanks on my arm, and I turn to face her.

"No, Jackson. I'm not going to let you do this. You're not going to run away again."

"Who says I'm running away?"

"You ran away the last time. You told me this could never happen again. Then you show up at my house and run away in the middle of the night. And now?" She shakes her head. "You're not running away from me this time. We're going to do this."

"Last time I checked, we *both* need to consent," I say dryly.

"Fine." She turns. "If it's so abhorrent to you to be here with me—"

I grab her, pull her into my embrace.

This is Mandy. She is so much more than this club. She's *everything*—everything *except* the club.

This is the one part of my life that I can never let Mandy into.

Now? She's interested. Seriously interested, and I...

Again the Pushmi-Pullyu from *Dr. Dolittle* invades my mind. Part of me wants to introduce Mandy to my lifestyle so much. I want her to enjoy what I enjoy.

And at the same time...I don't. I don't with every fiber of my being.

I don't want to taint Mandy. I don't want her to be one in my long list of women I couldn't commit to. I don't want to lose our friendship.

I hug her tightly, savoring the fruity scent of her hair, the feel of her body melted against mine, and then—

I let her go.

CHAPTER TWENTY-NINE

Amanda

"For God's sake," I say. "What is it now?"

"I don't want to lose you," Jack says.

"On what planet would you lose me?"

"If we... If we go down this road, Mandy. What if it doesn't work out between us? You know I'm not a commitment type of guy. What if..."

Right. I suppose he's right, ultimately. I've been in love with him for so long that I never imagined it *wouldn't* work out between us.

So here he is...afraid I'll go running from his preferred way of sex. Doesn't he know that he could be anything short of a mass murderer and I'd still love him?

And that's the whole issue. He has no idea how I truly feel about him.

"I *want* to go down this road, Jack."

"I do, too. And I also don't."

"What if I take a class?"

"What?" His eyebrows rise.

"The staff of Treasure's Chest, where I got the corset, said they give classes. Mary told me—" I widen my eyes.

No. No freaking way.

She's here. Mary is *here*.

"What's wrong?" Jack asks.

"The clerk from the lingerie store. She's here. At least I think that's her."

Jackson follows my gaze with his own. "*That's* her?"

"I think so." Nerves again. So many nerves.

"For the love of God…" Jack rubs his forehead.

"What's the matter?"

"Nothing. We've got to leave, Mandy. Please."

Jackson's eyes are haunted. Distraught. I don't want to leave, but—

"All right."

He leads me toward Claude's desk and out the door.

"What's this about, Jack? Do you know Mary?"

His eyes are glazed over, still haunted. "Yeah, I know her. Her real name is Mariah. In here she goes by Blossom."

I'm not sure what to say, so I say nothing. I just stand there, feeling the color drain from my skin.

"So you and Mary…"

"In the past. Not…recently."

Nausea crawls up my throat. I lean against the wall next to the door to the club. Costumed members come and go, and I wish for my blindfold.

I wish for a blindfold that can not only cover my eyes but change the last ten minutes.

"Mandy…"

"It's fine, Jack. Everything's fine."

But everything is so *not* fine.

I bought a corset from a woman who has had sex with the man I love.

My one true love.

Except can he be my one true love if he doesn't return my feelings? He can't. Which means I have no choice. I have *got* to work this man out of my system if we have any chance of saving our friendship.

I move away from the wall, force my legs to turn the jelly back into muscle.

"I want to go back in, Jack."

"Mandy…"

"Jack, this is something I need. And I swear to God, if you don't take me back in there, I'll find someone else who will."

CHAPTER THIRTY

Jackson

Mandy's silver gray eyes are on fire. And that gorgeous blush? It's on her cheeks, her neck, the tops of her breasts.

And here I am…guilty—and rightfully so—over what happened between Blossom and me. Upset that Blossom has made her way into Mandy's life. And the worst of it?

I'm so fucking aroused, I can't see straight.

Mandy… Mandy and her blush.

I breathe in, out, back in again.

An unaccompanied man wearing a *Phantom of the Opera* mask walks toward the door.

"What about him?" Mandy says. "He's alone. Perhaps he'll take me into the club. Sir…?"

The Phantom of the Opera looks toward us. "Yes?"

"I was wondering if—"

"Damn it, Mandy." I grab her a little more harshly than I mean to and lead her through the door of the club.

"Jack!"

"Quiet," I say.

We get past Claude as quickly as possible and into the club.

Then I turn to her. "What the hell do you think you're doing?"

"I think I'm getting into the club."

"You don't even know that guy."

"I didn't need to know him, did I? I'm in the club." She smiles at me. And damn it, her smile is full of cheekiness and... sheer beauty.

A few regulars glance at me, surprise in their eyes. For sure. I'm usually dressed in my black jeans, or at least in black pants, when I come here. Tonight I'm wearing regular blue jeans and a button-down.

But Mandy...

Mandy is wearing that black-and-blue lace corset, and I can't keep my eyes off her. And that black choker from Claude? I imagine it as a collar of diamonds and sapphires, sparkling around Amanda's slender neck.

"We're leaving," I say.

"Go ahead. I'm already in."

"You're here as my guest."

"Fine. I'll just go find the Phantom of the Opera, and I'll be *his* guest."

My God, she's going to send me to an early grave.

I breathe in, out, in again. *Take it down a notch, Jack*, I tell myself.

"All right, Mandy," I say. "What would you like to do?"

"I want you to answer my question."

I rub my temples. "What question?"

"Back at the restaurant, you said if I told you why I'm wearing a corset, you'd tell me why you came to my place last night."

Damn. She's right. I did make that promise.

"I needed to see you. Be with you." True enough.

But that's not enough for Mandy, nor do I delude myself into thinking it is.

She lifts her eyebrows. "Why?"

"Because you... You're my safe place, Mandy."

The blue-gray of her eyes soften then, and I know she won't push me. Thank God, because I'm not ready to tell her what happened with Blossom. As much as I want Mandy to run from this club, I don't want her to run from *me*.

We're here now. We're here because she wants to be, or at least she thinks she wants to be. "What do you want to do?"

There. The ball's in her court. She has to decide whether she truly wants to stay here.

I expect her to want to leave any minute now.

Instead, she pulls me over to the bar. "Two mineral waters, please," she says to the bartender on duty.

Good girl. She knows she's had enough to drink. She knows I've had enough to drink.

Our mineral waters slide before us, and I take a long sip.

Damn, I'm dehydrated. I feel like my blood is dried up into powder.

Mandy drinks hers slowly and glances around the club. "Tell me about this place," she says.

"You know about it. You've been here before."

"I have, but you can tell me anything. I'm bound by my nondisclosure agreement. How long have you been coming here, Jackson?"

"A couple of years."

"And you said it's by invitation only?"

"Yeah."

"Who invited you?"

What she's really asking is whoever it was, how did they know I'd like this place? She's asking about me. Why I enjoy this place.

"Does it matter?" I ask.

She takes another sip of her soda water. "No, I guess it really doesn't."

"What you're really asking is why I like to come here."

"No, I'm not asking that. I think I've already figured that out."

I raise my eyebrows. "Oh, you have?"

"This place is very freeing, Jackson. Everyone here is doing something they want to do without fear of being judged for it."

I'm taken aback. Wow. She does get it. That's not all of it, but it's part of it.

Is my Mandy Cake seriously not so pure and innocent as snow?

"Am I right?"

Part of me wants to take her in my arms, tell her yes, she's right, and I'm so happy she understands.

Part of me wants to yell at her. Tell her she's wrong and that she doesn't belong here. Part of me wants to protect her from this world.

But why would I want to protect her from this world? This is my world. A world I enjoy. It's part of what makes me *me*.

Except...Mandy being here...

It led to what happened with Blossom. Led to me losing control, and that can never happen again.

Which means...

Mandy can't be here.

"Listen, Mandy," I say. "This place isn't for you."

"You keep saying that."

"I'm saying it for a reason. The things that happen here are..."

"Dark? Sexy?" She pauses a few seconds. *"Taboo?"*

My God, I'm horny just hearing her say those words.

So much of me wants to take her back to a suite, tie her up, bind her, flog her skin until it's as rosy pink as that gorgeous blush on her cheeks, and then slide between her legs and thrust inside her.

Already I know what she feels like. She's like heaven on my cock. Paradise between her sweet legs.

I'm so fucked.

But maybe… Maybe she needs to see that side of me.

Maybe that's what will ultimately show her that this place isn't for her. She'll want to leave, and we can reclaim our friendship.

I set my glass on the bar and stand, meet her lovely silver gaze. "Let's go."

CHAPTER THIRTY-ONE

Amanda

J ackson's eyes.
That luscious combination of green and gold and amber brown.

Even in the dim light of the club, they sparkle. They call to me.

And right now? They're searing into me as if he can see through my body straight into my soul.

Fear slashes through me—but not in a bad way.

And I wonder... Is this why I've always been in love with Jack? Is this why no other man would do it for me? Because of Jack, because of who he is? Is it that I always knew, on some level, that he had a kinkier side?

Does that mean I have a kinky side, too?

I can't deny that this place intrigues me, turns me on, gets me to a state of arousal I never knew existed. But is that the place? Or is it Jack? Or both?

Jack takes my hand, and I relish the feeling of my fingers entwined with his. We've held hands before. We're best friends, of course. But tonight it feels different. I feel overshadowed by him, by his magnificence, yet I feel more myself than I have in a long time.

He lets me lead. He keeps his hand on my back, and he guides me, but he lets me lead.

If he's a Dominant, why is he letting me lead?

And then I know. I know as if I've always known. He's letting me set the boundaries.

Is that what Dominants do?

Or is that just what best friends do?

We pass through the door from the open area of the club to the hallway that leads to the big rooms and the smaller rooms.

How many rooms has Jackson been in? How many—

"Where would you like to start?" He drops into my thoughts.

"Wherever you want."

He shakes his head. "God, Mandy…"

"What? Did I say something wrong?"

He adjusts his crotch. "No, you said something *right*. Damn."

"How? How is it right?"

"It's what a submissive would say."

I tingle all over. He just used the word "submissive" to describe me—not exactly, but sort of. And I…I feel like the word *defines* me. Or at least it defines me with regard to *him*.

For the life of me, I can't understand why I feel so empowered by it.

He leads me to a room that's unoccupied, pushes the door open after keying in a code, and then closes it behind him.

Then he pushes me against the wall, sears his gaze into mine.

"The submissive has a lot of power in the Dominant and submissive relationship," he says in a raspy voice. "Something you'd do well to understand."

"Why would that be so difficult for me to understand?"

"Most people assume submissives lack power, and—"

"I'm an introvert, Jack. I prefer doing my work in my pajamas while sitting at my small table. I have very few friends." I look straight into his gorgeous eyes. "That doesn't mean I'm not an empowered woman."

He lifts his eyebrows. "I never said you weren't."

"You kind of did. Maybe I *am* submissive. What's wrong with that? If it's what I want, why shouldn't it empower me?"

He doesn't reply. Only a soft groan that I can feel more than hear coming from his chest.

He strokes my cheek with his fingers, traces my upper lip and then my lower. "How have I never noticed how beautiful you are?"

My legs turn to jelly. I'm actually quivering inside, and every quiver is surging straight to my throbbing pussy.

"Everything about you, Mandy. I've always loved you, but…"

I desperately want him to complete the sentence. I bite my lower lip, will him with my mind to keep talking. To tell me what I want to hear.

Instead, he says, "Are you sure about this?"

I nod.

"I need to hear you say the words. I need you to say, 'Yes, Jackson, I'm sure.'"

"Yes, Jackson, I'm sure." My voice doesn't crack.

"All right. What would you like?"

I give him what I hope is a teasing smile. "Whatever you'd like."

Then his lips are on mine, and he's kissing me, shoving his tongue into my mouth and twirling it with mine.

He tastes a little like sake, a little like mint, and a lot like the most delicious thing in the world.

I return his kiss. I return it with all the desire and passion in my soul.

I could kiss Jack forever and never tire of it. He kisses like no one. Sure, I've only had sex with two other men besides him, but I've kissed a few others. No one has ever kissed me like this.

Does he kiss all his women like this? Or is this special? Just for me?

I don't know. I will probably never know.

He deepens the kiss then, cupping both my cheeks. Holding my face, and it's so sweet and gentle but at the same time heart-pounding and arousing.

He burrows into me, and his hard cock presses against my belly.

He's turned on. As turned on as I am. Is this truly just physical for him? Or is there emotion?

I won't know. Not tonight at least. But that's not what tonight is for. Tonight is for me to learn. Tonight is for me to show him I belong here.

And then? Maybe he'll return my feelings and maybe he won't, but it's time for me to stop hiding in my apartment. Stop hiding behind my laptop and pajamas.

It's time for me to learn who *I* am. It's time for me to embrace my sexual identity, learn how to please a partner, and then I'll show Jack what he means to me.

If he doesn't feel the same way?

I'll be devastated, but I will go on.

Hell, I've been going on this long.

I let one of my arms drop, and I reach between us and cup his bulge.

Another groan from him. I swear to God, I feel it down to my belly.

He pulls away, breaks the kiss. My lips are stinging, and I absently bring my fingers to them.

"Mandy..." he growls.

"Jackson..."

"Are you sure? Are you really fucking sure?"

"Yes."

"I need your consent. And you need a safe word."

"What about the pager?"

"I may bind your wrists, but I won't bind your mouth. So tonight you need a safe word."

My tummy flutters. "Okay."

"If what I'm doing to you is uncomfortable in any way, you say the word. Do you understand?"

"Yes, Jack. I understand."

"Normally partners choose a safe word together."

I wrinkle my forehead. "I don't know what to choose. You choose one for me."

"All right. Your safe word is"—he drops his gaze to my chest—"blush."

"Blush?"

"It's the first word that came to my mind," he says. "Remember. If I'm hurting you, or if you're in any way uncomfortable for whatever reason, you just say that word. Blush."

"Blush," I whisper.

"Understand?"

"Yes"—I smile—"sir."

CHAPTER THIRTY-TWO

Jackson

Sir. Oh my God, my groin is on fire.

I didn't tell her to call me sir. Is she truly a natural submissive? And she's been here, underneath my eyes, the whole time? How did I never see it?

Except...maybe I did see it, and I looked away before I let it into my conscious mind.

This is Mandy.

My Mandy Cake.

Fuck. This is why she asked me not to call her by that nickname anymore. Because she's *not* so sweet and innocent.

She's not at all who I've created her to be in my mind.

She asked for a teacher. I've never taken that role. The subs I normally play with are experienced. I'd do anything for Mandy, and if this is what she wants? I will try...and hope that our friendship survives.

"Take off your clothes," I command.

She begins loosening the ties on her corset.

My God, I'm going to explode.

Once the corset is loose, she unsnaps the hooks. And then she parts it slowly...

So damned slowly that I'm aching.

Her beautiful tits fall gently against her chest, and her hourglass figure...

The only thing that stands between her and me is her pumps and jeans.

She kicks off the shoes, unsnaps and unzips the jeans slowly, and slides them over her hips.

I suck in another breath.

Pink lace panties. Boy shorts. So contrary to the black-and-blue corset.

And so fucking hot.

She flicks her fingers underneath the waistband, ready to remove them, when—

"No. Not yet. Turn around, Mandy."

She obeys me, and I take a few steps backward to admire her ass in the lace. It's not a thong, but in its way it's even hotter. The lace settles in the crack of her ass, and I imagine my tongue there, embedded between her flushed cheeks.

Oh my God...

I walk toward her, brush my hands over the silhouette of her figure until I'm touching the pink lace. "Hold still." I slide the panties over her hips, thighs, calves. I kneel, massage the globes of her ass. And then—

I swipe my tongue between them.

"Oh!" She shudders.

"Hold still, Mandy."

My tongue is between the cheeks of Mandy's ass. Her hole is taut and tight. I slide my tongue over it.

"Tell me," I say against her flesh, "how many other men have licked this beautiful asshole?"

She shudders again, and I feel it through my whole body.

"Am I the first?"

No response.

"Tell me I'm the first, Mandy. Tell me I'm the first man to

have his tongue on your ass."

"You're the first." She gasps in a breath. "This is…"

"This is what?"

"It's…"

"Forbidden?"

She sighs. "Yes. Forbidden. And good. Very, very good."

Yes, it's very, *very* good.

"My God, Jack. How can this feel so amazing?"

I should tell her not to talk. That's what I do with most of my subs when I'm doing a scene.

But not this time. I want to hear her. I want to hear every gasp of pleasure, every breath of desire.

I want to hear her say my name.

As if she's reading my mind…

"Jackson…"

"Yes?"

"I…"

"What?"

She shakes her head, doesn't complete her sentence or her thought.

That's okay. I'm busy eating her delectable ass.

I could munch on her all night, but after a few more moments, I stop. It takes everything I have in me to stop, because what I really want to do is stick my finger inside her, stretch her, get it ready to accommodate my cock.

But that takes more preparation. And even though I think she would let me do it if I asked, there's more I must show her first.

Anal can be done anywhere. This club is for other kinds of kink.

I rise, turn her around to face me, gaze at her body.

"So beautiful," I say.

Then she blushes. That beautiful blush that I've never seen on any other human being. It's a different pink. A pink like the blush on a sweet Rainier cherry. A pink that belongs only to Amanda.

"Hold out your wrists," I say.

She obeys instantly.

"Stand there."

I walk to the wall, pull off a set of fur-lined handcuffs. She's not ready for regular cuffs yet. I don't want to take the chance of chafing her delicate wrists. I bring the cuffs to her, lock them in place so her wrists are bound.

"Okay?" I ask.

"Yes, sir. Absolutely fine."

God, the word "sir" from her lips. It's like she was born to say it. Born to say it to *me*.

"Come here." I gesture, nodding to the leather table.

She walks toward me.

"Bend over the table, Mandy."

Again, she obeys without question. *Good little sub.*

Her wrists are cuffed, but I won't bind her to the table. Not yet.

I walk to the wall, choose a light flogger. Not a whip. I may never use a whip again after what happened with Blossom.

Instinctively, though, I know I'll never hurt Mandy. It's never my intention to hurt anyone, and—

Crap.

Mood killer.

I can't do this. I walk around to the front of the table and click the handcuffs off her.

"What are you doing?"

"I'm letting you go."

"No! You promised me. I want this, Jack."

"I know you do, Mandy. But I *don't*."

She frowns. And it's not a sad frown. It's an angry frown. As if something has opened up inside her. "You're not playing fair."

"To the contrary. I'm playing very fair. I'm thinking about

you. Not about myself."

"Did I ever ask you to do that? I want this. And if you want this, Jack, think about yourself."

"I don't want to hurt you."

"You won't hurt me. You gave me a safe word to guard against that."

She's not wrong.

Never—before Blossom the other night—have I distrusted myself here at the club. And what happened with Blossom was because of this woman before me. Because of Mandy. Because I was thinking of someone else instead of focusing on Blossom.

And that's on me.

"I swear to God, Jack, if you make me leave, I'll never speak to you again."

Her words cut me like a knife. We've had our scuffles before—sometimes knock-down, drag-outs—but neither of us has ever threatened to cut the other out of their life for good.

Mandy could be speaking from her libido. She's turned on, and she wants release.

Or she could be serious.

"Mandy..."

She faces me then, cups both my cheeks in her soft hands. "Please, Jack. I want to try this. And if you won't teach me..."

Someone else will.

Those are the words she doesn't say. She's right. I could walk out of this room and into the main area and find twenty people willing to teach her right now.

If she's determined... If she truly wants to try this...

I must be the one.

"All right, Mandy."

And inside, I say the words to myself that I don't say to her.

But you may not want to speak to me ever again after this anyway.

CHAPTER THIRTY-THREE

Amanda

I hold my wrists out to Jackson, and he secures them in the cuffs once more.

The fur is at once cool and warm against my wrists.

And I feel…at Jack's mercy.

It feels right. Oh so right.

"Bend over the table again," he says.

I do so, and the black leather of the table is cool against my skin. I suppress a shiver. For I know I will be warm soon.

Jackson is behind me. I feel his warmth even though I can't see him.

Something slides up my back. The flogger Jackson took from the wall earlier. He slides it over each arm, then down my back, over my ass.

Then—

I cry out as it comes down on my ass.

"Okay?" he says.

"More than okay."

The feathery leather comes down on my ass again. It doesn't hurt. Not at all. Simply tickles as intense sparks shoot through me.

Do I expect him to hurt me?

Do I *want* him to hurt me?

I think I do. I think I want to understand what he finds here. Perhaps I want to find it for myself.

"Harder," I say.

"I decide how hard, Mandy. I make the decisions here. Is that clear?"

"Yes, sir." I smile as my nerves sizzle beneath my skin.

The instrument hits my ass once more, and this time a bit harder.

I'm not sure this thing can actually hurt a person.

I want to tell him to flog me harder again. But I don't. I stay silent. I let him guide me. He has my best interests at heart. He always has, and I have no reason to believe that he doesn't now.

A couple more flogs to my ass, and then his lips feather along my heated skin.

His lips are on the cheeks of my ass, his tongue in my crease as it was before.

Never in my life have I given my ass a sexual thought.

But now?

I want it all. I want what he wants. And he wants to lick my ass.

Clearly he's enjoying it. And my God, it's amazing— forbidden and amazing.

I sigh, press myself into the leather of the table, and just enjoy what's happening to me.

My wrists are bound, and I wish...

I wish I were actually bound to the table, so I couldn't move. So I could just enjoy what he's doing to me and not move with or against it.

Now, though? I'm undulating my hips, and it's so difficult... So difficult not to turn around, even with bound wrists, and throw my arms around him and kiss him.

He moves away from my ass, and I let out a soft whimper

at the loss.

"You like that, Mandy? Do you like to have your ass licked?"

"Yes. Yes, I love it, Jack."

"Good. You have a sweet cherry-pie ass, Mandy. Sweetest ass I've ever tasted. Now turn around, sit on the table, and spread your legs."

I turn, but I can't hoist myself on the table because of my bound wrists. Doesn't matter. Jack lifts me onto the table, and then I bow my head as I spread my legs.

He scoots me to the edge of the table, kneels, and tongues my pussy.

And I shatter.

One touch to my clit, and it's over.

The orgasm rips through me with the force of a tornado. "Jack! Oh my God!"

He continues eating me, and then…inside me goes his finger. Two fingers, and he touches a spot that makes me break into shards of glass.

The G spot.

I know all about the G spot. I proofread romance—very graphic and explicit romance—for a living. I've tried to find it myself on occasion, but I've never been able to.

And of course neither of my previous two lovers had a clue.

But Jackson? He knows exactly where it is, and now I know for sure that I have one. Like the heroines in Lily's books, I'm having a clitoral and vaginal orgasm at the same time.

And oh. My. God.

I've never felt this good.

It continues, making me thrash as much as I can with bound wrists. Just when I think it's ending, Jackson hits the right spot. Finds a way to make me soar higher.

I'm not blindfolded, and I watch him. I stroke his hair with my bound wrists as he eats me.

The sounds—his tongue sliding, his lips slurping—turn me

on even more.

When he pulls away, removes his fingers, I'm still on the downward spiral of my orgasm. I finally hit the ground, and he rises, meets my gaze.

"Had enough yet?"

"Not even slightly, sir," I say.

He smiles then, his lips glistening from me. From my juices.

"Kiss me," I say. "Kiss me. I want to taste myself on your lips."

A growl then. A growl like a tiger getting ready to strike. Then his lips—his lips part my own, his tongue twirling with mine.

The tartness. The tartness and musk of my sex.

He breaks the kiss too soon, though. He gulps in a breath. "What are you ready for next, Mandy?"

I know my response by heart now.

"Whatever you want...*sir*."

CHAPTER THIRTY-FOUR

Jackson

Whatever you want.
    Sir.
Damn.

Damn. Damn. Damn.

How is she such a natural?

I flip her over, so her beautiful ass is in front of me once more.

I free my cock quickly and plunge inside her pussy.

All I've done so far is cuff her wrists. There's so much more to show her. So much more I yearn to show her.

But my need is too great.

I have to be inside her, and as I thrust, I only know one thing.

No one has ever fit me this perfectly, been a perfect cast for me.

I can't stop.

I should, but I can't. I thrust harder, faster, harder, faster...

Until—

I plunge inside her so deeply that...

That...

I swear to God I lose part of myself.

And that scares me more than anything.

I pull out, though I want to stay snugly inside her forever.

"You okay?" I ask.

"I'm wonderful," she says dreamily. She turns around, her gray eyes serene and gentle. "Show me more."

"Did you come?"

"That time? No. I'm not sure I had it in me after..." She blushes again.

My God, that blush.

"After all those... Or maybe it was just one... I'm not sure, Jack. Was it one huge orgasm or a lot of little ones?"

I can't help my lips curving into a smile. "It's whatever you want it to be."

She returns my smile, and I'm lost again. I've lost a sliver of myself in her beauty. It's a sweet beauty, yes. But no longer an innocent beauty. Seems I mistook the two things. Sweet doesn't necessarily mean innocent.

Still...when I compare Mandy to the women around here at the club. They're just...

Are they all that different?

I don't really know any of them outside of the club. That's always been the point. We don't exist in each other's day-to-day world.

This club—what I do here—is such a big part of me. Why shouldn't it be part of my everyday world? Why shouldn't I have a partner who shares my whole world?

Easy answer... I'm not cut out for a long-term partner. I eventually lose interest. Always.

And I can't do that to Mandy.

Besides, I really haven't shown her much.

I bound her wrists with fur-lined handcuffs, and I gave her a few whacks on the ass with the gentlest flogger.

She doesn't know what I crave.

She doesn't know that I would love to tie her up so she's at my mercy, flog her sweet ass until it's red as a candy apple.

Train her with an anal plug.

And…

Bind her with leather rope to the head of the bed, blindfold her, keep her quiet with a ball gag, and then…

Tantalize her with so many of the toys I've learned to wield with such efficiency. The toys through which I feel everything that she feels.

"Jack?"

"I think we're done for tonight, Mandy."

Her beautiful mouth turns down into a frown.

"This is new to you," I say. "Very new to you. I can't take the chance of frightening you."

"You gave me a safe word."

"I did."

The problem is that I'm not sure Mandy needs a safe word. I think *I* may need one, and I'm exercising it now. If we continue, I may go too far, and Mandy is too inexperienced to know when she's had enough.

It's up to me. I have to make that decision for her. That's what a good Dom does.

"So…" she prompts.

"Enough for tonight."

"Jack…"

"It's *sir*," I say with authority. "In the club, you will call me sir. And I decide when we've had enough."

She bites her bottom lip, and oh…that blush.

Then she drops to her knees, her wrists still bound.

"I understand, sir." She meets my gaze.

Normally, I would punish a submissive who meets my gaze without permission.

But Mandy? It only makes me want her more.

I pull her up to face me, remove the cuffs from her wrists. Then I massage her wrists gently. "Any pain?"

"No, sir."

I turn her around, take a look at her ass. It's pink, but

I'm pretty sure I didn't hurt her one bit. I give it some gentle massaging. "And here?"

"No, sir."

I turn back around, cup her silky cheek. "Good."

"Good?"

"Everything here is about pleasure. Yes, some of it will cause you pain, but it's ultimately about pleasure. This is all new to you, Mandy. You have to go slowly."

"May I speak freely, sir?"

I smile. A big, wide smile. My God, right here under my nose this entire time has been a natural submissive.

"You may."

"I don't want to go slowly. I've waited too long to discover this side of me as it is."

"That's not your decision to make," I say.

"Isn't it, though? I have a safe word. I can ask you to stop at any time. I have a pager. And I know you will stop, Jack—I mean sir. I know you would never hurt me."

I don't reply at once. I never thought I could hurt another human being...until Blossom.

Blossom understands. She forgave me, even though she certainly didn't have to. She knows me, and she knows I wouldn't purposefully do anything to inflict harm.

But Mandy? She's not an experienced submissive.

If I hurt her... Even if she asks for it...

She will not forgive me.

I will not forgive myself.

And I'll lose her forever.

Which, if we continue this, may happen anyway.

"You have to trust me, Mandy," I say. "You have to trust me to know what's best. If you can't trust your Dominant, you have no business being here."

She drops her gaze to the floor.

Finally, "I understand...sir."

CHAPTER THIRTY-FIVE

Amanda

J ackson threads his fingers through his sandy hair. He's still wearing his shirt, and I haven't seen his gorgeous chest. His jeans are unsnapped and hover around his thighs.

Sir.

The word drips from my lips as if it were created from the martini I had at dinner—harsh and pungent and oddly delicious.

He likes it when I call him sir. I can tell by his mannerisms, by the way his lips quirk up at the corners, the way he goes slightly rigid, the way his dick is still hard, even after he screwed me.

He says I should trust him.

I've always trusted Jackson. I've trusted him since we were little kids to have my back.

I know he'll have my back here. I know he'll never hurt me. He gave me a safe word, right?

Patience is not my strong suit. But I must have it if I want to go to all these places with Jack.

All this time, I had no idea this was the kind of sex Jackson liked. But now it all makes sense. He's only had a few relationships that I know of, and none of them have lasted long.

He gets his physical satisfaction here, at the club.

And perhaps...

Perhaps those relationships he had, those relationships that only lasted a couple of months at the most... Perhaps those women didn't like the other side of him.

But I do.

I like every side of him. Jack the man, with all his wonderful qualities and all his flaws. I've known him forever, and I know each one of them—especially now.

The one thing I didn't know about him was his preferences in the bedroom. Now that I know?

I think I love him even more.

I'm not ignorant. Just inexperienced. I read romance novels for living, and Lily likes to write some graphic and naughty sex scenes. Jack knows what I do for living, sure, but does he realize that a big part of my job is reading about sex?

What I do may be as foreign to him as what he does is to me. He works for Ben Black at Black Inc., and his specialty is marketing. I couldn't market my way out of a paper bag, which is why Lily hires someone else to market her books.

But I read a lot of sex, and though Lily doesn't write BDSM specifically, I've read many BDSM sex scenes. Part of my job is to stay on top of the genre and let Lily know what trends are coming and going.

The BDSM trend? It's always coming.

"We're done for tonight, Mandy."

I try not to let my disappointment show. "Whatever you say, sir."

He kisses my forehead, like he always does.

So that's it? We're back to being BFFs? I'm standing here naked, his pants are undone, he just had his dick inside me, and we're BFFs again?

Fine. I'll play this game. I'll go at his pace. It's probably best anyway, since I'm so inexperienced.

But that doesn't mean I can't take a class at Treasure's Chest. Then I remember. Mary.

She's here. She's here at Black Rose Underground.

I'll go see her tomorrow. I have no idea if she recognized me. I'll go in and sign up for the class. I'll suck it up and deal with her, even though she's been intimate with the man I love.

Jackson snaps up his jeans and hands me my clothes, including the corset. Because I never took it off after I left the shop, I'm not sure how to lace it up myself. Mary said I'd be able to do it with practice, but I've essentially had no practice. Do I dare ask Jack for help?

After donning my jeans and pumps, I wiggle into the corset, snap the closures, and take hold of the laces.

Jack walks to me, closes his hands over mine, and takes the laces. "Let me," he says gruffly.

I nod.

He tightens the laces gently, almost too gently.

"Jack, you can—"

He meets my gaze sternly. "Quiet."

I obey him. We're still in the club, after all.

He continues gently, inch by inch. Is he waiting for me to tell him when? Maybe he is. But he's going to have to speak first.

Finally he stops and ties the laces.

It's not nearly as tight as Mary secured it this afternoon, but I stay silent. After all, he did tell me to be quiet, and we're still in his place.

"There," he says.

I nod.

"Ready?"

I nod again, pick up my white sweater, and put it on around the corset.

"Come on, then." He takes my hand—his is so warm and big—and leads me out of the room, down the hallway, and back into the main area of the club.

It's happening now. The club is much more crowded than

when we got here. Apparently these clubbers like to start late.

So much I don't know. Sure, I read the scenes in romance novels, but they don't depict the clubs. Not usually, anyway. It's usually a bedroom. Or an at-home dungeon.

We breeze through the club, Jackson waving to a few people who say hello, and before I know it, we're in the stark hallway after saying goodbye to Claude.

"Everything okay, Mandy?"

I nod.

"Why aren't you talking?"

I say nothing. Did he forget that he told me to be quiet?

"Mandy..."

I lift my eyebrows at him.

"Why aren't you—" A broad smile splits his face. "You may speak," he says. "I'll take you home now."

I return his smile. "As you wish, sir."

"You don't have to call me that anymore."

"We're still at the club."

"No, we're in the hallway leading to the club."

We don't speak much as we get back to my apartment. Was it only last night that he camped out at my apartment? Only to leave before morning?

It certainly wasn't the first time Jack showed up at my place. It *was* the first time he ended up in my bedroom, staring at me.

Always the gentleman, he walks me to my door, takes the key from me, and slides it through the reader.

"You good?" he says.

"I am..."

Sir. The name sits so easily on my lips, but Jack told me not to call him sir outside the club.

Why do I want to?

It's the strangest feeling.

"Yeah?"

"I'm fine, Jack." I clear my throat. "Roger's going to go

nuts if we don't open the door soon. You want some coffee or anything?"

He reaches toward me, fingers a lock of my hair. "No. Not tonight."

"All right. Good night, Jack."

"Good night."

I walk in, give my dog a few scratches on the head, and then I unlace and unhook the corset, setting it on my table. Ah... sweet breath of air. I like the feel of the corset, but it's nice to take it off and relax. I grab a jacket, zip it up, and take Roger down for a quick pee and poop. When I return to the apartment, I shed the jacket. Topless, I amble around the kitchen and make myself a cup of chamomile tea. I need to relax.

I need to get Jack and the club out of my mind. If I don't, I'm never going to be able to go to sleep.

I sip the tea slowly, but then I jerk at the sound of my door opening.

I grab the corset and pull it around me, holding it in place by squeezing my arms, and then I inch my way to the kitchen and grab a chef's knife.

The door opens and—

"Jack!"

I should have known it was Jack, of course. Anyone else and Roger would be shrieking.

"I'm sorry." His gaze drops to my chest, barely covered by the corset I'm holding. "I smell chamomile."

"Yeah. I'm having some tea."

"Drop the corset, Mandy."

"Jack, we're not at the club. We're—"

"I said, drop the corset."

Without thinking, I obey, and the lacy garment lands on my rug with a soft plop. I'm standing topless, a chef's knife in one hand, a cup of chamomile tea in the other.

"Put down the knife, Mandy."

I obey again, setting it on the countertop. "I thought you were—"

"I know. I'm sorry I scared you."

"Why didn't you knock?"

"I thought you'd be in the shower or in bed."

"Oh."

It's a reasonable explanation. He has a key for a reason. Same reason I have a key to his place.

And all the times I've been to his place, all the times I've gone over uninvited whether he was home or not, I never saw one piece of evidence of this lifestyle he enjoys.

He must only do it at the club.

I guess he doesn't have one of those at-home dungeons like Christian Grey or Jonah Steel—two fictional Dominants.

He moves forward, cups my breasts as a soft groan vibrates from his throat.

"God...these tits." He bends down then, takes a nipple between his teeth.

And I let out a shriek.

His lips are soft, soft but firm as he tugs on my nipple, and he slides his fingers over the other one.

Is this why he's here? More sex?

He certainly didn't come back for chamomile tea. Jack hates herbal tea.

He came back for me.

Maybe not specifically to suck my nipples—though I'm not complaining—but he came back for me.

"Jack, I—"

My phone buzzes.

"Ignore it," he mumbles against my flesh.

"I can't. It's after midnight. If someone is calling, it must be important."

He nods. Lets go of my breasts.

I grab the phone. It's my future brother-in-law, Penn. "Penn, what's up?"

"Mandy, thank God you picked up. I can't get ahold of your parents. It's Frankie. We were in an accident."

My heart drops as my nerves make me nauseated. "Is she okay?"

"Yeah, we're at the ER at Mount Sinai. She cut her forehead pretty bad. She's lucid, but they're doing a CT to make sure everything's okay."

"I'll be right there."

"You don't have to come. I've got it."

"Are you kidding? She's my only sister. I'll be there." I end the call.

"What is it, Mandy?" Jackson asks.

"Frankie's been in an accident. She's okay, or at least Penn thinks so. But they're doing a CT on her head."

He grabs my purse and shoves my phone into it. "Go put on something other than a corset. I'll come with you."

And in that moment? I fall in love with him even more.

CHAPTER THIRTY-SIX

Jackson

Mandy and I leave the hospital at six a.m. Frankie's CT didn't show anything of concern, so they stitched up her head and they're keeping her a few hours for observation.

"Feel like some breakfast?" I ask Mandy.

"God, no. I just want sleep. Just take me home, please, Jack."

"Of course."

We don't talk during the drive, as we're both exhausted. When I drop her off, I do her the favor of taking Roger down for a quick walk around the block to do his thing. When I return, Mandy is already in her pajamas. I give her a quick kiss on the cheek and leave.

We don't make any plans to see each other again at the club or anywhere else. In fact, she seems...distant.

This is what I was afraid of.

Things are going to be weird between us now. I don't want to lose my best friend.

It's Sunday, so I head back to my own place, forgo the coffee, make some scrambled eggs, gobble them down, and then head to my bedroom.

I shower, put on a pair of boxer briefs, and flop on my bed.

Mandy had the right idea. We've been up all night and we need sleep.

...

I wake with a jerk.

My alarm is going off. It's four thirty...on Monday morning.

Oh my God. I did not just sleep for almost twenty-four hours.

Except that I did. What the hell is wrong with me? Sure, I was up for twenty-four hours. And I didn't get shit for sleep the night before because I was at Mandy's and left in the middle of the night.

Still...this is not like me.

What the hell is this woman doing to me?

I'm not myself.

Which means...this thing with Mandy is affecting me in ways it shouldn't. I've been slightly off my game at work and then what happened with Blossom.

But if I end it with Mandy, she'll say she's going to find someone else to teach her. And that will kill me. A slow, painful death by a thousand paper cuts.

That's what it will feel like, knowing someone else is doing things to Mandy that I should be doing.

Now what?

Of course my cock is rock-hard. I was probably dreaming of her—doing all those things to her she's not ready for but she thinks she is.

A cold shower it is. At least it'll wake me the hell up.

An hour later, after a cup of coffee and a protein shake, I'm on a run.

I try to run five miles every day. Sometimes I do it on the treadmill at the gym, but if the weather is good, I prefer to do it in the city.

Running early is the best. I love the yeasty aroma of the first bread bake at the neighborhood bakeries. Castiglione's is my favorite. They still use wood-fired ovens to bake their bread, and sometimes I see the bakers heading up from shoveling wood into the ovens. They always wear a white tank top, a hairnet, and their arms and neck are glistening with sweat and grime from the hot ovens. When I was a kid, I used to imagine myself working in a bakery when I was older. Then my dad made it big, and I didn't have to work as a teenager.

Sometimes, after my run, I head into Castiglione's and have a chocolate croissant. Sometimes an almond one—Mandy's favorite. Sometimes just a piece of baguette with butter.

Always the first bake, always warm, and always the best. More often than not, I grab an extra almond croissant and drop it off at Mandy's before I go home and shower. She'll pour me a cup of coffee, and I'll walk around the block with her and Roger.

Today, though, I don't stop. The scent of rising bread— its yeasty, golden-baked aroma—doesn't appeal to me today. Neither does stopping at Mandy's.

I run home, have another cup of coffee, shower, and then head into the office. It's early. Not quite eight a.m., so I'm surprised as hell to see Pendleton Berry waiting for me.

"Penn? Is Frankie okay?"

"Yeah, she's fine. They sent her home yesterday afternoon."

I heave a sigh of relief. "Oh, good. What can I do for you, then?"

"Can we talk in your office?"

"I have a meeting in half an hour that I have to prepare for."

"Oh. Sorry to bother you, then."

"We can talk for a minute. Come on in."

He follows me into my office, and I shut the door. I nod to one of the seats across my desk. "Sit."

He drops into a leather chair. "I think you should know

that Frankie is really concerned about Mandy."

I swallow. "You have my attention."

"She thinks Mandy is in love with you."

I widen my eyes but catch myself before I act too surprised. "She's mistaken."

"Maybe she is. I don't have a clue, to be honest."

Damn it. I knew we should've never had sex.

"Frankie's just worried," Penn continues. "Mandy's her big sister, and she loves her. She's afraid Mandy will never find another relationship because she's in love with you."

Emotion roils through me. And it's...*good* emotion. Which is bizarre because I don't do relationships.

You're the other half of me, Mandy.

"It's probably just a crush," I say, trying my best to sound dismissive.

Surely I'd know if Mandy had those kinds of feelings for me. Wouldn't I?

"Maybe it's just a crush. Maybe you're right." Penn stands. "I just thought you should know. Last night, at the hospital, well, I started to wonder if Frankie was right. And maybe you should...nip it in the bud or whatever."

"And Frankie's okay with you telling me this?"

"She's just worried about her wedding, I think. Mandy being her maid of honor and all. She wants Mandy to be happy. And..."

I resist an eye roll. "She doesn't want anything to ruin the wedding."

"Well...yeah. It's been a long time coming for both of us."

"Mandy is Frankie sister. She'll be happy at the wedding. Weddings are happy occasions."

Penn nods. His demeanor is...not exactly that of a happy groom-to-be, though. But that's none of my business. The only part of this that's my business is Mandy. Besides, the only reason I even give two shits about this wedding is because of Mandy. Penn and Frankie have been on-again, off-again so many times,

I'm still not convinced this wedding will occur.

"Thanks for your time," Penn says. "I just wanted you to know."

"I appreciate your candor. Don't tell Mandy any of this, okay?"

"Of course not. Gentlemen's club and all. Bros before hoes."

Bros before hoes? Did he really just say that? First of all, Penn and I are not bros. I tolerate him for Mandy's sake. And Mandy and Frankie are *definitely* not hoes. Penn is such an overgrown frat brat, as Mandy says. I sometimes hope they get into another fight and call off this farce. Mandy's sister deserves better. I'm almost as close to her as I am to Mandy, although in a totally different way. I was two when she was born, and there's a photo of Mandy and me sitting in an armchair and holding baby Frankie.

I simply nod and heave a sigh of relief when he shuts the door behind me.

Frankie thinks Mandy is in love with me.

A couple of months ago, that thought would've scared the hell out of me.

Now? It still scares the hell out of me.

But for a completely different reason.

CHAPTER THIRTY-SEVEN

Amanda

Treasure's Chest opens at ten a.m. on Monday, and I go in. My nerves are about ready to jump out of my body. Will Mary be here? Will she remember she sold me a corset? Will I be able to look her in the eye knowing she's been with Jackson?

My worries are for nothing, though, as Mary's not in.

"May I help you?" a salesclerk asks.

"Yes"—I eye the name tag on the blond woman's shirt—"Eileen. I was here a few days ago, and I understand you... have classes?"

Damn the inflection in my voice! I need to be empowered. That's why I'm interested in the classes, after all.

I clear my throat. "I understand you have classes."

There. That's better.

"We do. Come with me. I'll get you a brochure."

"I already have your brochure," I say. "I'd like to...enroll."

"Oh, awesome. Follow me, then."

I follow Eileen back to what I think is the dressing rooms, but then she takes me to an office.

"What kind of classes are you interested in?"

"The submission, I think. I'm pretty new at this."

"I understand. Let's see..." She types a few things into her computer. "We have a beginner class starting tonight, and I have room. I can put you down."

"That would be great. And Mary told me that since I spent over four hundred dollars..."

"Yes, you get the beginner class for free. Do you have your receipt?"

I pull it out of my purse and hand it to her.

"Perfect. All right, you're all signed up, Amanda."

"Mandy."

"Mandy...and you can call me Lena."

"Who will be teaching this class?"

"This one is...Mary, actually. So that works well. You already know her."

I bite my lip. "Mary. Okay."

"Is that a problem?"

Only that she's been intimate with the man I love. "No. Not at all." I use my best empowered voice. "Is Mary...submissive?"

"Mary is a submissive, yes."

"And...you..."

She smiles. "Me? I'm not in the lifestyle. I just like the clothes."

• • •

I haven't heard from Jackson all day, and I haven't reached out to him, either.

After checking in with Frankie and making sure she's all settled in at home and that Penn is looking after her, I finish up my work for the day, make myself a light supper, and then head to Treasure's Chest for my class.

It's after eight o'clock, so the shop is closed. I have to text them to let them know I'm here.

Mary answers the door, welcomes me, and leads me back toward the dressing rooms once more, to a room beside the office that turns out to be a large classroom.

And by large, I mean larger than the office but not really large at all.

"We're all here now," Mary says, "so we can begin."

Four others—three women and one man—sit in chairs. I say a quick prayer of thanks that I don't recognize any of them. Not that there's any probability that I might have. Working at home and being an introvert doesn't allow for meeting a lot of people, even in a huge place like New York City.

"I thought we would all introduce ourselves," Mary says. "Say a few sentences about yourself, first names only please, and why you're interested in this class on submission." She eyes me. "Would you like to start, Mandy?"

"Uh...sure. My name is Mandy. I'm a virtual assistant to an author, I'm twenty-nine years old."

What else is there to say about myself? At the moment, I feel like the most uninteresting person on the planet.

"What brings you in tonight, Mandy?"

"I read a lot of romance. In fact, the author I work for is a romance author. She doesn't specifically write BDSM, but I'm required to keep up with what's popular in the genre, and BDSM is very popular. I find it...intriguing."

Mary smiles. "I see. Do you have any experience in BDSM?"

"Very limited."

"Thank you, Mandy. Do you want to elaborate on your limited experience?"

"I've had my wrists bound with fur-lined handcuffs. That's about it."

I don't tell her about the soft lashing with the flogger. I also don't tell her that I'm in love with the person who dominated me—a person she has been intimate with. That's personal. *Very* personal.

"Good, thank you for your candor. And next, Jason?"

The one male in the room clears his throat. "I'm Jason, and I'm an accountant." Then he laughs. "I feel like I'm at an AA meeting."

Chuckles throughout the room.

"I've kind of always had the urge to submit to a beautiful woman. I'm not in a relationship right now, so I figured it would be a good time to explore these…inclinations that I have."

"Any experience?" Mary inquires.

"Just watching porn."

Another chuckle rolls through the audience.

"That's my only experience, too," one of the other women says. "I'm Liberty, by the way."

"What do you do, Liberty?" Mary asks.

"I'm a secretary. An administrative assistant, actually."

"And last but not least…Lakisha."

"I'm Lakisha, and I'm an attorney."

I resist the urge to widen my eyes. An attorney? Such a high-powered job, and she wants to submit? Interesting.

"And do you have any experience, Lakisha?"

"Yes, actually. I put myself through law school working as a professional dominatrix."

Collective gasps.

"Really?" Mary says. "And now you want to learn submission?"

"I actually already know a lot about submission," she says. "But I'm here because part of me always felt that I was in the wrong role when I was working. Believe me. I only did it for the money. I was good at it, too. I still have old clients who try to get in touch with me. I miss the lifestyle, but I don't miss my place in it. I want to be the one on the other side."

"That's a really interesting story," Mary says. "I think we're all going to learn a lot from one another."

I say nothing.

I'm not sure what any of them can learn from me.

"Okay," Mary says. "First things first. You have varying degrees of experience, but you all chose to come to this beginner class. Some of this may be a repeat for some of you. If at any time, you feel you should leave and seek more advanced training, feel free to do so."

Collective murmurs of okay.

"So," she continues, "let's talk about the power of submission. First of all, being a submissive does *not* mean you're a doormat to be taken advantage of. In fact, you have to have a pretty strong personality to be a good submissive. Some of you may know this already, but I am a submissive. I do not serve a Dominant during all of my life. I choose only to submit in a scene setting, meaning I participate in scenes at a club or at the home of a Dominant I trust who has requested a scene with me."

Has Mary been to Jackson's place? An image I don't want pops into my mind.

"I do not have a full-time Dominant in my life," Mary continues.

Liberty shoots her hand up.

"Yes?" Mary says.

"If you don't have one Dominant, how do you know who to play with? I mean…isn't the most important thing trust?"

"That's a good question, Liberty, and we'll get to that. That's the next thing. Trust is essential. A good Dominant will always give a submissive a safe word—or some other way of communicating if their mouth is bound—and the Dominant will respect it without question."

My safe word. Jackson gave me a safe word. Blush.

I trust Jackson. I trust him without question. It seems like he didn't trust himself.

"So submissive is easy to define. The person who is consensually obedient and compliant to the other partner and who is willing to give control to their partner during sexual activity or during all other parts of life. I personally, as I just said, do not live in a Dominant-submissive relationship. I exercise my proclivities only in scenes with Dominants I trust."

"But how do you know who to trust?" Liberty asks again.

"There's no easy answer to that question," Mary says. "But a good Dominant will show you that you can trust him."

Lakisha clears her throat.

"Or *her*." Mary smiles. "Sorry about that, Lakisha."

"I'm definitely interested in a Dominant 'her' as well," Jason says. "After many years, I've gotten used to the fact that I prefer the submissive lifestyle. It felt kind of emasculating at first."

"If I can interject?" Lakisha raises her hand.

"Of course, Lakisha."

"When I was working as a dominatrix, I had many clients who were very, very masculine, Jason. High-powered men, men with muscles the size of the *Titanic*. There was nothing effeminate about them. The desires you're having are quite normal."

"Lakisha is right," Mary says. "What we enjoy in the bedroom is what we enjoy in the bedroom. How you present on the outside doesn't necessarily coincide with what you enjoy sexually."

Jason smiles. "Would it be wrong to say I wish you were still doing dominatrix work, Lakisha?"

A burst of energy passes between Jason and Lakisha. It's so filled with electricity, I almost feel it. The two of them are going to end up in the sack tonight after class. I'd bet money on it.

Maybe Lakisha will realize she's still a Dominant.

And oh God, there goes Liberty's hand again.

Mary nods to her.

"So how do you know you can trust your Dominant? You said a good Dominant will show you that you can trust them. How?"

Mary smiles. The woman has the patience of a saint. "We're

going to get to that. Bear with me. Submissives can take on many roles. Each encounter with your Dom is called a scene. It's up to the Dom to decide how the scene will play out, but it's up to the submissive—you—to let your Dom know if anything makes you uncomfortable. A good Dom knows his submissive's limitations. Limitations are called hard limits and soft limits. You should agree on these with your Dom ahead of time before you begin any scene. For example, one of my hard limits is gunplay."

"Gunplay!" Liberty gasps. "Why would anyone want that?"

"Some do. Gunplay is considered edge play, which I'll get to. But I'm just using it as an example. Another of my hard limits is breath play."

"Meaning..." Liberty prods.

My God, this woman is going to try my patience during this whole class.

"Like I said, we will get to edge play. Right now, we're just discussing hard and soft limits. One of my soft limits is anal play. I only engage in anal play with the right Dominant."

Anal play. Already my skin is tingling. Jackson paid a lot of attention to my ass.

I'll bet he likes anal play.

Will that be a hard limit for me? A soft limit?

Neither.

With Jackson, I already know I'll have no limits.

Liberty's hand goes up again.

"We're going to run out of time if we don't continue," Mary says. "I'm going to ask you guys to hold all questions."

Liberty puts her hand down with a slight pout.

I send a subliminal *thank-you* to Mary.

"Now I'm going to show you some of the instruments that may be used in introductory submissive play."

I recognize almost all of the things she pulls out, though I can't name them all. Most of them were hanging on the walls of the rooms where Jackson and I...

I listen with one ear until Mary says—

"At the end of this four-week class, if you'd like, we will visit an actual leather club. I have permission to bring people in before club hours. However, because it's a private club, you will have to sign nondisclosure agreements. If you're uncomfortable with that, you certainly don't have to participate."

Oh God.

Black Rose Underground.

She's going to take us to Black Rose Underground.

My breath comes rapidly. *No reason to have a panic attack, Mandy. She said it will be during off hours. Jack won't be there.*

Then Mary looks at me. Cocks her head.

She *did* recognize me Saturday night.

My blush makes my cheeks go hot.

Her cheeks redden as well.

I thought I could handle this, but I can't.

This will be my last class at Treasure's Chest. No way can I face her again.

Not when I'm in love with one of her Dominants.

CHAPTER THIRTY-EIGHT

Jackson

B lossom is teaching a class tonight. I still haven't forgiven myself for what went on between us, so I wait for her outside Treasure's Chest. I'm holding a glass vase of lilies, her favorite.

The door opens, and a gorgeous dark-skinned woman leaves with a tall and handsome blond man.

Then a young woman with black hair and creamy white skin.

The classes at Treasure's Chest are usually small, so Mary should be coming out at any time.

A few minutes and then the door opens once more.

And—

I drop the bouquet of flowers with a crash.

Mandy. Mandy is coming out the door, and she looks lovely with her hair in a ponytail and black leggings hugging that delectable ass.

She gasps when she sees me. "Jack! What are you doing here?"

Then she eyes the flowers on the ground and the shattered glass from the broken vase scattered over the sidewalk.

Oh God...

I didn't know Mandy was here, and now she's going to think I'm here to meet another woman.

Which, of course, I am. But it's not the way she thinks.

"I'm...waiting for you?"

"Nice try." She glances at the flowers. "I don't even like lilies."

She's right. Amanda's favorite flower is a pink rose. Her favorite fruit is a sweet cherry. Her favorite color is red. Her favorite animal is a zebra, unless you count dogs, which are really her favorite.

I know all her favorites.

Blossom comes out next.

"Oh! Hi there, Jackson."

"Mary."

Blossom drops her gaze to the broken vase of flowers on the concrete, and then she looks at Mandy.

I can almost see the equation formulating in her mind.

"Always nice to see you." She turns to Mandy. "See you next week in class or maybe in the store." Then she hurries off.

She knows. Blossom knows those flowers were for her, and she knows I was with Mandy at the club over the weekend.

She's a good person. She tried to save all our faces.

Unfortunately, it didn't work.

Mandy brushes by me. "See you later."

I follow her and step in front of her, bringing her to a halt. "That's it? See you later?"

"What more do you want me to say, Jackson? You obviously brought flowers for someone else. Someone who was here at the shop. I know it was Mary."

"It's not what you think."

"Really, it doesn't matter what I think, Jackson. You made it pretty clear the way you feel about me and what we shared."

"Damn it, Mandy. I don't even *know* how I feel about what we shared."

"Well, I do. I feel like…"

"What?"

"I feel like I want to learn, and you're not willing to teach me. So that's why I'm here. I came to a class."

"And Mariah—Mary—is your teacher?"

"She's willing to teach me more than you are."

Relief surges through me. If Blossom is Mandy's teacher, she'll learn well. Blossom is an experienced submissive. But Mandy will eventually go looking for a Dominant.

That harsh reality sits in my stomach like a freaking anvil.

"When's your next class?"

"Never," she says."

"Never? Why?"

"Because… I guess… This just isn't the right class for me."

"Don't lie to me, Mandy. I know you better than you know yourself."

"You don't, really."

My visit with Penn this morning swings back into my mind. Frankie thinks Mandy is in love with me.

She does respond to me, but most women do. I'm good at sex. I'm good at dominating—except for that last time with Blossom, when I had my mind somewhere other than on my submissive.

I ought to get kicked out of the club for that. But Blossom is nothing if not discreet. She still trusts me, and she knows I'm not a danger to anyone at the club. In fact, she will probably play with me again. Except that she won't. Because *I* won't.

I don't want to play with anyone right now.

Except…

Except the woman whose path I'm blocking at the moment.

Fuck it all. What have I done?

"Mandy…"

"Get out of my way, Jack."

"Mandy, please. We can't leave things like this."

"What? What things, Jack?"

"God, I should've never…"

"Never what? Never what, Jack? I know. You should've never taken me to the club. Never fucked me. Never have—"

I can't help myself. I shut her up the only way I know how. I crush my lips to hers.

Her mouth is already open because she was talking. I take full advantage, sweeping my tongue against hers. Tasting her. Memorizing the smell and feel and touch of her.

She kisses me back, but only for a moment before she breaks the kiss and pushes me away with such harshness that I almost stumble backward.

"Stop it. Stop playing with me," she says.

Playing with her? Damn, she's right. I *am* playing with her. But somewhere…somehow… The lines between play and reality have become blurred.

So blurred I don't even understand them anymore.

Is Mandy truly in love with me?

If she is, how have I not seen it?

I just never thought of her that way, but honestly, playing with her was amazing. I felt things I've never felt before. And I almost feel like…

I almost feel like it wasn't play at all.

If Blossom was the teacher, that means Mandy was taking a submission class. Not a Dominant class. Not a bondage class. A submission class because that's what Blossom teaches.

Blossom has been a submissive for at least three years. I know this because three years ago, I became a member of the club, and Blossom was already there. In fact, Blossom taught me a lot about being a Dominant. She's good at what she does, so I imagine she's probably good at teaching submission as well. If Mandy learns how to be a submissive from Blossom, she'll be a damned good submissive.

God, just the thought of Mandy submitting to anyone else,

and I suddenly feel light-headed.

Am I actually in love with her?

No. I can't be. It's all wrong. Mandy and I... It could never work. It's purely physical, like it always is with me, and what I'm feeling will fizzle out in mere months.

But what if it's true? That she's in love with me? And what if she's only trying to learn to be submissive to please me?

God.

This has to stop. I don't want Mandy to be something she isn't just to please me.

Except part of me does. The submissive's job is to please their Dominant. But I can't allow Mandy to do this if it's not who she truly is.

I rub my stomach absently. "Can we please talk?"

She holds my gaze for several beats before her shoulders sag and she nods. "My place."

"Okay," I say. "Your place it is."

CHAPTER THIRTY-NINE

Amanda

I try not to think about the bouquet of lilies Jackson was bringing to Mary as I usher him into my living room.

I slide my purse onto a barstool as I turn to face him. And realize I have no idea what to say. Talking to Jackson has always been the easiest thing in the world. Like breathing. So why do I suddenly feel like all the oxygen has left the room?

"Umm. Are you hungry? I can make you a sandwich."

He seizes the distraction. "Yeah, kind of. Ham on rye?"

"Of course."

I know everything about this man. His favorite sandwich is ham on rye. His favorite drink is Tanqueray and tonic, except when something's bugging him. Then it's bourbon. His favorite sushi roll is a simple spicy tuna. His favorite color is blue, and his favorite fruit is the same as mine. Sweet cherries.

I head to the kitchen, grab the stuff out of the fridge, and make him a sandwich. Dijon mustard. The only mustard he likes. He doesn't like spicy deli mustard, and he doesn't like regular yellow mustard. He hates any kind of mustard that's been sweetened. Dijon only. Grey Poupon if possible.

Which is why I always keep Grey Poupon in my refrigerator.

To be honest, I hate the stuff.

"Coffee? Tea? Herbal tea?"

Then I have to laugh. Jackson hates herbal tea, which is why, when he came back up the other night and mentioned the chamomile, I knew something was off.

He wanted to see me. The only problem is that I don't exactly know why, and then Penn called.

Things are strange now. He's seen me naked, and he's had his tongue…in places. His dick in other places. How would his cock feel in my mouth?

I've never given head before.

Then I laugh out loud.

"What's so funny?" Jack says from the couch.

"Nothing."

Nothing I can tell him, anyway. Here I am, taking classes on how to be a submissive, when I've never even had a man's cock in my mouth.

I'm willing to bet submissives give a lot of head.

Yeah, the class was a mistake. Good thing it was free. If I'd paid for it, I'd have to take the loss.

I'm not even sure I'll go back to the shop, even though I love my bras, panties, and the corset. Manhattan has many more lingerie stores. It's a shame, really. I like Mary. I like her a lot. She was a great salesclerk and an even better submissive teacher.

I may miss her, but I certainly won't miss Liberty and her constant questions. I kind of liked Lakisha and Jason, who I'm pretty sure are hitting the sheets right about now. The electricity between them was so thick, I could cut it with a knife.

Me, I won't be hitting the sheets anytime soon. Not with Jackson or anyone else. Somewhere between the mustard and the meat, I decided I really didn't want to hear why Jackson was bringing another woman flowers. Ever.

I place Jackson's sandwich on a plate, walk to the couch,

and hand it to him. "Here you go. Stay as long as you need. If you leave, please lock up. I'm going to bed."

Then I turn and walk away from my best friend.

CHAPTER FORTY

Jackson

I stayed at Mandy's for a few hours, took Roger out twice, but then I ended up leaving. Sleeping on her couch felt all wrong. Just as wrong as leaving her with everything still unsaid between us.

I wanted to be next to her, sleeping in her bed. Beside her. I want to wake up and grab her and hold her in my arms and kiss her.

Those thoughts scared me, so I got the hell out of her place.

After a crazy day at work, where I nearly had my ass handed to me on a platter by Braden Black because of someone else's mistake, I finally left the office at ten p.m. and headed straight to the club.

If there was ever a day where I needed to wind down, this is it.

But then I find Blossom.

She's standing out in the hallway, wearing jeans and a black T-shirt—far from her usual club attire—her fiery hair flowing over her shoulders.

"Hey, there," she says.

"Hey, love. Those flowers last night..."

"Listen, Jack, everything's fine. You don't have to apologize anymore."

"All right. If you're sure. Why are you standing out here?"

She shrugs. "Just waiting for someone."

"Anyone I know?"

"Someone from one of my classes. Alfred's bringing her down."

Her? My heart does a ricochet against my sternum. "Not..."

She shakes her head. "No, not Mandy. Boy, do you have it bad."

"If I had it that bad, would I be here alone tonight?"

"You know," Blossom says, "there's always been something about you, Jack. Something about the way you dominate."

"What the heck are you talking about?"

"Nothing bad. It's just...you never have any emotion involved."

"I don't come here for emotion, love. I come for sexual gratification and satisfaction. But I do my best to please my submissive."

"I know you do. You're great at it. That's not what I'm talking about. Most other Doms I've been with show some— even if it's very little—emotion during the play. But not you. You're very matter-of-fact. You take care of your submissive very well. You make sure all their needs are met. But you don't have any feelings for them."

"How can you say that? I like you a lot. I like all the people I play with or I wouldn't play with them. I'm not going to play with someone I don't like."

"You're misunderstanding me again. Sure, you like me. We have fun together. I please you, and you please me. But what's missing is the emotional connection. The feeling that, during that scene, I'm the most important thing in the world to you."

"That's not true. I focus fully on my partner during any scene."

"That's not what I mean, and we both know it."

"I've never been looking for anything more than physical," I say. "I'm not good at relationships. I lose interest after a few months. That doesn't mean—"

"You're a good Dominant, Jack. I'm not saying that I haven't enjoyed every scene we've done together. Well... except..."

"Right."

"And I'd be willing to bet you were thinking of someone else that night."

She's right, of course. "I was unfocused, love, and you got hurt. I don't know how I'll ever be able to forgive myself."

"You *have* to forgive yourself, Jack. I forgive you. But I won't play with you again."

"I understand."

She shakes her head. "I don't think you do. I'm not going to play with you ever again not because I fear that you'll hurt me. I don't. In fact, if we went in the club right now and set up a scene, I'd be willing to bet that you will focus so intently on me that you won't play hard enough, the way we both like it."

I don't disagree with her.

She continues, "I won't play with you because it's very clear that you have feelings for someone. Feelings for someone that you've never had before. At least not for anyone in this club."

I shake my head. "You don't know what you're talking about."

She raises her eyebrows. "Don't I? Guess who didn't show up for class tonight?"

I don't have to guess.

"It's her, isn't it? Mandy. You have some kind of history with her."

"It's not like that," I say. "She's my best friend. I've known her almost my entire life."

"I get it now. You've known her for so long that it's almost impossible to try to think of her in the way that you're thinking of her."

Damn.

"Open up, Jack. I think maybe you've had feelings for her for a very long time, and you just let them lie dormant. And I think... I think that's why you don't allow yourself to form an emotional connection with anyone you play with."

"I assume most people don't come here to form an emotional connection, Blossom." There's no bite to my words.

"Scenes aren't always permanent relationships, Jack. But they *are* relationships. Submissives play with you because you're a good Dom. You know how to give them pleasure. Most of us aren't looking for anything permanent at the moment. But we do notice. We notice when there's no emotional connection on the part of our Dom."

I clear my throat. "I'm not sure what I'm supposed to say."

"You don't have to say anything. Just know that we know. I'm the only one who knows you're in love with Mandy. The other subs don't, so you'll still have plenty of people to play with inside the club if you choose to do so. But I have a feeling that you won't play again. Not with anyone, and not for a long time."

She's wrong. "Thank you for your forgiveness," I say.

She smiles. "I wish you well. And I hope... I hope with all my heart you find what you're looking for."

I nod, give her a chaste kiss on the cheek. "See you inside."

I open the door, whisk past Claude, and head into the club.

CHAPTER FORTY-ONE

Amanda

"I hear you're looking for an invitation downstairs."

The voice is low, deep, sexy.

And it's not Jackson's voice.

Alfred the bartender raises his eyebrows at me and smiles.

I turn around.

"Oh!" Zorro—or someone who looks exactly like him—stands in front of me. He's wearing a black mask and a black cape. His hair is slicked back, and his eyes are a brown so dark, they're almost black.

"I don't expect you to trust me," he says, "but I will never harm you. If you choose to come with me, I will take good care of you, and we don't have to do anything but talk." He pulls a chain-mail choker out of his pocket. "You'll need to wear this."

I nod. "A collar."

"Only for tonight, and only for your own protection."

"I understand."

"May I put this on you?" Zorro asks.

"Yes. Please."

He clasps it around my neck, and his fingers are warm. "You look amazing in that corset."

"Thank you."

The corset is still the only sexy garment I own. I'm wearing jeans and my pumps. The usual.

"I'll need to blindfold you."

"I understand."

"Good. Club rules, not mine."

"Can you tell me your name?"

"Just call me Zorro, and I'll call you my beautiful Elena."

I shiver. He arouses me. Not in the way Jack does, but still… I have to learn to take what I can get.

I'm never going to have Jack, so I'll look for love elsewhere. In the meantime? I'm not laboring under any delusion that Zorro is offering me love. But he can at least offer me some instruction and guidance.

Which I'd better make clear.

"Zorro?"

"Yes?"

"I want to learn. I want someone to teach me submission. How to please a Dominant."

"I've taught many submissives," he says. "I'm happy to offer my services."

"I'm not sure I want to…get intimate right away."

"Absolutely. Your comfort is the most important thing." He pulls me up from my barstool, his hands warm on mine. "Come."

The path is familiar to me, even though I can't see.

I've walked this way with Jackson twice.

Will he be here tonight? I don't know. Maybe *I* should have worn a mask.

Still, Jack would know me. Wouldn't he? I knew him as soon as I heard his voice. He tried to disguise his eyes, most of his face, and his hair by darkening it and wearing it in a completely different style.

But as soon as I heard his voice, I knew it was him.

Would he know me by my eyes? After all, a mask does

not hide the eyes. Jack wore colored contacts so I wouldn't recognize his distinctive golden-green eyes.

Except...

He doesn't feel the same way I do. He doesn't smell my breath in his bathwater. He doesn't see my face in his dreams.

"Okay?" Zorro asks.

"I am."

"Are you sure? You got kind of tense for a moment."

Of course I did. I was thinking about Jack and how he doesn't share my feelings.

"I'm fine."

"All right. We're going in now."

"I've already signed all of the forms."

"I know that. I checked before I agreed to come here when Alfred asked."

"Am I being completely naive? Ridiculously innocent? Going into a club with a strange man?"

"It would be irresponsible of me to tell you that you're not, because you are. But I can promise that you have nothing to fear from me. This club makes everyone's safety the first priority. You've been here before. You've probably seen the emergency buttons lining the walls."

"No, I haven't." Funny that Jack didn't show me those. Then again, he knew I was never in danger with him.

"I'll show you when we get in. You can have a pager, too. And of course a safe word."

I like this club more and more. It's a safe place.

"Are you ready?" Zorro asks.

"I am, Zorro."

"Then come with me, my lovely Elena. Let me make you quiver."

CHAPTER FORTY-TWO

Jackson

The club holds no interest for me tonight. After I have a quick gin and tonic at the bar, I head back and find an empty suite. I go alone. I sit down on the bed.

And I wonder...

Do I have these feelings for Mandy?

If I do... Is Frankie right? Is Mandy in love with me as well?

So many years we've put into our friendship. I cherish it, and I don't want to lose it.

I lie down. It's selfish of me to take up a suite when I'm not doing a scene, but right now I don't care.

I need to think.

I should go home and think, but this place... This place is where I am my most authentic self. This is where I want to be at this moment.

I like sex. I've always liked sex. I'm good at it, and the kinkier the better.

It took me a few years to recognize this in myself. But once I did, I knew it was who I authentically am in the bedroom.

I'm a Dominant.

I love being a Dominant.

Perhaps there's a reason why—though I'm good at it and I enjoy pleasing my partner—I've never allowed any emotion to form with a submissive.

Thinking back…

I'm not sure I've ever allowed emotion to form with any woman.

I love you.

I've never said those words.

Not even to my high school girlfriend, who I considered marrying. I was so young that I had no idea what marriage was, except that I thought I could have it with Serena—my only relationship to last longer than a couple of months. It lasted the duration of our senior year in high school.

Serena was the homecoming queen to my king.

The head cheerleader to my most valuable player on the football team.

We broke up after graduation, each going our separate ways. Serena fought me on the breakup. She wanted to stay together, to eventually get married. I considered it. Serena was everything I thought I could ever want in a woman. She was blond, buxom, smart, and athletic. Tall and beautiful. I believe I did care for her very much. But I never said the words.

And then there was Mandy.

Mandy, who showed up at every one of my games and cheered the loudest. Mandy, who was the last person I said goodbye to before leaving for college. Not Serena but Mandy.

Mandy with her warm brown hair and eyes like the night moon. Mandy, with a curvier hourglass figure compared to Serena's tall and athletic form.

Mandy…who I never thought of that way.

Who I never *let* myself think of that way.

That's the key.

I've been so focused on protecting my friendship with Mandy that I never allowed my feelings to go anywhere else.

And then... When she wrote that damned Lustr profile, and I was frightened for her, wanted—no, *needed*—to protect her. Because that's what we do. We take care of each other.

I thought I could scare her off Lustr. Scare her off—

Fuck. Who the hell am I kidding?

I would do anything to protect Mandy.

Even from *me*.

CHAPTER FORTY-THREE

Amanda

"Would you like something to drink?" Zorro asks.

"Sure."

"I don't recommend having alcohol, but if you need one drink to relax a little, that's fine."

"I think I can figure out whether I want to drink on my own."

"That's why I asked, Elena. But perhaps I should give you your first lesson. You don't speak to your Dominant in that tone."

Funny, his reprimand irks me, which is interesting because I didn't feel that way when Jackson did it.

Maybe submission isn't for me after all.

"I'm sorry."

"The correct response is, 'I'm sorry, sir.'"

Well, I asked for a teacher.

"I'm sorry, sir."

The words feel all wrong in my mouth. Jackson is sir. I don't want to call this stranger sir.

"May I ask a question, sir?"

"You may."

"Would it be okay if I call you Zorro instead of sir?"

"Of course, Elena. Zorro is fine."

I nod. "Thank you."

"Thank you, *Zorro*."

Seriously? "Thank you, Zorro."

I'm here to learn, after all. To determine if my enjoyment of this place—this lifestyle—is because I'm trying to please Jackson...or myself.

And if I want to learn, I need to please Zorro. Jackson will never be my Dominant. He's made that abundantly clear. Zorro may not be my dream Dom, but he *is* willing to teach, so I must learn where I can.

"So...the drink or not?" he asks.

I agree with him. I need my full faculties here. If I do need to grab a pager, I want to be able to do it quickly.

"Just some water, Zorro. Thank you."

He orders drinks from a topless bartender. Water for both of us.

"I don't like to drink when I'm doing a scene with a submissive for the first time," he says. "It's best that we both remain hyperaware and focused."

I simply nod.

"Yes, Zorro," he says.

"Yes, Zorro." I echo.

"I'd like to show you what I like to do," Zorro says. "You may need to remove your corset. Are you okay with me seeing your breasts?"

Not really, but I know the correct answer. "Yes, Zorro."

"Good. I'm glad, because, my beautiful Elena, I can't wait to see those beautiful breasts."

I gather my courage and finger the laces of my corset. "Would you like to see them now?"

"In good time." He leans toward me and kisses my cheek.

"Zorro?"

"Yes, my Elena?"

"Tell me what you want to do to me, please."

"I want to touch you. I want to look at your beautiful body, touch you all over. Then I went to bind you intricately with shibari rope, spread your legs so you're open for me."

"Will you flog me?"

"I'd like to very much."

I swallow. "Whatever you want, Zorro."

"We can't do everything I want this first time, Elena. Not until we've gotten to know each other a little better. But I promise that you will not be left wanting this evening."

I look at Zorro. Truly look at him. His face is covered by the black mask, but his dark eyes are on full view. Is he wearing colored contacts like Jackson did the first time we came here?

No. There is nothing fake about those eyes. They're dark and intense and searing into me.

His jawline is sculpted, and black stubble peeks out. His hair is also dark and his skin tanned, slightly darker than Jack's.

Even masked, I can see he's a beautiful man. Any other woman would be tingling right now, sitting next to him, having him tell her he's going to make her feel wonderful.

And while I truly want to feel those things, I just can't.

But that's okay. I'm here only to learn—to learn if I like being a submissive.

Or if I just like being Jackson's submissive.

After one night with Zorro, I will know.

"Dear Elena, you seem to be comfortable baring your breasts here. In the main room of the club."

Am I? I was being flirtatious before. Am I an exhibitionist?

I'm not sure. I guess there's only one way to find out.

"Yes, Zorro. I mean… I'm not sure, but I'd like to find out."

"All right. If at any time you're not comfortable, tell me. I'll put my cape around you, and we'll go somewhere private."

"Yes, Zorro."

I see what he's doing. We're staying out in the open because we don't know each other well enough yet. He wants me to feel safe.

He's a good man. A good Dominant.

I appreciate that so much. So I'm not tingling for him. What does that matter? That'll make this even better. I can focus on learning—learning to be the best submissive I can be without my libido distracting me.

And there's one thing I *really* need to learn.

"Zorro?"

"Yes, beautiful Elena?"

"Would you be willing to teach me something special tonight?"

"That depends on what it is, my love."

"Zorro, sir...would you...teach me how to give a blow job?"

As soon as the words leave my mouth, I realize I made a terrible mistake. I came here hoping to discover if this is a lifestyle I'd choose for myself. And maybe it is.

But only with Jackson.

Only this realization comes too late...because Zorro's twist of his lips signals that he's definitely interested in teaching me how to suck his cock.

CHAPTER FORTY-FOUR

Jackson

Zorro, sir...would you...teach me how to give a blow job? Those words, that voice...

I curl my hands into fists, and I advance on the creep dressed in a cheap Zorro Halloween costume.

Who is he, anyway? I know most of the members here. How the hell is he here with Amanda?

"He will *not*," I say, my voice trembling with rage.

Zorro glares as he assesses me with his dark eyes. "This is the person you were with the other night, isn't it, my sweet Elena?"

My sweet Elena? Mandy is not Elena, and she's not *his*.

She stares at me, her gaze defiant.

He continues. "But the lady is with *me* tonight."

Damn it all to hell. She's wearing this bastard's collar.

I do it. I know I shouldn't, but I do it anyway. I rip the fucking mask off his face.

Mandy's pretty mouth drops open as we both stare at Ben Black.

And he's smiling. Fucking smiling.

"What the fuck? Ben?" I stiffen. "I thought we were friends, man. This is low."

I may as well say whatever I want. I'm sure I just lost my membership at the club, which is owned by his brother, and my job, at the company he owns *with* his brother. I don't even care. If he touches Mandy, I will pummel that smile right off his face.

"It's all right," Ben says to the security guy. "I was just proving a point to Mr. Paris."

"If you're sure." The guard frowns at me.

"Yeah, I'm sure. Just give him a minute. He's a sensible guy."

I don't feel sensible. I feel like my whole world is collapsing in on itself. My two closest friends were going to play a scene together—even though Ben suspects I might be in love with her. And damn it all to hell, I may never forgive him for that alone.

I draw in a breath. Then another. I turn toward the bar, grip it, my knuckles going white.

A glass of water slides toward me. I grab it and drink it all.

Ben is next to me now, ordering two more waters. "It's okay, bro. She's fine, and you know I'd never hurt her."

"I can't believe you were going to fucking touch her," I say under my breath. "I ought to kick your ass into next year."

"I wasn't going to do anything with her."

"Right."

"Honestly," Ben says. "I knew you were here."

Mandy looks to Ben, to me, and then to Ben again.

"Why didn't you tell me who you were?" she demands of Ben.

"Hey, I'm not the bad guy here. I was trying to prove a point to both of you. And as for you"—he turns to me—"I had permission for everything I did, and I knew if I didn't collar her and bring her down, neither of you would admit what's really going on here."

Mandy whips her hands to her hips, causing the corset to push her breasts up even more.

My God, her tits are delicious, and they heave with her angry breaths, her gaze narrowed on Ben.

"If the two of you are going to have it out, we should get out of the club," she suggests.

That seems to knock some sense into Ben. It's a weeknight, so the club isn't very crowded, but still… We are making a scene.

Of course, Ben's brother owns the damned place, so he can do whatever he wants.

Mandy looks between us again and shakes her head. "I'm leaving."

"Not without me you're not," I say.

"See you at work tomorrow," Ben says.

I'm too focused on catching up with Mandy to give more than a passing thought to the fact I apparently still have a job. Fuck work. Mandy is walking away from me. Again.

Once Mandy and I are outside the club in the hallway, she turns on me.

"What was that all about?"

"You know damned well what that was about. What were you doing with him?"

"I didn't know it was Ben."

"For God's sake, Mandy, he's my boss."

"Hello? Did you not hear me? I said I didn't know that, Jack. What do you care? Why would you care *who* I play with at the club?"

I seethe in anger. In rage. But the rage…it's morphing into something else. Shame.

"Mandy—"

"No, Jack. I can't keep doing this." She takes a deep breath and holds my gaze, her voice breaking. "What's going on? You brought flowers to another woman, but you don't want me to be with another man?"

CHAPTER FORTY-FIVE

Amanda

Jackson opens his mouth, closes it, and finally opens it again. "Mandy..."

I stand, my arms wrapping around my middle.

He immediately removes his jacket and arranges it across my shoulders. "I'm sorry. You must be cold."

His jacket smells like him—like pine and musk and cinnamon and man. He's had that smell as far back as I can remember.

Once I'm covered, he whispers, "Let's get the hell out of here."

Seriously? He really thinks I'm going to just fall into line and be his amenable little bestie, his sweet and innocent submissive?

"No. I'm not going anywhere, Jack." I unclasp the collar around my neck. I grab one of Jack's large hands and place the color inside his open palm, close his fingers around it. "Please give this back to Ben. I'm done with both of you for tonight."

"Don't, Mandy—" His mouth comes down on mine again.

It would be so easy...so easy to melt into him...into his kiss... In a moment, I could be somewhere else in my mind, not in an empty hallway next to a BDSM club.

I could float away on a cloud of love and lust and promise, kissing Jackson with all my passion, all the love I feel for him.

So easy...

He deepens the kiss, and I welcome his tongue with mine. We kiss, we kiss, we kiss...

Until—

I break it with a loud *smack*.

"Jackson, why can't you play fair?"

I sniffle, but damn it, I will *not* cry for this man. He's put me through too much in the last week.

But I will give him one last chance. "Are you going to answer my question?"

He doesn't reply.

Not that I thought he would.

"What's it going to be, Jack? Do you want something with me or not? What's going on here?"

This time, he at least parts his lips, and as I watch his neck, I see his vocal cords move. He's getting ready to say something... But then he closes his mouth.

"Fine. I'm leaving. Do me a favor and don't call me."

"Mandy..." He pulls me to him. "I can't let you leave. Not without..."

Hope ignites in me. "Without what?"

He pulls the blindfold out of his pocket. "Without this."

• • •

One month later...

More than four weeks have passed since Jackson placed that blindfold over my eyes, led me back up to the bar, left his jacket on me, and put me in a cab.

I slept with his jacket that night, with his spicy scent enfolding me.

The next day? I threw it in the dumpster.

I've had work and Frankie's wedding to keep me busy. Though every night I think of Jackson. Does he miss me as much as I miss him? At least I know he hasn't been in the club. Before we'd left, the guard had said Jackson was suspended for a month after ripping off Ben's mask.

Lily has had two releases in the last month, so work has kept me busy. Plus, I've been dealing with Isabella and Gigi and Frankie's shower. They asked me to plan the shower since they were doing the bachelorette party and luncheon, and I couldn't exactly refuse. I am the maid of honor, after all, and Frankie's sister.

Tonight is the bachelorette party. Isabella and Gigi wanted to fly to Vegas, but Frankie said no. Surprised the heck out of me, but I'm just as glad. I don't have the excess cash to fly anywhere right now.

Besides, the last time I was in Las Vegas was with Jack. He surprised me after I finished my master's degree. Vegas would simply be another painful reminder that he and I haven't spoken in a month—the longest we've ever gone. Sure, in the past we've gone weeks, even months, without seeing each other sometimes, but we've always talked every few days.

But here we are, both living in the same city, and more than a month has passed since we've spoken.

I miss him so much. Sometimes I feel like I've lost a limb. But damn it, I refuse to cry for that man.

I haven't been back to the club, either. Going to the bar and soliciting someone to take me into the club was a huge mistake. Only now am I realizing how lucky I was that Zorro turned out to be Ben Black. What if it had been someone who wasn't so nice? Wasn't so respectful?

I let a strange man put a collar on me.

Maybe Jackson is right. Maybe I *am* too innocent for that lifestyle.

At any rate, it's time to get dressed for Frankie's bachelorette party. We're going to a male revue show featuring the Long Island Playboys, a Chippendales wannabe act.

And of course, I have nothing to wear.

Until—

I spy the black-and-blue lace corset in the back of my closet.

I took it with me to the dumpster the day after I last saw Jackson. I had been planning to throw it away along with Jack's coat, but at the last minute, I chose to keep the corset. After all, I paid good money for it. In the end, I couldn't bring myself to toss three hundred bucks in the trash.

Hiding it in the back of my closet isn't a lot different from throwing it in a dumpster. I'll wear it to Frankie's bachelorette party. I'll show Frankie, Isabella, and Gigi that they aren't the only hotties in this circle. Plus, if I'm not going to get rid of it, maybe wearing it will help exorcise the memories of my sexy times with Jack from my mind.

I take a cab to the locale instead of the subway. Getting on the subway wearing the corset doesn't feel right to me, but I've started watching my pennies. Having Jackson absent from my life made me realize just how many meals we share that he pays for. Consequently, I've been spending my cab money on food for the last month.

When I arrive at the club where the Long Island Playboys are performing, I pay the cabbie and hope I'll be able to hitch a ride home with Frankie or one of the others.

Gigi and Isabella reserved a few tables up front. I walk toward them after telling the house that I'm with the bachelorette party.

"Mandy!" Frankie yells. "We weren't sure you'd make it. The show's about to start."

"I'm here. No worries."

Not that any of them were worried. I'm hardly the party animal they are.

A very good-looking and muscular waiter who's wearing a bow tie but no shirt saunters up to me. "What can I get you to drink?"

"Sidecar, please."

"You got it." He winks.

He has several dollar bills shoved in the waistband of his pants. Is he one of the dancers? Probably not, but apparently some feel the need to tip him in his waistband for bringing them a drink.

Whatever.

Isabella and Gigi are counting out their dollar bills.

"We each brought a hundred," Gigi says.

"A hundred?" I gasp.

"Yeah," Frankie says. "You brought loose bills, didn't you?"

"Uh...I didn't, actually."

"Mandy, don't you know anything?"

"Sure I do. I've just been busy. I forgot."

It's not a lie. I did forget. And yes, I know you're supposed to tip when you go to a male revue, but frankly, I can't waste any money right now.

Frankie pushes a pile of money in front of me. "You can owe me."

I roll my eyes. "No thanks."

"Oh, forget it. It's a gift, okay? You don't owe me anything. This my bachelorette party, Mandy. Have some freaking fun, why don't you?"

Fine. Fun.

When the hunk in the bowtie and no shirt comes back with my sidecar, I shove a dollar bill into his waistband, which is actually a lousy tip, because the drinks here are about fifteen bucks a pop. I should be giving him a three dollar tip at least.

Frankie told me ahead of time that the party was already paid for and that I could have as many drinks as I wanted. She's being a little dense, telling me that, since Isabella, Gigi, and I paid for the whole thing.

Yeah, I'm pretty strapped this month.

I take a sip of my sidecar, savor the sour and sweet.

Then I nod to Hunky Waiter. "Another," I say.

He nods and smiles. Shimmies his hips a little at me.

I'm going to need at least two drinks to get through this evening.

CHAPTER FORTY-SIX

Jackson

After more than a month of no communication with Mandy, I finally broke down. I called Pendleton Berry to find out if maybe he knew what was up with Mandy and Frankie.

Turns out tonight is Frankie's bachelorette party.

And also Penn's bachelor party, to which he granted me an impromptu invitation, which is how I find myself at The Lion's Den, a strip club.

I'm expected to get turned on by women who gyrate their booties for cash.

This doesn't turn me on.

I see naked women all the time at the club.

Of course…I haven't been to the club in a month.

Seeing Ben at work is more than enough right now.

Do I miss it? In some ways. I miss being around people who understand me. But going to the club and finding a submissive to do a scene with? I just have no desire.

I don't want to be with anyone right now, which is bizarre. I've thought of Mandy—a lot, actually—but each time, I consciously wipe her from my mind. My fears have come true. Our friendship has been ruined.

I've ruined it.

She hasn't called me, and though I yearn to call her, I can't. I won't put her in the position of having to talk to me when she doesn't want to.

What happened between us should never have happened. Frankie was wrong. Mandy's not in love with me—a fact that scars me in my soul. Am I in love with her? I can't even entertain the thought, not when I've ruined everything between us.

So here I am, sitting at a strip club with Penn, who I don't even like very much, as he gets a lap dance from a dancer who looks kind of like Morticia Addams.

She holds out her fake tits, and he latches onto her nipple.

That's a no-no. You're not supposed to touch the strippers. They can touch you, but you don't touch them.

However…many of them relax the rules when money is dangled in front of them.

Hey, no judgment. Everyone has to make a living. It's not the stripper I'm judging. It's Penn. He's about to get married, and he's sucking another woman's tit. Not cool.

A pretty stripper approaches me, dances in front of me. "Care for a lap dance, stud?"

She reminds me kind of…

Can't go there.

The thought of Mandy dancing around a pole…

Except it kind of excites me.

What the hell is wrong with me?

"No thanks." I stuff a twenty in her thong. Maybe she'll leave me alone now.

Penn's friends are buying him beer after beer. I've been nursing the same gin and tonic since we got here.

I was a last-minute invite, to be sure, which says a lot in itself, since I've known Penn for the six years he's been dating Frankie. I'm Amanda's plus-one at most family events, so Penn and I have been thrown together a lot over the years. Has Mandy been blackballing me in her family?

I shouldn't care.

I *don't* care.

Yeah, I've become very adept at lying to myself over the last month.

I finally finish my drink. It's after midnight, and this party shows no signs of breaking up. Penn is between lap dances at the moment, so I rise and go to his chair.

"Thanks for the invite, man. I'm going to head out."

"Jack, buddy, the party's just starting."

I smile, pat him on the back. "Congratulations, man. I know you and Frankie will be really happy."

He snorts. "Yeah, sure thing."

Then another stripper straddles him.

I'm out of here.

This is his last hurrah. If this marriage even happens. I have no right to judge him. He's far from the first guy who sowed wild oats with a stripper before the wedding. That's kind of the idea behind a bachelor party.

Still, the whole thing rubs me the wrong way. This is Mandy's sister.

What if it were Mandy? What if someone was going to marry Mandy and I saw him sucking a stripper's tit?

I'd flatten him. I'd flatten him so badly, he'd never walk again.

And honestly?

It wouldn't be because he was sucking some stripper's nipple. It would be because he's marrying Mandy.

Damn. I really am an idiot.

I head back into the bar.

"Hey, Penn," I say.

He's busy squeezing the globes of his lap dancer's ass. "Yeah, man? You decide to stay awhile?"

"No, I have a question. Where's Frankie tonight? Where's

her bachelorette party?"

"Some club over on Seventh. A male stripper show is playing there. The Long Island Playboys."

Male strippers. Great. Not that I should be surprised. It's a bachelorette party.

Easy enough to find. A quick search on my phone tells me exactly where the Long Island Playboys are performing.

I grab a cab.

And I hope to God I'm not too late.

CHAPTER FORTY-SEVEN

Amanda

These Long Island Playboys are friendly. Too friendly. Three of them wanted to climb onto my lap so far. I desperately shoved dollar bills in their G-strings so they'd find someone else more enthusiastic.

Isabella and Gigi are being their normal flirtatious selves, making out with any of the dancers who will have them.

At least Frankie's being good. She is engaged, after all, and her ring is on her finger.

I'm on my third drink. More than I normally imbibe, but I'm not driving. And after three sidecars, I'm not all that worried about paying for a cab to get home. So I use my credit card. So I don't pay the balance in full next month. Who cares? I'll get back on track soon enough.

Before I know it, though, one of the dancers grabs my hands and pulls me up to the stage.

Warmth and embarrassment surge through me, but after three sidecars... While I'm not exactly a willing participant, I don't put up much of a fight. Amazing how alcohol can evaporate shyness in even the most timid. And me.

He touches my hips, shows me how to move them to the

beat of the music. All the other dancers have pulled someone up as well, but I'm the only one from Frankie's party.

I glance back at Isabella and Gigi; both of them have giant grins on their faces as they cheer me on to follow him up.

The man dancing with me has long black hair, and it's pulled up in a man bun. Normally, I hate man buns, but this guy makes it work. He has tanned skin, no chest hair. Sleek as satin, actually. He probably manscapes. A guy with that dark of hair must have chest hair.

He's wearing only his G-string, and I have to admit his ass is very nice.

Not as nice as Jackson's, though. I shake my head.

Why do my thoughts always come back to Jackson? How do you fall out of love with someone?

Dancing with a male stripper is as good a start as anything. These guys are paid to act this way. He's not really attracted to me. He pulled me up because he saw the pile of bills sitting in front of me on the table, and he probably expects most of them will end up in his G-string. He's not wrong.

So I dance with him. I laugh because I've had a couple of drinks, and they've definitely taken the edge off. I laugh, smile, let him touch my hips and show me how to follow him. Then he trails my arms up until they're around his neck, and we gyrate together in a kind of dirty-dancing style. I drift with him, slide with him, angle my body with his.

It's kind of fun.

It would be more fun if I were doing it with someone who actually wanted to dance with me, but hey, a girl takes what she can get. Not my normal MO, but after three drinks? Whatever.

One glance toward our table, and I see Isabella and Gigi are still all smiles. Gigi is especially hooting the loudest for me to "get in there."

I laugh and look back at the hunk's face. He's quite handsome, of course. Brown eyes, a brown goatee, and the long brown hair and man bun. Add a sculpted jaw line and I let myself go. I move with him, slide into the dirty dancing...

I can't help myself.

I look toward the table once more, just to revel in the fact that Isabella and Gigi are jealous of—

Uh-oh.

My heart flips at the beautiful face I see.

Jackson is here.

He's glaring at me.

What occurs next happens so quickly, I can't quite put it together in my mind.

One second, I'm dancing onstage.

The next...Jackson's imposing presence makes the dancer back off and move away from me.

"Get down from there," Jackson says.

I can't actually hear him over the loud music, but there's no mistaking the movement of his full lips. Though he's being dominant and ridiculous, I can't help myself.

I obey him.

No communication in a month, and I obey him.

I obey him without question, even against my better judgment, as my heart races and I tremble. Jackson is here. For me. Is he *finally* ready to admit there's something more than friendship between us?

Once I'm off the stage, he takes my arm and leads me through the crowd.

When we're outside the club, Jackson covers me in his jacket—a new one, since the old one's in the dumpster behind my building.

"What were you doing up there?"

"Dancing."

He scoffs. "I'm not sure that's what I'd call it."

"It's a male revue. I'm supposed to have fun." I let out a huff. "For God's sake, Jack, it's Frankie's bachelorette party."

He grips my shoulders. "Damn it, Mandy."

"It wasn't my idea. The guy pulled me up to the floor."

"You didn't have to go."

"You're right. I didn't. No one held a gun to my head. Maybe I wanted to go, Jack. Did you ever think of that?"

"This isn't like you."

I move one of his hands off my shoulders and shrug free of the other one. "How do you know what's like me and what's not? I haven't heard from you in a month, Jackson. A month." I can't help the break in my voice on the last word.

"The phone works both ways," he says softly.

I hold his gaze. What was he saying? He was waiting on me to call *him*?

He drops my arm, and a look of—I'm not sure—sorrow? crosses his features, landing in those gorgeous green-gold eyes.

He's quiet for a few seconds, until— "Do you still want to go to the club?"

I'm so shocked, I can only blink up at him. It's nearly one in the morning, so the club is probably still open. But *do* I still want to go with him? If the pounding of my heart is any indication, I know the answer.

I nod as I text Frankie that I'm leaving. I don't want her to worry.

Jackson hails a cab, and before I know it, we're settled into the back seat and pulling away from the curb.

He pulls a velvet choker out of his pants pocket. "You'll need this." He secures it around my neck.

"Maybe I don't need it." I hesitate a moment. "Maybe I *want* other men to pay attention to me at the club."

"Damn it, Mandy. You really have no idea what this is all about, do you?"

I rest a hand on his arm. "You don't give me enough credit for knowing my own mind," I say. "When will it stop, Jack? I don't hear from you in more than a month and—"

"The phone works both ways, Mandy."

What, is he stuck on repeat? His words only frustrate me further.

"You're the one who should've reached out. You're the one who refused to answer my question that night."

He seems to have no answer for that, for which I'm grateful. We spend the rest of the cab ride in silence.

Continuing in silence, we exit the cab, and I'm still wearing Jackson's jacket. It's a brisk night, and he must be cold.

And you know what? I don't give a damn.

He pulls the blindfold out of his pocket next.

"Mandy—"

"Yeah, yeah. I know the freaking drill. Put the damned thing on me."

I don't know why it matters. Does he really think I'm going to tell someone about this club? How to get into it? I signed their nondisclosure agreement.

By now the path is familiar to me. Through the back of the bar, down a flight of stairs, through a narrow hallway.

And then—

Into the club.

He slides the blindfold off me and I look around. The club is busier than I've ever seen it.

It's a Saturday night, but it's very late on a Saturday night. People are dancing, people are making out, one woman sits on the bar, a man's head between her legs. He's eating her. Eating her right here in the public part of the bar.

Not public, actually. It is a private club.

"Is this what you want?" Jackson nods toward the couple at the bar. "You want me to eat you out in public?"

Is he still trying to scare me away? His gaze is inscrutable, and for the first time, I honestly have no idea what he's thinking.

"Yeah, I do, Jack. If that's what you want."

"Dear God." His eyes blaze with heat, but he makes no

move to touch me. "If you only knew what you were doing to me. What you're doing to every man in this club right now. With that corset. Even with my jacket on, your boobs... Those tits... Those sweet, luscious tits..."

I shed his jacket, let it land on the floor. "You like what you see?"

"This isn't a game, Mandy. You're playing with fire here."

The idea actually turns me on. Fire. Candles. Wax play. Yeah, I've done some research.

"Or maybe you *do* know what you do to me. Still want to learn how to give head, Mandy?"

"Maybe I do. Or maybe I want to get burned."

Jackson's whole body stills for one beat, two, and then—

"Damn it all to hell," he growls and pulls me to him, crushes his lips to mine.

I try to keep my mouth closed. I'm determined to keep my lips sewn shut. I want to. He doesn't deserve a kiss from me, not after ignoring me for a month.

But he's still Jackson Paris.

And...I still love him.

Zorro—or Ben Black, as it turned out—didn't make me tingle like this. The hunky dancer at Frankie's party didn't make me tingle like this.

Neither of them made my body warm in a sizzling flush.

I try. I try so hard...

But Jackson's will is stronger than mine.

I part my lips, and I let him kiss me deeply.

My legs turn to jelly, and my whole body beats with the pounding of his heart.

We're on display in the open part of the club—I wearing my corset, Jack wearing only a button-down shirt.

And we're making out. Making out next to the bar, where only ten feet away, a woman is getting her pussy licked.

This isn't reality. It can't be. I'm kissing the man of my

dreams while a woman gets eaten out next to me.

I want it.

I want it all.

I want Jack to show me everything that happens in this club. After all, that's what he thinks I'm not ready for.

So I open to his kiss, let his tongue sweep deeper into my mouth. I kiss him back. I kiss him back with all the tingling in me that his nearness evokes. With all the love in my soul that I feel for him.

And with all the deep, dark passion of this place, with what this place conjures in me.

What Jackson conjures in me.

In the end, it's Jackson who breaks the kiss.

Jackson who gazes at me with his beautiful hazel eyes.

"Come with me, Mandy. Come with me to the dark side."

CHAPTER FORTY-EIGHT

Jackson

Only one suite is available, and it's just been vacated. Employees are sanitizing, so I stand outside the door with Mandy while they finish.

"Are you sure about this?" I ask her.

"I'm sure."

"Be very sure. Once we go inside, I'm in charge."

She swallows. It's not audible, but I see the movement in her neck.

"I understand, Jackson."

"Do you?" I touch her cheek gently. Does she know what I'm after?

She smiles slightly. "I understand...sir."

God, she sounds just like a submissive. Dare I hope?

The jealousy that invaded me when I saw her dancing with that stripper felt like razor-sharp knives cutting my flesh open. I've never felt anything like it, and damn, I never want to feel it again.

Except I *have* felt it before.

When I caught her with Zorro at this very club.

The night my friend Ben betrayed me.

He apologized the next day. I forgave him, of course. He's my employer, but even more than that, he's my friend. He was trying to show me that I felt something more for Mandy than I was willing to admit. I threw his accusations into the back of my mind and took a break from sex, from the club.

From Mandy.

And now, a month later? Seeing her up onstage with that dancer?

I finally have to admit it.

Mandy is more to me than just my best friend. Perhaps she always has been.

I love her.

I fucking love her, and I've never loved any woman.

I have to find out. I have to find out if we can be together, because if we can't? If she can't be a willing participant in the kind of lifestyle I enjoy?

I have to make a decision.

Do I give up my lifestyle? Or do I give up Mandy?

I already know the answer.

And it scares the hell out of me.

The room we're about to enter is the ultimate suite. Inside is not a simple bed and bondage table.

Inside this suite are several chairs. The first, and simplest, is a spanking bench—a leather table where the submissive lies on their belly with a lower stool to rest their knees. The ass sits slightly elevated from the rest of the torso. I get hard just imagining Mandy's sweet ass spread before me on that chair, but it's only as long as the torso. Poles perpendicular to the bench leave her open for business.

The second is a Tachigaeru bondage chair, this one in red leather. With a split seat so only the thighs are held in place and a long split back complete with wrist and ankle restraints, the chair is perfect for any kind of punishment where you want your sub facing you and fully bound.

Both chairs offer endless possibilities for pleasure and pain.

But neither of them is what I'm looking for tonight.

No, I cast my gaze to the third implement in the room—the padded BDSM bench that features five pads at varying heights, all with leather bindings. The large and highest pad is for the torso, of course, and the four lower and smaller pads correspond to each limb. The sub can be bound into the doggy-style position at exactly the right height to please the Dominant.

I can adjust the height so that Mandy's mouth will be at the perfect level for my cock.

She wants to learn how to give head? She'll learn tonight. She's beautiful, her cheeks that gorgeous blush of pink, her tits squeezing out of the corset and her lips trembling, but only slightly.

This equipment is a lot for her innocent eyes to take in, but she's being a trouper. A brave trouper, and I love her even more for it.

"Come here, Mandy."

She approaches me, and I lock the door of the suite.

"Do you remember your safe word?"

"Yes, sir." She bites her lower lip. "My safe word is 'blush.'"

"Good. Don't be afraid to use it."

I gaze at her. The corset, simple jeans, simple black pumps.

The most beautiful supermodel in the world tied into the most intricate leather BDSM attire is no more delectable than my Amanda.

"Are you ready, Mandy?"

"Yes, sir."

God, my cock is hard. I'm not sure how I'll get through this.

I advance on her, take the laces of her corset between my fingers, and loosen them. I unclasp the hooks and remove the corset, and her beautiful breasts fall against her chest.

I want to touch them. Cup them.

So I do just that. I take them, hold them in my palms.

They're mine now. No one else's.

She sighs softly.

I bend toward her, kiss one nipple and then suck it between my lips. "Mine," I murmur against her soft flesh.

Another soft sigh, and my cock nearly explodes.

I lick and tug on her nipple while I pull at the other with my fingers. She's like silk, and her blush spreads over the tips of her breasts as her nipples harden further at my touch.

I could spend two hours just on her breasts, but it's late, and I have a plan—a plan that includes the BDSM bench and Mandy's sweet lips around my cock.

I breathe in, breathe out, breathe in again.

I let the tension flow out of my body, drop her nipple, and kneel down before Mandy to unsnap and unzip her jeans and move them slowly over her hips. I remove her shoes one by one and then her jeans.

She stands wearing only black lace boy shorts.

I suck in a breath.

The urge to rip them and expose her treasures is strong, but I hold back. I'll leave her this tiny bit of cover. She'll be exposed enough when I tie her to the table.

I take her hand, and together we walk to the BDSM table.

"Do you know what this is?" I ask.

"No, sir."

"This is how you're going to learn to give head, Mandy."

Her eyes widen, but she says nothing.

She's bound and determined to be here, to prove something to me.

Or perhaps to prove something to herself.

Either way, she has a safe word that I will honor, and if she can't speak, she'll have a pager, which I'll also honor.

"Lie down on your stomach, Mandy, and place your arms and legs on the lower pads."

She obeys, and already she looks like decadence on a platter.

"I'm going to secure your wrists now. Is that okay?"

"Yes, sir."

I secure her delicate wrists with the silver hoops and leather bindings, and as I do so, I feel what she feels. I feel the leather on her flesh, the coolness of the silver hoops.

"Now your ankles."

"Yes, sir."

I get a good look at her ass from this angle. The black satin and lace is crawling into her crack, so beautiful. That ass that tasted like cherry pie under my tongue.

But tonight is not about me taking her ass. It's not about me fingering and sucking her beautiful nipples.

Tonight is about Mandy—about Mandy learning how to give head, how to give head the way I enjoy it.

She has beautiful lips, my Mandy. Pink and full and luscious.

I want to disrobe. I want to take all my clothes off and be naked with her, but I cannot. It's an element of control, of my dominance, that I stay clothed when she is not.

So I simply unbuckle my jeans, unsnap them, lower them around my thighs, and damn, there's already a spot of wetness on my boxer briefs.

I'm so fucking turned on now, so fucking hard.

I palm my cock, stretch the cotton around my hard length, and Mandy's eyes widen.

"I could use a spider gag on you, Mandy," I say. "Do you know what a spider gag is?"

"No, sir."

"It's a metal gag shaped in a circle. It holds your mouth open while I shove my cock into it. Do you want me to use a spider gag?"

"If you want to, sir."

Her voice cracks a little...but to her credit, only a little.

I have no intention of using the spider gag tonight.

I want only her lips around my cock.

I mentioned it for one reason only—to exert my dominance. To make sure she truly understands who's in charge here and what that entails.

"I don't think I'll use it tonight."

"Whatever you like, sir."

"I've adjusted the table to the height of my cock. However, you still will need to move your neck.

"Whatever you want, sir."

"If you're uncomfortable at any time, please let me know. I've placed a pager near the fingertips of your right hand. If you can't speak, use the pager."

"Yes, sir."

But there's a tone in her voice. An indignant tone I was afraid of. She will not tell me she's uncomfortable. No. But that's okay. A submissive is allowed some discomfort.

Perhaps she's not just doing this to please me.

Perhaps she's a natural submissive after all.

My God...

I'm getting ahead of myself. Only time will tell.

My boxer briefs come down, nearly of their own accord. My cock springs out, hard as a rock.

Mandy doesn't react.

She's seen it before, of course. She's felt it inside her.

God, her pussy was paradise—perfect paradise for my cock.

"Show me what to do, sir. Tell me how to please you."

My balls quiver. Damn. I'm about ready to blow my load already. Maybe this head thing wasn't the best idea. But she wants to learn and, if I'm being honest, I want to teach her.

"The head is the most important part of the cock. The most sensitive part," I say.

"Yes, sir. I know that, sir."

Of course she knows that. She's a novice, but she's not ignorant. She knows theory. She's here to learn the substance behind the theory. Part of being a good Dominant is assessing what your submissive knows and doesn't. Already I'm failing.

Already I'm thinking of her as Mandy Cake.

Which I cannot do. Not anymore.

"I'm going to nudge the head of my cock between your lips now."

"Yes, sir."

I move toward her, inch by inch, until the head of my cock is touching her lips.

My balls are scrunching, and I fist the base of my cock to steady my urge.

Will she swallow?

She will if I tell her to. Already I know this.

How far can I go with her?

I fear she'll let me go as far as I need to, as far as I want to. I need to make it clear again that she can stop at any time.

I open my mouth to do so, but then I shut it.

I *have* made it clear. I must be the Dominant that I am if she's going to understand what she's getting into.

Her soft lips already feel so luscious against my cock head.

"Part your lips, Mandy."

She obeys.

"Take your tongue and swirl it around the head."

Her beautiful pink tongue slides out of her mouth, touches the head of my cock, and she moves it in a snakelike motion.

I suck in a gasp. *Easy, Jack. Relax.*

"Now take the head of my cock between your lips," I say. "Suck on it gently."

And a flaming dart shoots through me, landing right in my balls. A growl escapes my throat.

She moves her lips slightly. I feel it. It's what a smile would be if she didn't have her lips around me.

She likes my growl.

And I like that she likes it.

"Suck gently, Mandy, or this will be over before we start."

I feel the smile again. She knows she's in control of my pleasure, and she likes it. She likes it a lot.

"All right, Mandy. I'm going to fuck your mouth now. I'm going to move slowly into your mouth. Your wrists are bound, but if I go too far, if you feel like you're going to gag, I want you to touch the button on that pager with your right hand. I will keep my eyes on your hand at all times."

I move my cock slowly into her mouth.

And damn, it's more difficult than I thought to keep my eye on her right hand. I want to close my eyes. I want to savor the ecstasy of this moment. I'm fucking her virgin mouth.

I may not be the first cock in her pussy, but I'm the first cock in her mouth, and my God, I'm thrilled.

Fucking thrilled.

So thrilled and ecstatic that I'm ready to blow my load right down her throat.

But I keep my gaze seared on that hand. And inch by inch, I glide into that beautiful, warm mouth.

I stare at the hand.

Waiting for her to move a finger, to touch the button.

Waiting…

One more inch, one more, one more. I'm dying, going to an early grave. Only about an inch and a half of shaft left.

Surely she can't—

There goes the pager.

I withdraw.

She took almost all of me on her first try.

She's going to be a fucking master at giving head.

I will be her willing recipient.

"My God," I groan.

Her lips are still around the head of my cock, so she doesn't speak.

But I feel the smile again.

"All right. Now I know how much of me you can take. I want

you to suck my cock. Suck the head and continue the sucking motion as I move in and out of your mouth. Use your tongue and lick me. Do what feels right to you. I know how much you can take now, so I won't be watching your hand."

I withdraw all the way, instantly missing her mouth on me.

"Do you understand all of that?"

"Yes, sir."

"Good." I thrust the head of my cock between her gorgeous lips once more.

Despite the animal urge to plunge into her sweet mouth, I go in slowly again, to the point where she can take it, and then I withdraw.

Back in to the sweet and warm suction of the inside of her mouth.

My God, she sucks me so sweetly. She sucks me so well.

I plunge in again, pull out, back in. I go a little faster and then faster still.

Until I'm fucking her not quickly exactly, but at a pace that makes me feel like I'm ready to burst.

We didn't talk about swallowing.

And with any other submissive, I'd assume she swallows.

But Mandy is so new at this.

I continue to fuck her mouth, over and over and over, in and out, the wet suction pulling on me harder and harder, until—

I withdraw and fist myself as I come and spurt right onto her face as my entire body releases all the pent-up frustration of the last month without her.

If only I'd come in her mouth. Or in her sweet and tight pussy... I'm lost in the revelation of my love for her when—

"May I speak, sir?"

My eyes are closed as I continue milking my cock. "Yes, Mandy."

"Why didn't you come in my mouth, sir?"

I open my eyes and meet her gaze. God, she looks so

delectable. "I didn't want to alarm you. We should've talked about that beforehand."

"For future reference, sir, I would like it if you would like it."

I growl as I head to the bureau in the room to get a cloth to wipe my semen from her. This is going to be a night for the books.

CHAPTER FORTY-NINE

Amanda

I never imagined.

I don't have a lot of friends other than Jackson. I don't have girlfriends—people to dish with—like Frankie does, so my knowledge of blow jobs comes from reading romance novels and watching a few porn videos here and there.

The woman always looks like she's enjoying it immensely. I had my doubts, but I loved it.

Was it uncomfortable at times?

Yes. My jaw hurts, and my neck is a little stiff.

But I pleased Jackson. I could tell by the look on his face, by the soft groans coming from him. By the way he grabbed my head, the way he went faster as he continued.

I feel so much satisfaction—almost as much as if I'd had an intense orgasm myself.

And I realized then. I realized the power I have. The power of the submissive.

I want to learn more.

"All right, Mandy." Jackson wipes himself from my cheeks and chin with a soft cloth. "The next time, I'll finish in your mouth."

The idea makes me hot. To take that part of him into my body.

It's like sharing something I've never shared with another man. I've never had any cock except Jackson's in my mouth.

I want it to stay that way. I want it to stay that way forever.

But I can't get ahead of myself. He may not be thinking in terms of forever. He probably isn't. He's made it quite clear where he stands with me.

I need to think of this as a lesson. As a lesson only with a willing instructor.

The problem? I don't want to use what I've learned with anyone else.

"I want to do something special for you, Mandy," he says.

"I'd like that, sir."

"I need to get something from the bar. Will you be okay here for a few minutes? If you want, I'll unbind you."

"I'll be fine, sir."

"If you're sure."

"I'm not worried, sir."

I'm not. I feel more myself bound here for Jack's pleasure than I have in a long time. Maybe ever. He adjusts his jeans and leaves the room, clicking the door locked.

Nerves skitter over me, but I'm not sure whether it's from apprehension or anticipation. I don't have a lot of time to dwell on it, though, because Jack returns quickly, and in his hand is a ceramic bowl filled with—

I gasp. Sweet Bing cherries.

"I got lucky," he says. "I didn't dare hope they'd have fresh cherries. I was going to get maraschinos, but this is so much better. Your favorite fruit and mine." He turns his back then, takes a few moments to do something I can't see.

When he turns back toward me and approaches, he holds a cherry out and places it against my lips. "Taste, Mandy. Taste this cherry that is almost as sweet and succulent as you are."

I take the cherry onto my tongue, chew, ready to discard the pit, when—

There's no pit. That's what Jack was doing. He pitted the cherries. For me.

And this is the sweetest fruit I've ever tasted.

Jackson then does something that surprises me.

He removes his shoes, his pants, his underwear.

And that means he's going to...

A smile of satisfaction curls my lips.

He moves behind me, and I shudder when I feel his fingers softly caressing the globes of my ass.

"Have I made it clear how beautiful your ass is, Mandy?"

How well I remember. How well I remember the amazing feeling of his tongue licking me there. "Yes, sir."

"Would it surprise you to know that I'd like to fuck you there?"

I shudder. "No, sir."

"I'm going to rip these black lace panties from your body, Mandy."

I suck in a gasp.

"Don't worry. I'll buy you another pair. But these? These will be in shreds when I'm done."

He pulls my panties hard, giving me a freaking atomic wedgie.

But he succeeds in ripping them.

I can't help a soft chuckle. Mary told me how well the Treasure's Chest garments were made. Not well enough to stand up to Jackson Paris.

And I love it.

Then his hands, the warmth of his hands is on my ass.

"Beautiful," he breathes. "So very beautiful."

His finger slides into my pussy, and I gasp softly.

"So tight and warm, Mandy. My God..."

His voice isn't even his own anymore. It's a mixture of sighs and growls and moans.

And God, I love it. I want to hear nothing but this voice for the rest of my life.

"Does that feel good to you? To have my finger inside you?"

"Yes, sir. You have no idea."

He chuckles then. "I think I have a bit of an idea. Would you like to know how it felt to have my cock in your mouth, Mandy?"

I warm all over. "Yes, sir."

"The only thing better was having my cock in your pussy. That's how wonderful your mouth felt. It felt like…"

"What, sir?"

He doesn't reply.

Home.

That's what it felt like to me. Is it possible that Jackson is feeling the same?

His finger goes in and out of my pussy slowly, and when he adds another, I quiver.

It's a strange sensation, not being able to move. I want to undulate my hips, but I'm trapped.

I want to move with his finger.

But I'm trapped.

And I realize that's the point.

He wants me trapped here. At his beck and call. Laid out for his desire and his desire only.

And that is powerful indeed.

I didn't expect to feel as empowered as I do.

After all, I can't move. But oh my God, I have a power over Jackson. Power I never wished for, but power I don't want to give back.

The power of submission.

For the first time, I understand those words Mary said.

I wipe Mary from my mind then. I don't want to think about anyone else Jackson has been with.

He's with me. Here. Now. It may not happen again, but it's

happening now.

And I will embrace it.

"Do you have any idea how much I want to fuck you?" Jack asks.

"Yes, sir."

"Good. And I will. But not quite yet." He continues to move his two fingers slowly in and out of me.

Then he hooks them and grabs onto the anterior, pushing on that beautiful spongy spot.

Then his tongue... His tongue is between my ass cheeks.

He licks my asshole while I come from his fingers.

I'm flying. No stimulation to my clit, and I'm freaking flying like a shooting star.

"That's it, Mandy. Come for me. Come for your Dominant."

Your Dominant.

If possible, I just soared higher.

This is wild. Wild and primal and ecstatic all at once.

I can't get enough. I can't get enough of being here. Of being here with Jackson. Of learning. Of the pleasure and pain and pleasure yet again.

I slowly come down from my orgasm as Jackson withdraws his fingers.

But I draw in a sharp breath as something enters me, propelled by Jack's fingers.

"All that cream," he says gruffly. "It would be a shame to waste it."

Something else enters me and then something else again.

"Cherries and cream," Jackson says. "What could be more decadent?"

God, the cherries. The freaking cherries. How many are inside me now?

"Now relax, Mandy. Let them drop back into the bowl."

I'm not sure what's happening to my body, but I do my best to obey his command. A moment later, he's in front of me, the bowl of cherries in his hands. He kneels so that he meets my gaze.

Then he seductively brings a cherry between his lips, chews, swallows. "Cherries and cream. Nothing like it."

My body is throbbing. He's playing me like a concert violin, and he's not even touching me.

He eats another cherry and then another. "Would you like to taste one?"

"Yes, sir," I say, my voice a cracking mess, and I'm surprised at the truth of the words.

I want to taste a cherry that's been inside my pussy, that's drenched in my juices.

He places a seeded cherry between my lips, and I let it fall onto my tongue. The flavor is the same but more intense. Whether it's because it's been inside me or whether I know it's been inside me, I'm not certain.

Most likely it's because I'm looking at Jackson licking his full, glistening lips.

I chew, swallow, and he feeds me another. Then he eats one more himself and rises.

He sets the bowl down, walks to the wall, and takes down what looks like a black leather flogger. He brings it back and slides it over from the back of my neck, over my shoulders, my torso, and then my ass.

"So beautiful. My beautiful little submissive."

Whack! The flogger comes down on my ass.

Then—

The flogger hits the carpeted floor with a light thud.

And—

Smack!

This time it's Jackson's palm on my ass—his flesh spanking my flesh.

And it's unbelievably erotic.

"So beautiful. So red. So much like the blush on your lovely cheeks and breasts."

Smack!

The sting of pain, but then… Oh God, the pleasure.

Then the pressure of his lips—soft and firm—over the areas where he smacked me.

"Now I kiss it and make it all better."

I shudder. Flashes shoot through me—electric currents and boiling syrup and everything wonderful all at once.

I whimper, moan, cry out softly.

"Everything okay?" he asks.

"Yes, sir. Oh God, yes, sir."

Smack! Smack! Smack!

"Good. Your ass is so beautiful. I'm going to put some lube on it, because I want very much to finger you, Mandy."

He wants to finger my ass? I suppose that makes sense, since he wants to fuck me there.

I go a little rigid.

"You have a safe word," he reminds me.

"I'm fine, sir."

"Good. Because I'm very much looking forward to this."

He walks again to the bureau, removes something. I strain my neck to see but can't quite move that way, as I'm bound to the table.

Something cold and slick slides over my asshole.

"This is the lube."

He massages me with his finger. And it feels…good. It feels so good.

And then—

I gasp as he breaches the rim.

"Easy," he says. "The hardest part is getting past the rim. I won't move for a moment. Get used to the feeling of the invasion. I will listen to your body."

"Yes, sir."

Within a few seconds, I no longer feel the pain of the breach.

He seems to sense my relaxation, and he moves his finger in and then out. And it feels...

Strange. So strange and jabby and unthinkable.

"So tight and warm in there, Mandy." He groans. "Tell me. Tell me, does that feel good?"

"Yes, sir," I say, and I'm flabbergasted to realize I'm not lying. It *does* feel good. It feels different. Feels forbidden.

And I like it. I like it all.

"Good," he says. "I want you to feel good, Mandy. There is pain in this room. But this room is more about pleasure than anything else. Pleasure not just for me but for you as well."

"Yes, sir." I sigh.

When he withdraws his fingers, I whimper at the loss.

"You know what's great about this table, Mandy?"

He doesn't give me time to answer.

"I adjusted it at the beginning, so your mouth was at the right height for my cock, and it made your pussy the right height for my cock as well."

Then he plunges into me with one swift, unexpected thrust.

Such complete fullness. How he eases the aching emptiness inside me.

I can't turn my head and see him plunge into me. Can't rise up to meet his thrusts. Can't participate in any way.

All I can do is take everything he's giving me, his body slamming into mine over and over and over again.

And my God...I've never felt so free.

"You feel so good to me, Mandy."

"Yes, sir."

Then I gasp.

His finger is back in my ass, and he's fucking me in both holes.

I can't help it. I cry out his name.

"Jack! My God, Jack! Feels so good!"

"Good, my little sub. My beautiful little sub." He moves

faster. Fucks me faster, harder, faster, and harder.

Then, presumably with his free hand, he reaches underneath me, grabs my clit, plucks it, and—

"My God!"

This orgasm—this one that rips through me at lightning speed—is different. So different.

I'm not sure how different until Jackson plunges into me, releasing.

He leans down, kisses the skin of my back.

In the ether, words float around me. Words I've never heard, and even now in my orgasm-induced haze, I'm not sure I hear them correctly.

But I choose to embrace them, embrace them in the glow of my climax.

I love you, Amanda.

CHAPTER FIFTY

Jackson

Thank God I didn't say those words out loud.

But I thought them.

When I came inside her, when everything swirled with perfection, my finger in her gorgeous ass, my dick in her pussy feeling so complete and gloved...

For a moment, everything in my world seemed to make sense. Not just everything in this room, not even everything in my life.

But everything in the *whole world*.

Everything was in balance for those few moments of my orgasm, and that's something I've *never* felt before.

I'm not a novice at this, as Mandy is. I've had my share of sex—my share of *kinky* sex.

And even though what I did tonight with Mandy wasn't as kinky as I've ever gone—far from it—it was the most satisfied I've ever felt.

More satisfied than my best scenes.

More satisfied than the first time I discovered, at age twelve, what I could do to myself.

More satisfied than my first time with Serena.

Even more satisfied than the previous times with Mandy.

And damn it, those were hard to beat.

Am I truly ready to give my life to one woman?

This woman?

For the first time, I'm hoping what Penn told me is true. That Frankie's right. That Mandy's in love with me.

How could I not have seen it? Perhaps the woman of my dreams has been under my nose this entire time.

I never imagined she would enjoy the kind of lifestyle I enjoy, but then...I never gave her the chance.

I just assumed that she was too sweet, too innocent, too naive.

I can teach her so much, and so far, she's been a more-than-willing student.

But to have her *here*—with the other members staring at her. Funny that I never worried about that with anybody else I brought here. Most of the time, I find a submissive to play with who's already here. Before Mandy, I only brought a few women here. One of them ran away screaming, and I never saw her again. Another enjoyed parts of it and we had a relationship for a few months, but I wasn't in love with her, and I was bored after a few months, as usual.

But Mandy...

Mandy is the one who has always been in my life. Who would drop everything if I needed her, as I would for her.

Mandy...

The last person I said goodbye to before I left for college. Not my parents. Not Serena. Not my coach, who was like a second father to me.

Mandy. My Mandy Cake. Amanda Rose Thomas. My best friend. The other half of me.

"May I speak, sir?"

I jerk out of my reverie. I'm still embedded inside Mandy's lush body. I withdraw, fighting it every inch of the way. "You may."

"That was the most amazing thing I ever felt in my life. I never even imagined."

Warmth flows over me like chocolate syrup. "Me too, Mandy. Me too." I unbuckle her ankles, massage them, and then take care of her wrists.

I help her off the table and walk her to the bed, where I lay her facedown. I begin at her shoulders and massage the tenseness out of her from being bound. I pay special attention to her wrists, making sure there's no chafing, and then I move to her thighs and calves, paying special attention to her ankles. I end by massaging her feet.

I always take care of my submissive. It's my duty as a Dominant.

With Mandy? I don't want to just take care of her today.

I want to take care of her for—

Oh my God.

The words. I *did* say them out loud.

Perhaps she didn't hear me. She's made no indication of it.

What if Frankie and Penn are wrong? What if she *doesn't* feel the same way?

What if she doesn't want to lose our friendship? I don't want to lose it, either. It's been the one constant in my life for nearly all my twenty-nine years. I don't know what I would do without it.

What if I can't commit to her? I feel like I want to, but what if it's not possible for me? If it were possible, surely I'd have been able to do it before now.

I lean down and kiss the side of her neck. She shudders beneath me.

"Are you okay?" I ask. "It's tough on your body to be bound in a certain position for so long. I want to make sure I'm taking care of you."

"I'm fine, Jack."

"You sure?"

"I'm so very sure. I don't think I've ever felt as fine as I do right now."

"Good. I'm glad."

"Do you know what would make me feel even better?"

"What's that?"

"If you would take off your shirt and lie next to me. Just hold me."

Holding my partner isn't something I do after a scene. I take care of her, yes. But holding—snuggling—that constitutes an emotional bond, something I've never wanted.

The truth is, though, I *am* emotionally involved with Mandy. I love her. I always have.

As much as I ache to give her what she desires, I can't. Not until I know where this is heading. I absolutely cannot give up my friendship with her, and if we're not on the same page—if she can't accept that I may not be able to commit to her long-term—I can't allow it to continue. I would rather go back to being friends.

Best friends.

"I'm sorry," I say. "I can't."

"But you just said—" She stops abruptly.

God. I'm right. I said it out loud.

"We need to talk," I tell her.

"Do we?"

"Do we what?"

"Do we need to talk, *sir*?"

The snide tone of *sir* isn't lost on me.

This is my own fault. I left the scene before she did by saying the words, by unbuckling her. I brought her to the bed and took care of her without explaining what I was doing.

I left the scene. But so did she. She addressed me as Jack instead of sir.

And now I'm getting all Dominant on her again.

"I can't do this," I say.

"Can't do what exactly?" She pauses a moment. Then, *"Sir."*

Okay, I had that coming.

She continues, "Why not talk here? It's us, Jack. Mandy and Jack. We've always been able to talk."

"I know that. That's what makes it all wrong. This isn't a place where I talk, Mandy. This is where I..."

She drops her gaze. "Oh. I see, sir."

"You can drop the *sir* now."

"No, sir. I cannot possibly, sir. Here, in this place, you are the brave Dominant and I am but your meek submissive, sir. I would never ask you to do anything like talk to the likes of me, sir."

She rises, and I can't help but stare at her delectable red ass as she walks toward her clothes. Her panties are of course shredded, but she wiggles into her jeans and pumps and picks up the corset.

"You can't leave the suite without me," I say.

"I wouldn't dream of it, sir."

She's trying to piss me off, and she's succeeding. Except I understand. She heard me say those words, and she thought I meant them.

I *did* mean them.

But I have to be sure.

Can I truly give up my best friend? Because if I'm not capable of a committed relationship—if this somehow ends—I lose so much more than a lover.

I lose so much more than a submissive.

She tightens the strings of her corset and then whips her hands to her hips and meets my gaze. "I'm ready, sir."

"Fine." I shuffle into my clothing as quickly as possible. I do want to talk to her, but I don't want to do it here.

The velvet choker around her neck is all wrong. It's one of the standard issue here at the club that Dominants use to keep their guests protected.

I don't speak to Mandy again as I lead her out of the suite, down the hallway, and through the main area of the club past Claude and out the doorway.

I don't speak as I adjust the blindfold on her face and take her back up through the bar. I don't speak as I remove the blindfold, walk her through the bar, and then outside to hail a cab.

I still don't speak during the cab ride, and finally, when we reach her building, "I'll walk you up."

"Don't bother," she says.

"Mandy, I've always walked you up, and I'm not going to stop now."

"Fine, sir." She gets out of the cab without waiting for me or the cabbie to help her out.

"Mandy," I say. "That's not necessary—"

"Isn't it?" She glares at me. "Why won't you talk to me, Jackson? You said you loved me and then—"

"Mandy, please…"

"Just don't." She walks into her building, up the stairs.

I follow her.

I take her key from her as I always do, open the door for her, and follow her when she walks inside. Roger is barking and squealing to go out.

"You can leave now," she says. "I have to take the dog out."

"I'll do it," I say.

She gives Roger a quick scratch behind his ears and then points to his leash on the table. "Suit yourself."

Yeah, I asked for that. I leash Roger. "Come on, boy. Let's go do your business."

I walk Roger for a few blocks, bag up his poop, and hit the nearest trash can. Twenty minutes later, we're back at Mandy's place. I let myself in.

Mandy sits on the couch, wearing yoga pants and a T-shirt. She's already scrubbed her face of her makeup.

My God, she looks beautiful.

"He's all set. He should be good until morning." I let out a soft scoff at my own words. It *is* morning. Early morning, but still morning.

I unhook Roger's leash, and he runs to his bowl and takes a sip of water.

"I'm ready to talk now, Amanda."

"Are you? That's interesting, because I'm not."

"Mandy..."

"Jackson, I'm tired. I can't do this with you right now. Call me tomorrow, okay?"

She's right. This is better left until we're both fully rested and fully out of the clouds of that orgasm.

"Okay. I'll call you. Sometime before noon."

"Fine."

I want to go to her. I want to at least give her a kiss on the cheek. Hug her. Pull her close to me and whisper that she's my best friend and I need her.

But she's sending off waves of anger. Wistful anger. Exhausted anger.

So I'll wait.

I'll wait until tomorrow, and I'll call her. We'll meet somewhere. Not here or at my place but on neutral ground. Somewhere quiet where we can speak privately.

"Good night, Mandy."

"Good night, Jackson."

I give Roger a quick pet, let him lick my face, and then I leave, making sure her door is locked securely.

I reach my hand up to hail a cab when I realize I'm not ready to go home. I just need to walk, to blow off the steam that's boiling inside me. I'll walk to my place.

When a dive bar comes into view, I go in. I want to sit, have a drink of some kind of rotgut, and think about where my life is heading.

"Last call, friend," the barkeep says to me.

"That's all I need. Bourbon, please."

"Brand?"

"The worst rotgut you've got."

"Been that kind of night, huh?" He pours me a shot of something that doesn't even have a label on it.

"You don't know the half of it."

"A woman?"

"You got that right." I shoot the bourbon, letting the smoky rawness crawl like acid down my throat. "Could I bother you for another?" I slide a fifty across the bar. Money talks.

He pockets the bill. "Sure. But this time it's really last call."

CHAPTER FIFTY-ONE

Amanda

The clock ticks.

Okay, the only clock in my apartment is on my phone, and it doesn't technically tick, but I hear it in my head—a bizarre sound that makes me tenser with every minute that passes. It's nearing one p.m.

Jackson promised to call before noon. That we'd talk.

Like a fool, I believed him.

Damn it. I *heard* him say the words. I heard him say that he loves me. Clearly, he spoke only in the heat of the moment. Must've been a great orgasm for him, too.

Are we back to this again? Are we going to go another month without speaking? Just because he got into something that he can't deal with?

As much as I love him, and as much as I know I will always love him, perhaps he truly is not the right man for me.

Maybe it's time...

Maybe it's time to update that Lustr profile. If a relationship is what I want, I have to face the fact that it may not be with Jackson.

I was looking for a teacher, and Jackson at least gave me that.

I know a lot more than I did two months ago, for sure. I know I enjoy a little bit of kink. I know I enjoy being submissive in the bedroom. I have some ideas about how to give blow jobs. I'll be able to do even better if my hands are available to me.

After getting in a few hours of work, I decide to call Michael to book another training session at the gym. I sure as heck paid for that last one. It was awful. I hurt for a week, but like a moron, I didn't go back and continue the training. I let my body heal, and now I have to do it all over again and be in pain.

If I keep working the same muscles, the pain will go away, and I'll be stronger.

Frankie kept telling me that, and I knew she was right.

And Michael told me that, too.

He also asked if he could see me outside of the gym, but he never called.

So I call him.

"Mandy Thomas," he says into my ear.

"How do you know it's me?"

"Your name comes up on my screen. Like it does for all my contacts."

The warmth of my blush. Embarrassment swirls through me. "Oh. I guess I didn't realize you had plugged in my name as a contact."

"I plug in everyone as a contact."

"Oh. Of course."

"What can I do for you?"

"I'd like to book another session at the gym with you."

"It's been more than a month, Mandy. I figured you weren't interested."

"I am. I need to get in shape. I should've come back after the first session. My bad."

"I get it. You were probably in a lot of pain."

"You don't even know."

He laughs. "Of course I know. Everyone knows the pain of

a new workout. Especially trainers."

"I guess I'm going to be in pain again because I want to try again. This time I want to commit. I need to make a commitment to bettering myself. Stepping out of my comfort zone."

"Getting stronger will always enrich your life," he says. "But it does come with pain."

This time I laugh. "You're not kidding."

"I have some time next weekend. Or I'm open a couple evenings a week as well if you want to come in after work."

"I actually work from home, so I'm flexible. I was thinking maybe sometime in the morning."

"Looks like I have Monday morning free. Ten o'clock?"

"That'll be great. What do you suggest for breakfast?"

"I'd keep it light. Some protein and some good carbs. Maybe an egg and whole grain toast. Maybe some avocado."

"Sounds good. I'll see you Monday at ten."

Good. I'm going to better myself, beginning with a workout on Monday. Now what the heck else am I going to do today?

Turns out I don't have to wait too long to decide, because Frankie calls.

"You're not going to believe what happened," she says. "The bridal shop just called. The designer has discontinued the bridesmaid dress I ordered."

"And they couldn't tell you that a month ago when we ordered them?"

"Some snafu with the manufacturer. I don't know. But now we have to choose a new one. Can you come today? This afternoon? They're opening up special for us on a Sunday."

Why not? Not like I have anything else to do, since Jackson didn't call.

"Sure. I can be there, Frank."

"Great, I really appreciate this, Mandy. Three p.m. at the shop, okay?"

"Got it."

...

At three o'clock on the nose, I walk into the shop. Frankie is already there.

"Where are the others?" I ask.

"Neither could make it on such short notice," Frankie says. "We have all their measurements. You know, from the last time."

"Yeah, but that means they won't have any say in what we choose."

"I guess they trust my taste."

Frankie does have amazing taste. Plus, this way, I'll be able to steer her toward something that looks amazing on my body as opposed to Isabella's supermodel lithe body and Gigi's healthy posterior.

The owner of the shop, Martha, hurries toward us. "I just want to apologize again, Francesca. This hardly ever happens."

"It could only happen to me," Frankie says dryly.

"We will find you something just as spectacular. More so, even."

"All I ask is that we stay in the same price range. I've already cleared the price with my other bridesmaids, and I don't want any issues. My parents will be paying for Mandy's dress."

I widen my eyes. "They will?"

"Did I forget to tell you? Sorry about that. Yeah, Mom and Dad are footing the bill for the entire wedding. Including your expenses."

"They don't need to do that."

Though it does help, since I'm a little tight from the last month.

"I've got some potential dresses laid out for you," Martha says. "Come on back to the fitting room."

The first dress is a light-pink sheath that doesn't fit well at all. "If you like this design, we can alter it to fit your figure."

"It's up to Frankie," I say, "but honestly, this isn't really me."

Frankie bites her lip. "It's beautiful, but I have to agree. I want Mandy to feel comfortable."

"It's your wedding, Frank."

"You're my sister. If you're not comfortable, I won't be happy."

Sometimes my little sister surprises me. She really is a good person, and she deserves so much better than Pendleton Berry.

But I keep that little gem to myself.

The next dress is light pink and cocktail length, with a wider skirt, cinched waist, and a beautiful sweetheart neckline. It's definitely a bridesmaid dress—not one of those dresses, like Frankie's original choice, that you can wear again, unless you go back in time for your high school prom.

But honestly, this dress flatters me in all the right places.

Frankie sucks in a breath. "Mandy, you look gorgeous!"

"I love it," I say. "But it's nothing like what you originally chose."

"I know. It's sure not." She laughs. "Isabella will absolutely hate it. But Gigi will look adorable in it."

"I do like it," I say, "but it's up to you."

"You know what? Let's go with it. It's totally not what I had in mind, but maybe that even makes it better."

"Perfect," Martha says. "I actually have these in stock in all of your bridesmaids' sizes. The tall one will probably require some alterations, but Mandy here and the other bridesmaid should have no problem with their regular size."

"Perfect. Thank you so much, Martha, for opening for me."

"Of course. This is totally our fault. Well...the manufacturer's fault. I don't normally like to pass the buck, but I will on this one."

"Snafus happen," I say. "And this dress...the color, the design. I have to tell you it's not what I originally had in mind, but I love it."

"I'm so glad, Mandy," Frankie says. "Oh...and I need to apologize to you."

"What for?"

"For Penn and his big mouth. I'm so sorry that he said that stuff to Jackson."

My stomach bottoms out. "What stuff?" I choke out.

Frankie clasps her hand to her mouth. "He didn't tell you?"

"Not that I know of."

"Just forget I said anything."

"Oh, no. You're not going to open up that can of worms and not tell me what the hell you're talking about."

"I swear, Penn has the biggest mouth."

"Just tell me, Frank. What did Penn say to Jack?"

"Apparently, this happened a month ago, but he didn't bother to tell me until yesterday. He might've told Jackson that...you're in love with him."

I freeze. She didn't just say what I think she said. Wasn't I just thinking wonderful thoughts about my little sister?

"Frank, how could you?"

"It was just..."

"We've never even talked about that."

"I know. But I just always suspected... I mean, isn't it true?"

"Does it even matter if it *is*? Why would you talk to Penn about that?"

"It was just casual conversation. I had no idea he was going to go to Jack with it."

Everything is finally making sense. Why Jackson is being such an ass. Why he didn't call me this morning after he promised.

"Damn it, Frankie. What the hell am I going to do now?"

"If Jackson hasn't said anything to you, just do nothing. Pretend you don't know. Pretend it's not true."

"It's not."

"Mandy..."

No. I am not going to cry. I'm not going to cry over Jackson

Paris, who gave me the most amazing time of my life last night, told me he loves me, but then neglected to call me this morning when he was supposed to. Now I get it. He thinks I'll read too much into his postcoital words. How many others has he said those words to in the throes of orgasm? I feel sick. Really sick.

"I have to go," I say abruptly.

"Mandy, I'm sorry."

"That doesn't really help me right now."

"I wish I hadn't mentioned it. I just assumed Jack had gone to you about it, and the two of you had a good laugh."

"I'm really sick of people assuming things about me," I say, but there's no bite in my words.

All these years, Jackson assumed I was some sweet and innocent schoolgirl with whom he couldn't share his deepest fantasies. And now Frankie assumes I'm in love with my best friend. She's right, of course, but it's not like she had any way of knowing.

Do I really wear my heart on my sleeve like that? Do I have "I love Jackson Paris" tattooed on my forehead?

I may as well.

I step out of the bridal shop, head to the subway station, and get on the train.

Only to have a woman with two grocery bags bump into me and knock me to the dirty subway floor.

"Oh my God, I'm so sorry, ma'am."

I pick myself up, not bothering to wipe off the dust, and grab a pole. "Not a problem. This is actually the highlight of the day I've had."

. . .

Monday morning, and Jackson still hasn't called. After getting a few hours of work in and eating my light breakfast, I head to the gym for my appointment with Michael.

"Let's chat a bit," he says.

"What about?"

He cocks his head. "About your goals and objectives, Mandy. What did you think I wanted to talk about?"

God, the embarrassment, the warmth of the blush. Either he forgot he wanted to see me outside the gym, or he changed his mind.

"I don't know where my head is this morning. Okay. Goals and objectives. Just to tone up a little before my sister's wedding in two months."

"You don't actually want to lose weight?"

The blush again. "Do you think I need to?"

"No, but a lot of women think they need to look supermodel thin." He reddens. "I'm sorry. I don't mean to imply—"

"Stop. I know I'm not supermodel thin. I just want to tone up. I'd like my tummy to be a little flatter, my arms and legs to be a little more defined."

"You look great, but there certainly are a few exercises we could do. I can definitely help you get a little more definition in your arms. And, as for your stomach, we'll just work on your core strength. That's important for your whole body, and it will help tone up your abs as well."

"Sounds great. Let's get started."

"You're going to hate what I have to say first, though."

I roll my eyes. "I know. Cardio. A freaking half hour of cardio."

"Right. And the elliptical is your best bet, Mandy. It actually works muscle groups as you move, which the treadmill and bike don't really do, other than your legs."

"What the heck. If I'm serious about this, I need to take your advice. Lead me to the damned elliptical."

After Michael kicks my ass for an hour, I head home and finish my work for the day. For dinner, I make myself a Lean

Cuisine. Good enough. Now for a night of Netflix bingeing.

It's been that kind of day.

It's been that kind of couple of days.

My phone rings, and I don't recognize the number, so I let it go to voicemail.

Who cares anyway?

I fall asleep on the couch with Roger curled in my arms.

• • •

I jerk awake, still on the sofa, as my phone alarm blares at seven a.m. I rise, still in my workout clothes, and take Roger out for a quick walk around the block to do his business.

When I return, I grab my phone and notice I have a voicemail.

The call from last night.

I tap in my code.

"Hi, Mandy, it's Ben Black. I'm wondering if you've heard from Jackson. He didn't show up for work today, and he didn't call, which isn't like him. He's not answering his cell phone or his landline at his place, and I got your number from his emergency contact form with personnel. Give me a call if you hear from him, please. Thanks."

Jackson didn't go to work yesterday?

That's not like him.

My heart thuds in my stomach.

That's not like him at all.

CHAPTER FIFTY-TWO

Jackson

Brain mush. Bits and pieces come back to me in fragments. My name.

They keep asking me my name.

I think it begins with J.

You've had a bad concussion, sir. You're in the ER.

You may need surgery, sir. We're sending you up for an MRI.

Good news, sir. You don't have any bleeding in your brain.

How did I get here?

Brain mush.

And then sleep. Blessed sleep.

Except they keep waking me up. Checking my vitals, looking into my eyes with that damned bright light.

Sir, do you know where you are? Do you know your name?

I open my mouth to respond, but nothing comes out.

Then sleep again.

Until they wake me again.

Sir, is there anyone we can call?

Call? I don't know. What's my name? I don't know.

"Mandy," I say.

"Mandy? Is that your wife?"

I say nothing more. I think my name begins with J.

"For now, he's a John Doe," someone says. "No ID on him."

No ID. My wallet.

Someone took my wallet.

I think I was walking. Late at night. Early in the morning. The bakeries hadn't opened yet. No yeasty smell of the first bake...

But then everything goes dark. And I don't know.

I'm here. Somehow, I'm here.

They don't let me sleep for long. Someone is always squeezing my arm with that blood pressure cuff, checking my vitals, my pulse ox, and then of course the dreaded light in my eyes.

"They still look good," someone says.

They? What are *they*?

"We're going to do a repeat CT," another voice says. "Just to make sure you don't have a slow bleed that we couldn't see earlier."

Into the tube again. MRI? CT? I'm not sure which one.

I think my name begins with a J.

"Mandy," I say inside the tube. "Mandy."

Back in my room. I think there might be another guy in here with me. I'm not sure.

They check me again.

"Good news, sir. No brain bleed. Just a tiny bit of swelling, which should go down on its own. Do you remember yet? Do you remember your name?"

"Mandy. I need to see Mandy."

"Is she your wife? Do you have her number? You didn't have any ID or phone on you when you were brought in, sir."

"Mandy. Mandy Thomas."

"Try to find Mandy Thomas," the person examining me says to someone else.

"That's a pretty common name."

"It's all we have to go on. Get the police involved. They'll be able to find her."

"Sir, who is Mandy Thomas? Is she your wife?"

"Not married."

"Your mother? Sister? Girlfriend?"

"Everything. Mandy is everything."

My eyes close, and I'm left in the dark.

CHAPTER FIFTY-THREE

Amanda

I hastily call Ben while my heart rages against my chest.

"Black," he says.

"It's Amanda—Mandy—Thomas."

"Thank God. Have you heard from Jackson?"

"No, and you've scared me half to death. What's going on?"

"He didn't show up for work again this morning. It's unlike him. But you know, we all have emergencies, right? Except he's not answering my texts or my phone calls."

"He was supposed to call me Sunday morning, and he didn't. I...I didn't call him to check."

"Why not?"

"I thought he was blowing me off."

"Jesus Christ, the two of you..." He sighs. "It's been more than twenty-four hours, so I'm calling the cops."

"Can you please keep me posted? Please?"

"Yeah. Absolutely. Thanks, Mandy."

He doesn't sound overly sincere. Probably thinks it's my fault for not checking in with Jackson. What has happened to him? To the man I love?

Ben Black has all kinds of resources. He'll find him.

In the meantime, though, I need to do what I can.

It's Tuesday morning. Where would Jack be, besides work, on a Tuesday morning?

And the answer is that I don't freaking know. He's my best friend. I should know. But Jackson doesn't miss work unless he's at death's door. He's very dedicated.

I could call his gym, but Ben probably already did that.

Mary. Maybe Mary at Treasure's Chest... They know each other.

I should be working, and the shop doesn't open until ten. Now what?

I could go to the club, but it's closed. They wouldn't let me in anyway.

My God, Jack. Where are you?

I try to calm myself by posting on social media for Lily, but I can't focus.

I take Roger on a long walk, then, for an hour, trying to relax. He nearly gets into a fight with another little Chihuahua, so I'm anything but relaxed.

When I get back to my place, my phone is buzzing.

It's Ben's number.

"Found him," he says. "He's at Mount Sinai. He was attacked early Sunday morning."

I gulp.

My God. That's why he didn't call me.

And of course I thought the worst.

"I'm on my way."

· · ·

Jackson lies in his hospital bed, his eyes closed. His gorgeous skin is pale, and he looks so weak.

"Are you family?"

"I'm his friend. Mandy."

"Mandy Thomas?"

"Yes."

"He's been asking for you."

"Have you contacted his parents?"

"We haven't. We don't have any information. He didn't have any ID or phone on him when he was brought in."

Poor Jackson has a black eye, a swollen jaw, and probably more bruising under his gown that I can't see.

"Can you tell me anything?"

"We can only give that information to family."

"I'll call his parents." I pull my phone out to give them a call. I don't want to alarm them, but these people won't give me any information. "Can you at least tell me if he's all right? Before I scare his mother half to death?"

"His prognosis is good." The nurse smiles. "I'll get his doctor for you. She's right next door with another patient. I know she'll want to talk to Mr. Doe's parents."

"He's not Mr. Doe. He's Jackson. Jackson William Paris. He's—" I choke out a sob.

"Ma'am, it's okay. He's going to be okay."

I nod, shaking, as I call Jackson's mom.

"Hello, Mandy," she says.

"Mrs. Paris—Noreen— I..."

"Mandy, what is it? You don't sound good."

"I'm fine. And Jackson... He's going to be okay."

"Going to be okay?" Her voice goes shrill. "What are you talking about? What happened?"

"I..."

A doctor comes scurrying into the room. "Are you Ms. Thomas?"

"I am. Are you Jackson's doctor?"

"Yes. I'm Dr. Hodges."

"I have the doctor," I say to Jackson's mom into the phone.

"I'm going to let her explain."

I hand Dr. Hodges the phone, and then I collapse in a chair next to Jackson's bedside. Here and there, words make their way into my brain.

Attacked, probably from behind. Clubbed on the head, robbed. No internal bleeding, no bleeding in the brain. A fairly serious concussion, but he's coming out of it. He knows his name now. And he knows Ms. Thomas.

Pause.

I will myself to focus. I need to hear about Jackson.

"No surgery is necessary. We watched him very carefully, and he's progressing nicely. He'll probably be able to go home tomorrow. He had a bit of amnesia at first, but now he knows who he is."

Pause.

"Yes, ma'am, that's why we didn't call you sooner. He didn't have his phone or his ID, and he couldn't remember his name."

Pause.

"Yes, it's very common. His prognosis is excellent."

Pause.

"Not at all, ma'am. We'll keep you posted." Dr. Hodges hands the phone to me.

"Noreen?" I say.

"Yes, Mandy. Thank God you're there with him."

"He's going to be okay," I say, more to myself than to Jackson's mother.

"Bill and I will get there right away. He's out on a jog, but I'm going to call him. Tell Jackson we'll be there within an hour or two. As quickly as we can."

"I'll tell him."

"Thank you, Mandy. Thank God he has you."

I end the call and shove my phone into my pocket. Then I sit down next to Jackson.

"Jackson? Are you okay? I'm so sorry."

He opens his eyes. "Mandy?"

"Yes, I'm here. Just sleep. Get your rest."

"It's funny," he says. "I remembered you before I remembered myself."

Warmth envelops me.

"I'm so sorry, Mandy."

"For what?"

"Everything. I guess I didn't call you like I promised."

"It's okay."

"Even when I didn't know who I was, I always knew who you were, Mandy. The other half of me," his says, his thumb idly moving along my hand as I hold his. "I remembered you before I remembered myself. That's got to mean something."

"It means we're forever friends, Jack. We always have been, and we always will be." I lean forward and kiss his forehead.

Jack is here. Jack is alive. Jack will be okay. I may never have him the way I want to have him in my life, but he's here. That's all that matters.

I can live with us being forever friends.

As long as he's alive.

CHAPTER FIFTY-FOUR

Jackson

No. That's not what I meant.

Mandy's not getting it. Maybe she's not in love with me. Maybe Frankie's wrong.

I'm wrong. I got the wrong signals.

So much I want to say to her. So much I can't find the words for with my brain still not working properly.

"Mandy..."

"I'm here, Jack. Your parents are on the way."

I close my eyes and sigh. My parents. Good people, and I love them, but I can't talk to Mandy about our relationship with them here.

Hell. I can't talk about it here anyway. Not with nurses and doctors and techs walking in all the time, checking on me.

No. It will have to wait till I'm out of here.

Tomorrow.

I close my eyes.

...

When I open my eyes, my parents are here. My mom is sitting where Mandy was, her hand holding on to mine.

"Jack, you're awake. Thank God."

"How are you feeling, son?" my father asks.

"I can't lie. I've been better, Dad."

"Have you filed a police report? Who did this to you?"

"My mind is still fuzzy. I don't remember a lot of it."

"Did they have a gun? A knife?" Mom this time, the lioness in her coming out.

She wants all the answers, so she can personally go after whoever did this to her only child.

"I'd tell you if I could, Mom. They attacked me from behind."

"Fucking cowards." This from my father.

"It was late. Or should I say early."

"You shouldn't be out on the streets alone at night," Mom says.

"I wasn't in a seedy part of town. I've walked the same route thousands of times." My eyes close.

"Let him rest, Noreen. He's okay. That's all that matters."

"Where's Mandy?" I ask, my eyes still closed.

"We sent her home. We're here now."

I yawn.

As much as I love my parents, I want Mandy here.

Always.

I want her by my side always.

As more than a BFF.

I want her for everything—as my wife, my lover, the mother of my children. I won't have any trouble committing now. I figured it out. I figured it all out.

Mandy, why did it take this? Why did it take this to realize what I have?

"When will she come back?" I ask, this time opening my eyes, turning my head, and meeting my mother's gaze.

"I don't know. She didn't say."

"I'll call her later."

"You will get your rest," Mom says in her *I'm your mother and I know what's best* voice.

"I need to talk to Mandy."

"You can talk to her tomorrow, once you've been released. I'll make sure she comes over."

"All right. Thanks, Mom."

I surrender to the fatigue, close my eyes, and fall into slumber.

CHAPTER FIFTY-FIVE

Amanda

I wake up the next morning, ready to get back to the hospital to see Jack, but his mother calls and tells me they're bringing him home later in the afternoon. I'm so happy he's okay. I can deal with the fact that we'll never be anything more than friends.

After getting some work done and taking Roger on his walk, I decide to take the rest of the day off. I head to Jackson's with supplies.

I let myself in using his code and walk into his apartment. He has a wonderful kitchen plus a living room, dining room, and two bedrooms. Much nicer than my tiny little one bedroom.

I don't come here often. He always picks me up, takes me home. He spends more time at my place than I spend at his, which makes no sense, since he has a lot more room, but whatever.

I find a vase in one of his cupboards and arrange the flowers I picked up from a vendor on the street. I throw some cinnamon bark in a pot, bring it to a boil on the stove, and set it to warm.

Then I get to work on my mom's special chicken soup.

I boil the chicken I picked up at the butcher, add chopped onions, chopped celery, and chopped carrots, along with thyme, sage, and garlic, bring it to a boil, and then let it simmer. The scent of the simmering broth merges with the cinnamon, and Jack's apartment smells like Christmas.

After the broth has been simmering an hour, I remove the chicken, skim off the fat, and let the meat cool until I can shred it with my fingers without burning them.

I taste the broth, add salt and white pepper until I'm satisfied, and add the shredded chicken and the noodles. Jack should be home any minute, and the soup will be ready for him.

I sit down on his sofa, fire up my laptop to do a little more work, when I hear the door clicking.

First to walk in is Noreen. She gasps when she sees me.

"Mandy, you scared me for a moment. What are you doing here?"

"I came over to make sure things were nice for Jack when he got home." I nod to the flowers. "I've got homemade chicken soup all ready for him."

"Oh, goodness. You needn't have bothered. I was going to go to the deli and get some chicken soup."

I smile. "Now you won't have to."

The Parises live on Long Island. They have a long drive ahead of them.

Jackson comes in a moment later with his father.

His black eye looks worse than it did yesterday, which means it's healing.

"Hey, Mandy Cake." Then he widens his eyes. "I mean… Mandy."

"Mandy Cake is fine. You call me whatever you want to, Jackson. I'm just so glad you're okay."

He inhales. "What smells so good?"

"My mom's famous chicken soup. Without homemade noodles, though."

"I can get some at the deli with homemade noodles if you prefer," Noreen says.

"No, Mandy's chicken soup is great. I can't wait to have a big bowlful. Thank you, Mandy."

"It's ready whenever you are."

"I'm going to make myself comfortable in the extra bedroom," Noreen says. "Bill, would you get my bag from the car?"

"Yes, dear." Bill heads out the door.

"Mom, you don't have to stay here."

"Nonsense. Of course I'm going to stay here. You'll be needing some help."

"I can stay," I say.

"Don't you have a dog at home?" Noreen says.

"I do, but he loves Jackson. I'll just go get him. If Jackson needs someone here, I'm happy to do it."

"Please, I'm his mother. This is my job."

She's right, of course. "I understand." I gather my laptop and my purse. "Jack, you know where I am if you need me."

He turns then, grabs my forearm. "Mandy. Please don't leave."

"Of course I'll stay if you want me to."

"At least have a bowl of soup with me."

"All right." I walk to his kitchen, grab two bowls out of the cupboard, and then turn to his parents. "Noreen? Bill? Would you like to try some soup?"

"No, thank you," Noreen says. "And Bill will be getting on the road as soon as he brings my bag up."

"Okay." I ladle two bowls for Jackson and me and bring them over to his dining room table. "Do you want yours on a tray? So you can eat on the couch?" I ask Jack.

"No. I can sit at the table. I'm fine, you guys. Really."

He sits down, and I serve his soup with a spoon and a napkin.

"I'm just so glad you're okay, Jack. I was worried sick. I don't know what I would do without my best friend."

He touches my forearm again, and I try to ignore the tingles that shoot through me.

"Mandy, you will never know the answer to that question."
I smile.

He leans forward and whispers, "I need to talk to you. I need to talk to you so badly, but my mom…"

"I understand," I whisper back.

Noreen comes bustling out of the extra bedroom. "Jackson, what happened to those Egyptian cotton sheets I bought for you?"

"They're on my bed, Mom."

"Oh. Of course they are. Do you have an extra set?"

"Check the linen closet in the hallway. If you don't find something you like, take the sheets off my bed and put them on the extra bed. I don't care."

"Goodness, I would never do that." Noreen walks away, and I hear her pawing through the linen closet.

"I love my mother, Mandy, but I wish you were staying here with me."

"I do, too, Jack, but you'll be fine." I can't help myself. I reach toward his face, gently touch him right below his eye. "Does it hurt?"

"Actually, it feels a lot better. Looks worse than it feels at this point."

"I'm glad. And your memory?"

"Sharp as a tack. I woke up this morning, and I didn't have a foggy feeling anymore."

I smile.

"Did I tell you that I remembered you before I remembered myself?"

Warmth coats me. "You did."

"It made me realize something—"

"All settled in." Noreen comes bustling back into the room like a tornado. "Jackson, I have to organize your linen closet. It's a mess."

"It's fine, Mom."

Jack's father comes back with the bag. Noreen takes the large navy duffel from him, gives him a kiss on the cheek. "Drive safely, Bill. Call me when you get home."

"Will do."

Then he looks at Jack. "You okay, son? Anything you need before I leave?"

"No, Dad. Thanks."

Once Bill is gone, Noreen starts messing with the linen closet.

"Mandy," Jack says. "I really need to talk to you."

"All right. What is it?"

"Wait a minute." Then he yells, "Mom?"

Noreen walks in. "Yes, dear?"

"Could you go to the deli for me after all? I really want a ham on rye."

"All that sodium wouldn't be good for you right now."

"Okay. Turkey then. Turkey on rye. Have them add some avocado. With Grey Poupon."

"Of course, Jackson. Right away." She grabs her purse from the coffee table. "I won't be more than ten or fifteen minutes, I hope." The door closes behind her.

"So my soup isn't enough for you," I say, joking.

"Mandy, your soup is all I'll ever need. I don't want a sandwich. I just wanted to get my mom out of here so I could talk to you."

I swallow, and my stomach flutters with nerves. "Oh. Okay. What do you want to talk about?"

"Us, Mandy. I want to talk about *us*."

CHAPTER FIFTY-SIX

Jackson

I grab her hand.

She jerks, tries to pull away, but I hold firm.

"Mandy...I'm in love with you."

Her eyes pop into circles.

Even I am amazed at how easily the words came. Those words I've never said to another woman.

"Jackson?" Her voice shakes. Either from fear or hope, I have absolutely no idea.

I rush on. "I haven't seen what's right in front of me. I didn't want to think of you that way. I guess it took a literal bang on the head for me to figure out why I've been fighting this."

She's blushing. That beautiful pink blush. "I don't know what to say."

I brace myself against the nervousness that's so new to me. I'm all in now. "How about *I love you too, Jack*?"

"I do. I do love you. I've always loved you. But I finally... I finally made peace with the fact that you and I... That we won't happen that way."

"But we *can* happen that way." I entwine our fingers together. How perfect her hand feels in mine. "I was afraid. Afraid of relationships because I've never been able to make one last, and I couldn't risk losing you in my life, so I figured I could never take that route with you, but I figured it out while I was lying in the hospital, wishing for you."

"Figured what out?"

"That I *can* have a relationship for more than a few months. I'm already in one. With you."

She wrinkles her forehead. "I don't understand."

"You're why it never worked with anyone else, Mandy. It was you. It's always been you." I draw in a breath. "Somewhere deep inside me, I've always known what you meant to me, but I was afraid. Afraid of losing you. I still am, but at least I know it's not because I'm incapable of a long-term relationship. I've been in one—with the one woman who means more to me than I ever realized. The one woman I have loved as far back as I can remember. My best friend."

She doesn't speak for a moment, just gazes at me, until I finally can't stand it.

"You've got to say something."

She smiles then. "I've loved you for so long, Jack, but when I found out you were missing... And then I saw you in that hospital bed... It didn't matter anymore. All that mattered was that you're alive. And if what you need is a best friend, that's what I will always be."

"I do need that, Mandy. I don't want to lose that. That's what's been keeping me from admitting my feelings for you for so long. We can be both. We *have* to be both. You'll always be the other half of me. It will work between us. I committed to you a long time ago. I just didn't realize it."

She smiles then, and tears well in her eyes. "You mean it? Really, Jack?"

"I do. I mean it with all my heart."

"Oh my God. I love you too. I've always loved you. I will always love you. But I don't want to lose what we have, either."

EPILOGUE

Jackson

A month later...

After a particularly satisfying scene, I kiss Mandy on the back of her left shoulder—right on the tattoo of two sweet cherries she got after our first scene at the club as two people in love. We visited the tattoo parlor together, and after getting some color enhancement on my eagle, I got the same cherries on my ankle, with Mandy written under them.

We dress and head back to the main room of the club, until Mandy tugs on my arm. "I want to go into one of the big rooms."

"The exhibition rooms?"

"Yeah. You're still my teacher, after all. I want to see what else we can do here."

Damn. I'll be ready to go again in mere minutes. This woman never ceases to amaze me.

We enter hand in hand. A quick scan of the room shows three different scenes.

Mandy holds my hand, squeezes it, and then nearly cuts off my blood supply. "Oh my God!"

"What is it, love of my life?"

She doesn't reply. Her gaze is fixed upon the scene in the

corner—a man and woman, both dressed in leather, the woman bound and strapped to a pole and the man taking her hard from behind.

He looks familiar.

Very familiar.

"Shit. Is that...?"

"It's Penn," Mandy says dryly. "My sister's fiancé. Their wedding is in a month. And that woman he's screwing? Is not Frankie."